MY SAVIOR

BEWITCHED AND BEWILDERED

ALANEA ALDER

PUBLISHER'S NOTE
This is a work of fiction. Any names, characters, places and incidents are the product of the author's imagination or are used fictitiously, and any resemblance to actual persons, living or dead, business establishments, events or locales is entirely coincidental.

The scanning, uploading, and distribution of this book via the Internet or via any other means without the permission of the publisher is illegal and punishable by law.

Please purchase only authorized electronic editions, and do not participate in or encourage piracy of copyrighted materials. Your support of the author's rights is appreciated.
www.sacredforestpublishing.com
P.O.Box 280
Moyock, NC, 27958
Digital ISBN- 978-1-941315-06-4
Print ISBN- 978-1-941315-07-1
Sacred Forest Publishing

Cover Design and Interior format by The Killion Group
http://thekilliongroupinc.com

DEDICATION

~Omnia Vincit Amor- Love Conquers All~

To Peggy, thank you for all your support, as always I couldn't have done it without you.

To Sabrina Stopforth, thank you for your amazing dedication. Your work sharing My Savior with everyone truly made some of the long days bearable, because I knew someone believed in the book already.

And to my readers, every single one who purchases my books and dives into my worlds. Thank you for loving my characters as much as I do!

PROLOGUE

Thirty years ago

"Do not be afraid; I am with you." Amelia smiled up at the very tall, golden prince. She swung her arm, and their clasped hands swayed between them. All around them, small, winged sprites sang and danced in mid-air. The warm sun overhead cast the clearing in a soft, honeyed light. The air around them seemed to sparkle and shine as the animals walked through the woods, completely at peace. The perfume of the gardenias and passionflowers made her feel lightheaded and content. She looked around in wonder. Even though she had never been here before, she knew she was in the very heart of the fae garden in the mystical city of Éire Danu.

"I know you won't hurt me; you're my mate."

The prince looked down at her, his lavender eyes kind and gentle. "That I am, little one."

Amelia sighed. "We have to wait until I grow up before we can mate, huh?" Even she knew that you couldn't get mated when you were six years old.

He nodded. "But do not worry; we are tied together by the light of our hearts. Someday we will find one another."

Amelia stared down at the ground. "What if you forget?" She knew it would be *forever* before she would be a grown up. What if he forgot her between now and then?

Her prince placed a hand over his heart for a moment before extending his arm. When he opened his fingers, a small orb of golden light pulsed in his hand. Smiling, he lifted the orb to her chest where it flared brightly before disappearing. Immediately, she felt its gentle presence surround her heart.

"Now there is no way that I will forget you, for you carry a piece of my light with you," he explained.

She placed a hand to her chest and beamed up at him. She thought of the long years ahead and frowned.

He tugged on her braid. "What has you looking so sad? If it is something I can fix, I will," he promised.

She looked up, feeling hopeful. "Can you make me a grown up so we can be together right away?"

He shook his head and ruffled her hair. She loved the feel of his large, warm hand in her hair. He made her feel special and safe. She silently thanked Fate for sending her someone so tender and kind.

"I know to someone so young the oncoming years seem far away, but in reality, the time will fly by in an instant. Before you know it, I will be standing in front of you, and we will be able to start our life together."

"Promise?"

He knelt before her on one knee, cupped her face between his two large hands, and kissed her forehead. "I promise."

"I won't let you forget. You're mine," Amelia declared fiercely.

A delighted smile transformed his face from charming to roguish. She felt herself blushing; her mate was very handsome.

"And you are mine." He winked before standing. He reached out to take her hand, and she felt herself tumbling backward.

"No!" she screamed. She felt the ground give way and she was free-falling into the darkness, the beauty and warmth of the garden disappearing.

"I will be waiting. Do not fear," he called after her.

Amelia woke up gasping and looked around her room. Her pink dolls and stuffed animals seemed so ordinary after such an amazing dream. Grinning, she hopped out of bed and ran for the kitchen. She knew her brother, Caiden, would be making breakfast before he and her other brothers, Kyran and Tristan, had to report in for drills with the other unit warriors.

She skidded to a halt in front of their small, wooden table in the kitchen.

Caiden turned from the stove, a white apron covering his training gear. "Why aren't you dressed, young lady? You don't have much time to eat breakfast before we have to drop you off at the Armstrong's for classes."

The guest at their table snorted, eyeing Caiden's apron. "You know, Caiden, you look adorable in that apron. Maybe your brothers should get you a nice string of pearls to complete the look."

"Good one, Kendrick," Tristan said and lifted his fist to be bumped. Kendrick looked at it and raised an eyebrow. Amelia giggled.

Tristan rolled his eyes and let his hand drop. "Of course, you don't do fist bumps. You're Mr. Dark and Mysterious."

Kyran laughed. "I don't think someone with hair that red can pull off dark and mysterious."

Caiden dished out scrambled eggs and then looked over at her. "Well?" He jerked his head toward the hallway. "Go get ready."

Amelia hopped up and down. "School can wait. I have to tell you about my dream. It was amazing!" She was practically vibrating with excitement.

Caiden frowned and turned to Kendrick. "I thought you bound most of her powers? I don't want her setting off another earthquake."

"I did." Kendrick looked at Amelia. "What happened in your dream?"

"I met my mate!" she announced happily.

Around the table, Kyran and Tristan began to choke on their breakfast. Caiden dropped his frying pan, and Kendrick began to rub his chin.

"Wha-wha-what!?" Caiden roared.

Kendrick tapped his lips thoughtfully. "It makes sense. The binding spell wouldn't be able to block a witch's mating dream. Those are how we find our mates."

Caiden rushed around the table while Kyran and Tristan fumbled at their drinks and tried to clear their airways. He knelt down in front of her. "Are you sure? You're just a baby!"

Amelia put her hands on her tiny hips. "Yes, I'm sure, and I am *not* a baby!"

"You're my baby!" Caiden yelled.

"Our baby!" Tristan corrected. He and Kyran stood and crowded around her.

Remembering her prince, she sighed happily. "He was perfect, like a prince."

Caiden stood, his face like a thundercloud. He looked over at Kendrick and then pointed to her. "Fix this!" he demanded.

Kendrick looked at her oldest brother flatly. "Fix this how, exactly?"

Caiden began to pace in their small kitchen. Of the three, he was the most protective as he was both mother and father to her. Kyran, the second oldest, was her confidant, and Tristan was her playmate. Together, the three of them took care of her while her parents traveled the country.

"There is nothing to fix." She scowled at her brother. Of the three, unfortunately, she was the most like Caiden; they were both headstrong and stubborn.

Caiden walked back over and placed his hands on her shoulders, concern on his face. "Are you okay? Did he do anything weird to you?"

Amelia thought about it for a second. "He put his thing in me."

All four men froze.

The air around Caiden began to spark and crackle. "He did what?" he asked, his voice sounding odd and strained.

"He put his light in my heart, that way, he can find me later," she explained. She looked around confused when the men seemed to slump forward in relief. "What?" she asked.

"Nothing, baby." Caiden scooped her up and sat down with her on his lap. "I can't do this. She can never mate." He let out a long breath and cuddled her close. Kyran and Tristan sat back down in their chairs and rested their heads on the table.

Kendrick's smile was wicked as he stood. "Makes me eternally grateful I have a brother."

Behind her, she felt Caiden laugh. "As if you're any less protective of Keelan than we are of Amelia?"

At the mention of his brother's name, she saw Kendrick's eyes soften for a second before becoming hard again. "True," he agreed.

Amelia knew that nearly everyone in Storm Keep was frightened of the antisocial archivist, but since he was her brother's best friend, Caiden had made him her *Athair;* she had grown up around him. He might seem mean and prickly, but he had always been kind to her.

"Go get dressed, baby. For some reason, I can't wait to do drills today. Beating up on the Omicron Unit sounds very therapeutic," Caiden remarked, setting her on her feet.

Kyran stood. "Sounds like a good idea. We'll get the units started on basic drills while you drop Amelia off at school." He and Tristan kissed the top of her head and walked out the back door.

Kendrick sighed. "Try not to break too many bones. I have reached my limit of good deeds for the year. I don't feel like listening to the water temple beg for my help in healing any muscle-bound warriors who don't have the good sense to duck." Kendrick turned to the door.

"I'll keep that in mind," Caiden said, pushing her toward the hallway.

Humming, she skipped down the hall to her bedroom. She had met her mate, and he was a gentle, golden prince! She couldn't wait to grow up!

CHAPTER ONE

Darian watched his opponent carefully. In his mind, he identified the order of bones to break that would cause the most pain. They were standing in a damp, abandoned warehouse inside a caged fighting ring. The overhead fluorescent light bathed everything in an unforgiving, harsh light and cast stark shadows. To him, the world had faded to varying shades of gray so that even the blood running from his prey looked black.

It no longer shocked him to think of his opponents as prey. In his mind, the man before him was of no significance. Darian knew that his own soul was so damned that even these fights, which at one time held the rage at bay, could no longer help him control his murderous thoughts. It was another reason why he had been spending so much time away from Lycaonia and the Alpha estate. When he did finally lose control, he didn't want to be anywhere near his family.

"Come on, pretty boy, is that all you got?" the barrel-chested man taunted. Darian sighed. The tiny human disregarded his height and only saw his face. He was making the same mistake so many others had in the past. They saw a handsome face and long blond hair, and assumed he couldn't fight.

Without hesitation, he stepped forward, and time seemed to slow to a crawl. He easily dodged the other man's futile attempts to land a punch. Darian pulled his arm back and punched him in the chest. He smiled when he heard bones break upon impact. Around him, he could hear the jeers and screams of the spectators. They wanted a kill, and he would give it to them.

Like the gladiators of old, he circled the ring, taking in the deafening and inhumane demands for the man's death. He walked lazily back over to the man who was coughing up blood. He put his knee in his back and brought the man's head back so that it was bent at an odd angle.

"Darian, no!" A young male voice screamed from the back.

His hands ached for the kill, and before he could be stopped, he twisted and the man fell limply to the mat. Seconds later, he heard Keelan yell above the crowd.

"*Obliviscaris!*"

The crowd quieted around him, and everyone stood around as if in a daze. Keelan had wiped their memories of him and of this night. Darian shrugged, stood, and walked over to the door. He kicked it open and jumped down from the ring, grabbed a towel, and started to wipe off the sweat and blood as Keelan pushed his way to him.

When Keelan finally reached him, his face was a mask of panic and fear. "Gods! Darian you killed him; you really killed him! What in the hell is going on?"

Darian shrugged. "Don't get involved. It's nothing."

"Why?!"

"Because for a while, fighting helped with the anger." Darian threw the towel down and picked up his bag.

"Anger, what anger? Why didn't you come to us?" Keelan demanded.

"You know what is happening Keelan. Is it really something that you can help?" Darian turned toward the exit.

Keelan grabbed his arm and spun him around. The only reason his fist connected was because Darian wasn't expecting the smallest member of his unit to sucker punch him.

"You sonofabitch! You're just going to give up?" Keelan's face was flushed with anger.

Darian rubbed his jaw. The little shit could hit. "I don't have much time left, Kee. I'm doing the best I can so that when I finally turn, I'm not at home with Meryn and the other women."

Keelan turned and looked at the dead body in the ring. "Are you? Have you already?" He sounded like he was having a hard time getting the words out.

Darian shook his head. "Not yet. The ones I have been fighting in the ring are known criminals. That one"—he jerked his thumb back toward the ring—"spent a lot of money last week bribing a judge to avoid jail time, I just made sure he received justice."

"What'd he do?" Keelan asked.

"He raped a six-year-old girl. The judge said that since she was wearing a tank top and shorts to bed, she was tempting him." He shook his head and began walking to the exit.

"You mean he was a bad guy? That's great, Darian! You haven't killed any innocents. There's still hope." Keelan said excitedly as they walked to where both their cars were parked.

Darian turned to the youngest member of his unit. "Why did you follow me?" He had to know if he was doing anything at the estate that would give him away.

Keelan rolled his eyes. "The other three members of our unit are mated. What the hell else am I supposed to do?"

Darian unlocked his car and threw his bag into the passenger seat. "You could be out wooing your own mate," he suggested.

Keelan looked down at the ground. "Something isn't right. I dreamt of her, sure, but I have met her, and I'm still having dreams of her. None of the others did that."

"It's probably because you haven't claimed her yet. You better be thankful for those dreams; the last one saved her life. If you hadn't told her to get her brakes checked, she would have had the car accident you saw."

Keelan looked up and stared at the moon. Darian knew that all witches were tied to the moon in a way no other race was able to explain. When Keelan looked back at him, the young witch's eyes were serious. "I'm not attracted to her at all," he confessed.

Shit.

Darian sighed. He had been counting on Keelan mating next so he could move on to the next world knowing that all of his fellow unit members were safely mated. Now it looked like someone had thrown a wrench in his plans. He really didn't have time for this.

"Have you tried being attracted to her?"

"What the hell kind of question is that? Of course, I have. We've gone out on dates, we get along great, but it's like something is off."

"You have time."

"So do you. We're all finding our mates, Darian. I know you have been dreaming of yours, too. Why aren't you doing everything in your power to hold on for her?"

Darian just stared at his closest friend. Keelan was right; he had been dreaming of a woman. She was innocent and bright and pure. She was always laughing and smiling. He had no right tying her to someone like him. He would drag her down into the dark hell that was his future. He would rather give up his soul than let even the hint of a shadow fill her eyes. "I won't tie her to me, not at this point, Kee. It's too late for me."

"Fuck that! I'm not giving up, Darian, and you better not, either," Keelan yelled.

"Or what, my friend?" Darian pushed. He stepped closer to Keelan until their chests bumped.

Keelan's eyes darkened, and suddenly, Darian wasn't one hundred percent sure he could take the young witch. Something in his eyes was wild and untamed. "Don't make me bind you, Darian," Keelan warned.

"It won't come to that," Darian promised. Keelan's display had been warning enough. When the time came, he would be nowhere near the witch.

Keelan eyes lightened, and he smiled. "Good. We'll fight this together, Darian; we can do it." Keelan turned and got in his car, clearly misinterpreting his promise.

Darian would let him continue to think he had a chance; it would be easier on everyone that way.

"Because! If I don't leave this fucking house I am going to lose my mind and I'll take you with me!" a familiar female voice yelled. The next morning, Darian stopped in his tracks in the hallway just outside the dining room and debated how hungry he was.

"Coward." Gavriel joked as he and Beth walked past him and into the war zone.

There were very few things left on this Earth that made him smile; Meryn was one of them. On rare occasions, she managed to push back the darkness, but those incidents were few and far between now. Darian's stomach made the decision for him. Steeling himself, he walked in.

Meryn stood on one side of her chair and Aiden on the other. He had both hands held up in front of him as he tried to calm his mate down. Around the table, everyone else was calmly eating their breakfast. Even Penny was taking Meryn's threat in stride, her tongue sticking out of the corner of her mouth as she concentrated on spreading cream cheese on her bagel.

"Meryn, sweetheart, you have to calm down," Aiden pleaded.

"I am calm! But if I don't see something besides our bedroom, your office, or the dining room, I will start to get stabby!" She sat down and crossed her arms over her chest.

Aiden paled and sat down beside her. "Okay baby, let's go to The Jitterbug. You haven't seen Sydney or Justice in a while."

Meryn shook her head. "I want to go see the last *Hobbit* movie. It won't be in theaters much longer, and I can't miss it. I've seen all the other ones on the big screen. I am not waiting for the DVD to see the ending."

Aiden looked over to where Gavriel sat with Beth and then to Colton and Rheia. Both men's faces were unreadable. Everyone knew this was not a good idea, everyone that is, except Meryn.

Beth laid a hand on Gavriel's shoulder. "I'd like to see it, too. If fear of being attacked keeps us from doing the things we want, then they have already won."

Gavriel closed his eyes and leaned back in his chair. Darian looked over to Aiden. He also wore a defeated expression.

Darian watched as Keelan looked around the table, his eyes slightly haunted and his face drawn. "We could make this a group outing. I bet some of the guys in the other units would like to see what humans think elves look like." Aiden shot him a grateful smile.

Meryn shook her head. "Only if they stay like, I don't know, fifty feet away at all times. I don't want to walk around with a huge wall of bodies blocking out the daylight. I might as well stay home."

Aiden nodded. "You won't even know they're there," he promised. He looked at Keelan. "You should invite Anne."

Keelan shook his head. "Maybe next time."

Darian caught the questioning and concerned looks Aiden was shooting at Colton. Colton just shrugged. Knowing nothing would be answered if the questions weren't asked, he spoke up. "Keelan, are you okay?"

The women turned in unison to stare at Keelan; he flinched at their scrutiny. "I'm fine."

Frowning, Meryn stood and walked over to his chair. She placed a hand on his forehead and then a hand on her own. "I don't think he has a fever."

Rheia got up. "Maybe I should be the one to check that out." She walked over to Keelan and put her hand next to Meryn's. Keelan eyes darted around the table to the other unit members. Darian could almost sense his desperation.

Rheia frowned, and Meryn began petting Keelan's hair. Darian was willing to bet that in a couple more seconds the witch would bolt.

"Well, Rei?" Meryn asked.

Rheia removed her hand. "No fever that I can tell. Keelan, have you been sleeping?"

Keelan just shrugged.

"Poor baby." Meryn hugged Keelan's head to her chest.

Darian watched and enjoyed a rare moment of amusement. Aiden was growling, and Keelan looked like he was about to piss himself.

After a few seconds, Keelan disengaged from Meryn and looked up at her. "I thought you didn't like me."

She stared at him in shock. "Where did you get that idea?"

The men all looked away, hiding their smiles. They all knew that Keelan was Meryn's favorite lighting rod in the morning. Penny snickered.

Keelan shrugged again.

She ruffled his hair. "Of course I like you. In fact, you're one of the few people in the world I *do* like. If I didn't like you, I wouldn't talk to you at all."

"I think an outing is a wonderful idea. Meryn needs more fresh air," Ryuu said, walking in from the kitchen. He set a pitcher of orange juice on the table and looked at Rheia. "I would be more than happy to watch Penny for you if you would like to go."

Rheia's eyes brightened before she turned to Colton. "We've never been on a real date," she said softly.

Colton sighed and wrapped an arm around her shoulders. Just like that, Darian knew they would all be going to see the *Hobbit*. He stood and reached for his phone. He knew his commander, and before Aiden even had to tell him, he was already dialing Sascha.

"You got this, Darian?" Aiden asked from the table.

"Yes, sir." Darian headed to the family room. He sat down on the sofa to make security arrangements. After the second ring, he heard Sascha's greeting. "What?"

"And hello to you, too, asshole."

"I'm not awake yet, so it had better be good."

"The ladies want to go see a movie in Madison. Gamma unit has security detail." Darian didn't even try to sugar coat it.

"Motherfucker!" Sascha continued to cuss as Darian heard the man's feet hit the floor.

"I expect they'll try to make the matinee showing at ten a.m. Get the guys ready and meet us in town at the theater."

"We'll be there," Sascha grumbled.

"See you later." Darian hung up the phone and let his hand fall on the cushion at his side. He should have had more fun torturing Sascha, but he couldn't find the energy. Everything seemed so pointless lately.

Darian felt a tugging on his sleeve. When he looked down, he saw that Felix was watching him with a worried look on his face. Forcing his lips to move, he smiled.

"Hey buddy, what's wrong?"

Felix continued to stare.

"I'm okay, really," Darian promised.

Felix's bright green eyes filled with tears. "Go home soon?" he asked in his tiny voice.

"I would if I could." Darian let the smile disappear as his head dropped back to rest on the cushion.

Felix tugged on his sleeve vigorously. "I take."

Darian turned his head to look at his small friend and lifted his hand. Using his index finger, he gently rubbed the top of Felix's copper curls. "I appreciate the sentiment, but that option was taken from me a long time ago."

Felix dashed at his tears with his coat sleeve. "Your light is almost gone."

Darian closed his eyes. "I know."

"Alpha help?"

Darian opened his eyes and shook his head. "There nothing anyone can do. Promise me one thing, Felix. If something happens to me, promise you'll keep the women and Penny safe. The guys can look out for themselves."

Felix sniffed and tried to look manly, the effort ruined by the steady stream of tears rolling down his cherub-like cheeks. He nodded then reached inside his shirt. He twisted his pendant and seconds he flew away.

Of course, a sprite would be able to tell that he was fading. They were distantly related to the fae. Darian stood and put his phone in his pocket before heading back to the dining room. If these were his last days then he was going to enjoy every scrap of Ryuu's cooking that he could.

"I thought you knew the story!" Aiden exclaimed, wiping more tears from Meryn's face with some theater napkins.

She was blubbering so hard she couldn't form coherent sentences. People were shooting Aiden evil looks as they walked by assuming he was the reason she was crying.

He had to admit, it did look incriminating for his commander. Meryn was only slightly taller than a toddler and just showing a pregnant belly behind her cartoon t-shirt that made her seem even younger.

Beth and Rheia stood on either side of Meryn making shushing noises. Gavriel, Colton, and

Keelan looked just as distraught and helpless as their commander.

Darian thought about it for a moment before deciding on a course of action. "Meryn, would you like some ice cream? The shop across the street is supposed to have a really good selection."

Meryn stopped mid-sniffle. "Ice cream?" She used her coat sleeve to wipe her nose.

"Yes, and toppings."

Meryn turned to Aiden. "Can we get ice cream?"

Aiden nodded frantically. "Of course you can get ice cream." He looked over at Darian and mouthed the words, "Thank you."

Darian shrugged. The sooner Meryn composed herself, the sooner they could return to the Alpha estate.

"We'll go with you. You men wait here," Beth said, as she and Rheia looped their arms through Meryn's. Together the three of them crossed the street and disappeared into the ice cream parlor.

"Oh. My. Gods." Aiden rubbed his hands over his face.

"Thank fuck! I didn't know she could cry like that." Colton let out a long breath.

"I didn't know *anyone* could cry like that," Keelan admitted, looking pale.

"Pregnancy hormones," Gavriel said simply. The four men nodded together.

"Good battle scenes though," Colton declared, changing the subject.

"Made me want to brush up on my axe skills," Keelan admitted.

Darian turned his head and watched the door
to the ice cream shop close behind the women.
He turned and started scanning the area as the
men discussed the merits of using an axe over a
broadsword. He wished he could die honorably
in battle, defending his loved ones, but he knew
better. As things stood, he would turn and have
to be put down like a rabid dog, he just prayed
to Fate that he didn't hurt anyone in the process.

"For the last time, no, you cannot fly out here
and escort me home. I'm fine!" Amelia
Ironwood felt her blood pressure rising. Only
her brothers could affect her so much, so
quickly.

"There have been missing persons reported
in that area, baby girl. You're on your way
home anyway." Caiden argued.

"I'll be in Lycaonia by nightfall. I'll hit the
shops in the morning then be on my way to
Storm Keep. I'll be home before you know it."

"Come home now," Caiden ordered. She
paused. This wasn't like him; he sounded
anxious.

"What's really wrong?"

"I had a dream."

Amelia waited for him to continue. When he
didn't, she prompted him. "And?"

"And you fucking died!" Caiden exploded.
Amelia pulled the phone from her ear. "You fell
into darkness and died. This will happen soon.
In my dream, the calendar was for this year and
month, right before Imbolc."

This wasn't the first time that Caiden had a dream about her. Usually, it was for smaller things like which date to cancel or which job to accept. He had never seen her in danger before now.

"Listen, I can't travel much more today anyway. I'll make sure I'm in Lycaonia tonight and leave first thing. I'll call you when I'm on the road."

"Please be careful, baby girl," Caiden pleaded.

"Always," she promised. She ended the call and stared at her phone. Their conversation sure put a damper on her evening. She looked around. She was in the small human town of Madison outside of Lycaonia. When her eyes landed on an ice cream shop, she did a happy dance on the sidewalk. Grinning, she skipped across the street and pushed the door open. A huge dose of sugar always helped in situations like this. She'd indulge in enough calories to put a bear shifter into hibernation, call the council number Caiden had given her, and arrange for an escort into Lycaonia. With any luck, the shops would still be open for some late evening shopping! She had already booked an overnight stay at one of Lycaonia's best bed and breakfasts. If she got an early enough start in the morning, she could stay at the spa in Dallas longer than she had planned, especially if she was giving up visiting Lycaonia because of her brother's premonition. She smiled; she might even be able to get Caiden to pay for the spa if she played her cards right.

Lucky!

Humming to herself, she stared into the ice cream case.

"Can I get you something?" A male voice asked.

She looked up and smiled at the middle-aged human. "Yes, I'd like a triple scoop ice cream cone. Only I'd like the ice cream cone smashed up in a bowl with the ice cream on top. I'd like bubble gum, butter pecan and mint chocolate chip please." She happily pointed to the brightly colored ice creams.

When he didn't respond, she looked up. His eyebrows were knit together in a frown. "The two of you related?" he asked, pointing across the shop.

Amelia followed his finger to where three women sat eating their ice creams. Amelia was about to ask the human what he meant when she spotted a bit of pink in the smaller woman's bowl.

She hurried over to the group and looked down. "No way! Bubble gum, butter pecan, and mint chocolate chip?" she asked the woman, unable to believe someone else ate her own special creation.

"Yeah, why?" Green eyes narrowed at her.

"Cone crushed up at the bottom?"

"Yeah. Who are you?" The small woman edged closer to the blonde woman who was staring at her in disbelief.

"Sorry, my name is Amelia Ironwood and that is exactly what I just ordered. I have never met anyone else who liked that combination."

"Miss, your ice cream," the man behind the counter called.

Amelia looked at the women. "Be right back." She turned around, paid for her order, and returned to their table with her own ice cream. Without asking, she pulled up a chair and sat down with them. She picked up the spoon and took her first bite.

"Yummy."

"Why is she sitting with us?" the petite woman asked with a scowl.

The dark-haired woman in scrubs laughed. "Meryn, that's rude. She's just being friendly." She turned to Amelia. "My name is Rheia Bradley, this is Elizabeth Monroe, and the anti-social one is Meryn McKenzie."

Amelia nodded. "Pleased to meet you. Do you all live here in Madison?"

Elizabeth shook her head. "No, we live... a little bit outside the city."

Amelia stopped digging through her bowl for the bubble gum flavored ice cream and took in her words. "You wouldn't be from Lycaonia would you?" she asked, going out on a limb. She had read the map; there wasn't anything for two hundred miles in any direction from Madison.

Elizabeth's eyes widened. "Actually yes. Is that where you're heading?"

Amelia nodded. "I need to call a Rene Évreux to arrange for an escort into the city."

Meryn growled and stabbed at her ice cream. "Don't call him; he's a total douchebag. You can follow us. We're going to the Alpha estate. One of the guys can show you how to get to the city."

"That'd be great! Without having to wait for an escort, I'll definitely get some shopping in tonight. Whoo hoo!" She waved her spoon around.

Meryn watched her with a guarded expression. "You're too happy."

Amelia nodded. "So I've been told. It's just my nature."

"Are you on drugs?" Meryn asked bluntly.

"Meryn!" Elizabeth swatted at her arm.

Amelia laughed. "No, but I've been asked that, too." She turned to Elizabeth. "She said that you are going to the Alpha estate, do you have business there? Did you need a place to stay? I have a room at the Rise and Shine bed and breakfast in the city if you need a place to crash," she offered.

"No, we live there." Meryn frowned at her. "Seriously? You would ask complete strangers to share a room with you? What if you woke up in the bathtub with missing kidneys?"

Amelia grinned. "Wouldn't be the first time," she joked.

Meryn and Elizabeth stared as Rheia began choking on her ice cream.

"Seriously?" Meryn whispered, her eyes wide.

"No, but I had you for a second, didn't I?"

Meryn scowled. "There's something wrong with you." This time, neither Rheia nor Elizabeth chastised her.

Amelia shrugged. "I like people."

"I hate people," Meryn admitted honestly as she scrapped the side of her bowl.

"You're talking to me," Amelia pointed out.

"You're kinda making me talk to you. I don't know if I like it yet." Meryn put her bowl down.

Amelia turned to Elizabeth. "You all live there? Are you mated?"

Rheia nodded. "Our mates are members of the Alpha Unit. I'm mated to Colton Albright."

"I'm mated to Gavriel Ambrosios," Elizabeth said, putting her empty bowl down.

Amelia turned to Meryn. Meryn stuck her tongue out at her. "What?"

"You're so adorable." Amelia smiled and took another bite of ice cream. Meryn reminded her of a hissing, spitting kitten.

Elizabeth turned to her. "I thought so, too, right after I met her, so much so, I adopted her as my little sister."

Meryn grinned at Elizabeth and began to eye Amelia's ice cream bowl. Amelia took one last bite and pushed her half-eaten bowl over to Meryn.

Meryn looked at her in surprise, her eyes becoming unguarded. "Really?"

Amelia nodded and pointed at Meryn's belly. "You're eating ice cream for two unless I'm mistaken."

Meryn smiled wide and pulled the bowl close. "I'm mated to Aiden McKenzie, and yes, I am eating ice cream for two." She dug in with gusto.

Amelia put her chin on her hands and watched her eat. She really was just like a kitten. Angry one second and purring the next. She was envisioning late night shopping when a thought struck her.

"Wait, Aiden McKenzie. *The* Aiden McKenzie? The Unit Commander?" she asked.

Meryn nodded. "Yup."

"That's crazy. Your mate is kinda like my brothers' boss."

Elizabeth turned to her. "Who are your brothers?"

"Caiden, Kyran and Tristan Ironwood. They lead the Nu, Xi, and Pi Units in Storm Keep."

"What a small world," Elizabeth murmured under her breath.

"Truly," Amelia admitted.

"Ladies, I suggest we head out. If we sit here much longer, the men will launch an all out assault on this poor shop." Rheia said standing. She gathered the bowls, including Meryn's now empty second bowl, and threw them away.

"Thanks for the escort. I heard it can sometimes take hours to get someone from the city to guide you in." Amelia stood and walked out with them.

"No worries. I mean we're heading that way anyway," Meryn said, blushing.

"Too cute!" Amelia pulled Meryn in for a hug. She pressed her cheek against hers and swayed back and forth.

"She's hugging me!" Meryn complained.

Rheia laughed. "And yet, you're not dead."

With her ears turning red, Meryn muttered, "It's not so bad."

"Somehow I knew we'd be friends," Amelia said, letting go.

Meryn looked up at her. "How'd you know?"

"I'm half witch. We get flashes of intuition."

"It was the ice cream," Rheia and Elizabeth said at the same time. The four looked at each other and started laughing.

"Okay, maybe it was the stellar ice cream choices." Amelia bumped hips with Meryn.

"Let's go introduce you to the guys," Meryn said, pulling her hand.

They looked left, then right and stepped out into the street. They had only taken a couple steps when they heard the terrified shouts from the men. When Amelia looked to her left, she saw a car heading straight toward them. Seconds later, she felt the rush of magic and a small explosion blew the hood up on the car causing it to veer to the right where it rammed into a light pole.

Beside her, Meryn's knees gave out. Amelia quickly wrapped a steadying arm around her waist to keep her upright.

"Meryn!" A deep male voice shouted.

"Rheia!"

"Beth!"

As men surrounded them, a tall figure walked past them. The man she assumed was Aiden didn't wrap an arm around Meryn to support his mate; he simply lifted her off the ground and into his arms.

A blond man was holding Rheia, and an incredibly handsome, dark-haired man checked Elizabeth over.

A fourth man, with auburn curls, took her hand. His warm, honey-colored eyes looked frantic. "Are you hurt?" he asked.

She shook her head and stared at him in shock. "Keelan?"

He frowned. "I'm sorry, do I know you?"

She smiled wide. "No, but I know all about you. Your brother Kendrick is best friends with my eldest brother and my *Athair.*"

"Amelia? You're Amelia, right?" His face broke out into a huge smile. He pulled her into a spine-cracking hug. He stepped back, still smiling. He was so warm and open, completely opposite of his brother.

Bang!

"That's me. I'm glad I got to see you on my trip. I'm only staying a night. I have a reservation with Rise and Shine in the city." Amelia couldn't believe she had almost been run over in a human city. Damn her brother with his premonitions! He could have said watch out for cars!

The auburn haired man blinked. "You're going to Lycaonia?"

"Yes, then I'll be heading home in the morning."

"It's great to meet you, though I am sorry about the circumstances."

Bang!

"Aiden, the perimeter is secure. Let's get the ladies to the SUVs and back to the Alpha estate," a sinfully gorgeous blond said, walking up from their right.

The large man cuddling Meryn looked up. "Good idea, Ben." He looked around. "Where's Darian?"

Bang!

They all turned in the direction of the loud noise. Keelan buried his face in his hands. The handsome blond began to laugh and the three men with mates looked smug. Amelia watched in amazement as the tall warrior smashed a human's face against the large stop sign.

She took a moment to appreciate that the warrior had no problem keeping the somewhat portly man in the air. But what really impressed her was the fact that he had no problem keeping the man in the air nearly *three feet* off the ground so that his face could connect with the stop sign.

"I'm sorry, did that hurt? Let me do it again," she heard a deep voice rumble.

Bang!

"See this sign. It is red. Red is the universal color to stop. Are you color blind? No? Well, even if you were, there are four large, bright white letters on this sign that spell out the word 'stop'. Let's go over them, shall we?"

"S." *Bang!*

"T." *Bang!*

"O." *Bang!*

"P." *Bang!*

"Oh, dear," Elizabeth said, trying to hide a grin.

"Darian, fall back," Aiden yelled across the street.

The golden warrior turned and, without looking back at the man, dropped him unceremoniously to the pavement. He walked over, checking over their group. "Is everyone unharmed?"

Amelia felt her breath catch; she recognized that voice. Looking closer, she nearly fainted when she saw his eyes. *Lavender eyes*. He had lavender eyes! She took in every single detail of his handsome face. A face that she had memorized in a dream so long ago.

"You're my mate," she whispered, feeling her heart racing out of control.

He turned to her. For a second she thought she saw a flicker of recognition and then it was gone.

He shook his head. "I'm sorry, you must be mistaken." He turned to Aiden. "I'll be in the car." He walked away without looking back.

"But..."—she looked around—"but he is."

The men looked at her dubiously.

"Maybe he just looks like your mate?" Aiden speculated, putting Meryn down.

Amelia shook her head. "It's him. I know it's him."

Aiden looked at the other men. They shrugged, looking unsure of what to say.

Keelan turned to her. "We'll talk to him," he promised.

Meryn stepped forward. "Remember what we talked about in the ice cream shop? We're heading there now. *All* of Alpha Unit."

All? Amelia was confused for a second, and then it hit her. Meryn was telling her where Darian would be.

"If you could escort me to the city limits, I'll find my way to the bed and breakfast," she said, trying to keep her voice nonchalant.

Aiden nodded looking relieved. "Sure, no problem. I hope you find your mate soon."

"Me, too," she said.

"Aiden, Gamma will wrap up with the authorities here. We'll be along soon." The blond offered.

"Thanks, Ben." Aiden wrapped an arm around Meryn, and they headed toward their cars.

Rheia and Elizabeth nodded at her before walking away with their mates. Though they had just met, she knew the women believed her. Feeling like maybe she wasn't crazy and making the biggest mistake of her life, she jogged to her car to follow her new friends into Lycaonia.

You bet I'll be finding my mate real soon, like, right after I freaking park.

CHAPTER TWO

Amelia followed the SUVs in front of her and replayed her mate's rejection over and over again in her mind. Even if he didn't recognize her, fae could identify their mates by their aura. Was hers broken? Finally, after what seemed like forever, the cars turned onto a side road. She watched as Aiden pulled over and got out of the lead car. He walked back to the main road.

She slowly came to a stop next to him and rolled down her passenger side window.

He pointed forward. "Lycaonia is about ten minutes down this road. You'll have to park at the garage and walk into the city. Did you need someone to show you around?" She was touched at the look of concern on his face.

She shook her head. "That's okay. I can figure it out. Thanks for the escort in."

He smiled wide. "Anytime. If you need anything while you're visiting, here's my cell phone number." He handed her a small piece of paper with a number scrawled almost illegibly on it. "Normally, we have visitors go through the council, but your brothers are my unit leaders in Storm Keep. We take care of our own."

Amelia felt her chest swell with pride. Not every paranormal could be a unit warrior. It took dedication and discipline. The fact that all three of her brothers not only served, but were also unit leaders spoke volumes about her family.

"Thank you. My brothers speak very highly of you." She smiled at him and his cheeks tinted pink.

Adorable!

Aiden cleared his throat. "I never have to worry about the units in Storm Keep; Caiden runs a great program out there."

Amelia had to fight to keep the smile off her face. If the Unit Commander knew of the shenanigans that went on, pretty much on a daily basis, she bet he wouldn't think that. "It was an amazing way to grow up."

Aiden laughed loudly. "I bet." He looked up at the sky. "Well, I better get going. We have a few more hours of daylight left, and I want to join the other units for afternoon drills. Drive safe."

"Thank you, I will." Amelia waved as he walked back to the SUV. She waited until they were moving forward before she started her car. When the two SUVs disappeared around the bend, she backed her car up and turned down the side road. She moved forward slowly in case the Alpha estate was closer than she realized.

After a couple minutes, she saw the road opening up. She pulled her car over to the side as close to the tree line as possible.

"Sure, I'll go to Lycaonia, right after I claim my mate," she muttered to herself. She opened her car door and got out. She reached into the back seat and grabbed her tote bag and eased the door closed, trying to make as little noise as possible. She walked until she could see a large estate house. Next to the house was an open field where men were performing various drill exercises. Smiling to herself, she looked around. When she spotted a tall oak tree, she did a happy dance. She hoisted herself up, climbed as high as the branches allowed, then got comfortable leaning against the large trunk. Praying that the spell didn't blow her up, she whispered an incantation she'd learned from Sederick in the Omicron Unit. Seconds later, she could hear the men's coarse banter clearly.

Even though it was still January, the men were starting to remove jackets and shirts. She had never appreciated shifter's high body temperature more.

"Yum," she sighed happily and reached into her tote bag. She grabbed a small bag of chips and her bottle of diet Mountain Dew, her favorite road trip snacks.

"Okay mate of mine, where are you?" She popped a Dorito in her mouth and watched the door to the Alpha estate carefully.

She was just finishing her snack when the door opened and the men she had met in the street walked out. From the direction of the road, another group of men walked up, the man in front was tall, very built, and had snow-white hair.

"How'd it go with the humans, Sascha?" she heard Aiden ask.

Sascha growled. "The bastard was screaming how he was going to sue, well, he was until I convinced him otherwise." He gave an evil grin. The men laughed.

"Thanks for the help." Aiden turned to the other men assembled. "We're doing obstacle course runs until we run out of daylight."

"Again?" the blond to his right complained.

Aiden raised an eyebrow. "Everyone is doing regular obstacle course runs except Colton; he will be doing them backwards." He grinned at the blond. "Different enough for you?"

Colton's mouth dropped. "Seriously?"

Aiden turned to the men. "Are you waiting for engraved invitations? Get moving!" he barked walking onto the course. The men scrambled to get started.

Colton stayed by Aiden's side. "No, really, Aiden, backwards?" he asked.

Aiden smiled. "Think of how proud Penny will be."

Colton scowled. "Dirty pool, old man."

"Quit being a baby, and get out there." Aiden pointed to the course.

"Dammit!" Colton growled and jogged backward toward the starting line.

A dark-haired man who exuded power shook his head. "One of these days he will get even," he warned.

Aiden shrugged. "Then I'll get him back, it's how our relationship has worked for centuries."

She watched as her mate approached the Unit Commander. "Where's Keelan?"

"In his workshop. He said he was working on a project for Meryn." Aiden answered keeping his eyes on the men.

Darian shrugged and pulled off his long-sleeve black tee. "Gods forbid we interrupt anything for Meryn." He walked over to the starting line.

Aiden nodded. "Exactly."

Amelia felt her mouth go dry. She scooted forward on her branch. Her mate was so close yet out of reach. In her childhood dreams, he had worn an expensive, cream silk robe accented in jewel tones that shimmered in the light. That was nothing compared to the sight of the large expanse of exposed golden skin and low slung, black combat pants.

When Darian shot away from the starting line, she clutched at her chest. He was poetry in motion. Sighing heavily, she went to lean back and miscalculated where she was on the tree limb. One moment she was fantasizing about her mate, and the next, she was falling backwards.

She let out a yelp as her descent was halted abruptly. The zipper of her jacket dug into her chin as she hung precariously from a jagged tree branch five feet off the ground. She tried to unzip her jacket, but couldn't get the zipper to budge.

Approaching footsteps caused her to look up. It was the white-haired unit leader. Frowning, he stopped in front of her.

She smiled brightly at him. "Hello."

He smiled back. "Hello. What are you doing?"

"Oh, you know, hanging out. You?"

"Doing drills with the guys." He sniffed the air. "Witch?"

"Sort of, I'm half witch."

"Can't you float yourself down?" he asked, pointing to the tree.

"So I'm terrible at being a witch. Can you help me down now?"

"That depends. Why are you hanging out, right outside the Alpha estate?" he asked.

"I'm looking for this blond guy. He's about seven feet tall with long, golden hair."

Sascha frowned. "Which one?"

She blinked. "How many are there?"

Sascha looked up at the sky, his lips moving as he silently counted. He looked at her and answered. "Well, six active fae unit members, plus trainees. Then there is Elder Vi'Ailean, and his personal guard at his estate. So I would say around twenty."

Amelia laughed at herself. "I guess that's true. I've spent too much time among humans lately. I should have remembered the unit warriors. I am looking for Darian, the one with lavender eyes."

"Why?" Sascha asked, suspiciously.

"He's my mate."

Sascha stared at her. She stared back. He blinked. She blinked.

Shaking his head, he lifted her off the branch. "You know, before Meryn, this would have seemed impossible to believe. But now? Not so much." He set her down on her feet.

"Thank you. My name is Amelia Ironwood." She thrust out her hand.

Smiling, he shook it firmly. "I know your brothers."

"They are hard to miss."

"True. Let's walk back to the estate and get this sorted." Sascha pointed to the obstacle course.

"Can't I just watch for a bit longer?" She batted her eyes at him.

Sascha sighed heavily. "Oh yeah, you'll fit right in. Come on Peeping Tomasina, time to face your mate."

Amelia pointed to her tree branch. "Can you get my bag?" Her colorful tote was propped against the tree trunk, right where she'd left it.

When Sascha bent his knees and jumped, Amelia felt her mouth drop open. He had jumped vertically fifteen feet, landed on her branch, snagged her tote bag, and hopped down. She remembered hopping up and down in her kitchen in her old apartment trying to knock down her last box of Pop Tarts. After twenty minutes and two kitchen utensils later, she ended up getting her step stool, which had been five feet away in the closet the whole time.

He handed her the tote bag, and she glared at him. "Tall people suck."

Sascha grinned. "You better hope they do." He turned and started walking back.

She was grumbling under her breath about her Pop Tarts when it hit her what he meant. Her mate was one of the tallest men on the obstacle course. She stopped in her tracks and stared. When he turned around and raised an eyebrow, she broke out into giggles.

"That was bad." She jogged to catch up to him when he started walking again.

"I don't have a mate to keep me in line yet."

They walked up to the training course, and Aiden's eyebrows shot up. "You? I thought you were heading to the city."

Amelia smiled. "I took a tiny little detour."

Behind them, they heard cursing. "What is she doing here?" Darian demanded, walking up to them.

"I've come to convince you we're mates," she said.

"Not gonna happen." Darian turned and went into the house.

Amelia looked at Sascha and Aiden. "That went very well, didn't it?"

"Are you sure he's your mate?" Aiden asked, looking unconvinced.

Amelia nodded. "I'm sure. I've been dreaming of him since I was six."

Aiden stared. "Wait. Since you were six? Not recently?"

"Nope." She shook her head.

Sascha looked at Aiden. "He never said anything."

Aiden frowned. "Go see if he'll talk to you. If you are his mate, then this is something he can't avoid."

"Wish me luck," Amelia said and turned toward the house.

"She'll need more than luck. Darian is a stubborn sonofabitch," she heard Sascha mutter.

I can be even more stubborn.

Amelia opened the door and poked her head inside. "Hellllloooo?" she called out in her best Tim Curry impersonation.

She heard footsteps on hardwood before Elizabeth, Meryn, and a man in butler attire appeared from a hallway.

"Oh, it's Bubbles," Meryn remarked, before popping something in her mouth.

Elizabeth turned to her. "Bubbles?"

Meryn shrugged. "She's bubbly."

Elizabeth just sighed and turned to her. "Looking for Darian?"

Amelia nodded. "He just came in."

Meryn laughed. "That's what that was? I thought one of the walls had caved in. He sure was loud."

The man in the crisply pressed butler outfit stepped forward and placed his right hand over his heart before bowing at the waist. "Welcome to the Alpha estate. My name is Ryuu; I am the squire here. If you would like, I can show you to Darian's room."

"That would be great."

"I am assuming you will be staying for the evening meal. May I inquire about your lodging arrangements for tonight?" Ryuu asked.

Amelia hesitated. She didn't know.

"She's staying here. She's Darian's mate," Meryn answered for her.

Amelia turned to the small woman and pulled her into a hug.

"She's doing it again," Meryn protested.

"And you're still alive," Elizabeth teased.

Amelia gave a final squeeze and stepped back. "Thank you for believing me." She felt better knowing that at least someone else believed her story.

"Of course, we believe you. Why would you lie about being his mate?" Meryn asked, reaching into a bag and popping a small piece of beef jerky into her mouth.

"Why would he?" Amelia asked softly.

Elizabeth pushed her toward the stairs and Ryuu stepped in beside her. Elizabeth winked. "Why don't you find out?"

"Remember, if he gets growly, hit him with the back of his toilet." Meryn called after them.

Amelia waved at her and kept walking up the stairs beside Ryuu. "Does that work?" she asked the squire softly.

"Evidently bear shifters are susceptible to toilet decks," Ryuu explained.

"Ahh." Amelia had a feeling there was more to the story, but was too nervous about confronting her mate to learn about bear shifters.

Ryuu stopped in front of large door. Amelia turned to him. "Could you take this?" she handed him her large tote bag and coat.

Smiling, he gently took them from her. "If it is permissible, I could arrange for someone to get your vehicle."

"That would be great. I left it parked on the side of the road leading up to the estate. The keys are in my coat pocket."

"Remember, we're just downstairs if you need us." He placed a comforting hand on her shoulder before he turned and walked back to the stairs.

Amelia took a deep breath. She didn't bother knocking and turned the handle. Finding it unlocked, she walked right in and stopped. Darian stood in the middle of the room, a towel wrapped low around his waist. He hadn't noticed she had opened the door yet, since he was using a smaller towel to dry his long hair. She felt electricity race through her body.

Bad hormones!

It was only after she tore her eyes away from her mate's mesmerizing form did she notice his room. She had to cut herself some slack. The only reason she hadn't seen the jungle in front of her was because her mate was practically naked.

Everywhere she turned, live plants bloomed and seemed to sway with their own magic. She felt like she had stepped into a dense forest instead of a bedroom. Vines climbed the walls and cradled a large four-poster bed. The furniture was made from the plants themselves, and she could have sworn she heard live birds. When she looked up, she was shocked to see a canopy of treetops and open sky beyond that. She couldn't even fathom the amount of magic it had taken to create this paradise.

She shook her head to break free of the magic that sustained his oasis and steeled herself to face her mate. She shut the door behind her. His head whipped in her direction, and he immediately scowled. "Get out."

"No. I want to know why you are denying that I am your mate." She crossed her arms over her chest.

"Because you're not." He shook out his hair.

"I am your mate. I dreamt of you."

He shook his head. "That's just a byproduct of the council spell gone wrong," he argued.

"I dreamt of you before they cast that spell. I first dreamt of you when I was six years old," she whispered softly.

He turned, and for a moment, he had gentle look on his face, exactly like her prince from her dream. Quickly, his features changed into a mocking expression, his lips turned up in a sneer. "I think I would remember dreaming of my own mate."

"Evidently not," she rebutted.

He turned his back to her. "Just go. Even if you are my mate, it's too late for me now." He walked over to the bed and picked up the pair of grey slacks that had been laid out. He glowered at her. "Do you mind?"

"No, I don't mind," she grinned at him. He shrugged and dropped both towels.

"Oh. My. Goddess," she gasped. She had grown up with three brothers and had spent more time at the training field at Storm Keep than was probably healthy for a small child. She had seen the unit warriors in various states of undress, but those brief stolen glimpses were nothing compared to the side view of her mate's sculpted back and firm ass. It felt like her heart would beat out of her chest as his manhood seemed to be playing a torturous version of peekaboo with her as he turned and lifted his legs getting dressed. His golden skin was flawless and was just begging to be touched. Just when she was about to throw dignity out the window and jump the man, she heard a masculine chuckle.

"What?" she demanded, her voice cracking.

"You amuse me; that's a rare thing nowadays. We could have some fun before you leave the city." He pulled on a royal blue sweater and turned to face her.

She stuck her nose in the air. "As if I'd cheapen our mating with a booty call."

His eyes hardened. "It wouldn't be a booty call. It would be a pity fuck."

She felt tears spring to her eyes. Clearing her mind, she stared at his chest. Slowly, she envisioned the mental trunk that housed her gift opening.

Her power caught her off guard and flared out of control. She quickly reined in her abilities and focused on her mate.

He frowned. "What are you doing?" He rubbed his hands up and down his arms.

She had always been able to feel other's emotions. She was the only one in her family who was an empath. Growing up, she had hated it, but now she was counting on it to show her what her mate was really feeling.

She was bombarded by the swirling depths of anger, but they weren't directed at her. He was filled with self-loathing. He hated himself for his words, for deliberately hurting her. But deeper down, past the anger, was an overwhelming, urgent sense of fear. He was drowning in an ocean of dread. He honestly felt that he was beyond redemption and would do anything to keep her away from him, even break her heart.

"You're afraid," she whispered, looking up at him.

His eyes widened in shock. "You're an empath?"

She nodded. "You're afraid of hurting me. You're afraid that our mating will destroy me." She took a step closer, and he took a step back.

"Stay away. I don't want to hurt you."

"You won't hurt me. The fact that you have a mate means that you're not lost."

"Men with mates have turned feral before."

"You're my prince, and you won't hurt me. I can prove it."

Darian froze. "What did you say?"

"I said, I can prove you won't hurt me." She walked up to him.

"No about being a prince..."

She didn't get to hear the rest of his question; she was already in motion. She brought her leg up and kneed him solidly in the groin. She smiled down at her mate as he hunched over taking gasping breaths.

"See, if you were really lost, you'd have hit me."

Darian tried to talk but words didn't come out. He shook his head. He tried again. "Do you know why I haven't hit you?" He choked the words out still bent over.

"Because I'm your mate," she said smugly.

He turned his face up and she stepped back. Maybe kneeing her seven-foot plus mate in the groin hadn't been such a good idea.

"No, because I can't move. When I can..." His eyes darkened.

"Shit." She took a step backward.

"Run," he growled.

She turned and bolted for the door. As she raced down the stairs, she screeched at the top of her lungs. "Ryuu! Aiden! Help!" She hit the foyer as Ryuu came racing from the back of the house as Aiden and the others came out of the front room. Behind her, she heard the heavy footsteps of her mate as he chased her.

Aiden stepped in front of her, a concerned expression on his face. "What happened?"

She scrambled up his back and held on for dear life.

Darian stalked toward them. "Give her to me."

Aiden stepped back and held up his hands, keeping Darian at bay.

"Maybe you should calm down first," Sascha suggested from the front room doorway.

"Calm down? She kneed me in the balls. I can still barely feel my legs, it's a miracle I'm standing!" he roared.

Aiden turned his head to her. "Why'd you do that?"

Amelia grimaced. "I was trying to convince him that he wouldn't hurt me."

Aiden's eyes widened. "So you kneed him?"

"Well, I figured if he didn't hurt me after I hit him in the balls, he'd know I'd be safe around him." She paused. "Not a good idea?" she asked.

Aiden shook his head. "No."

The three of them turned at the sound of laughter beside them. Sascha was leaning against the doorway, his arms wrapped around his stomach. He was laughing so hard tears were streaming down his cheeks. "Why is it that the Alpha females are crazy?"

Meryn shrugged. "She made sense to me."

Colton turned to Meryn. "You also set Aiden's car on fire when he ignored you."

Amelia looked at Meryn. "Sounds reasonable."

Meryn grinned. "I know, right?"

Her comment sent Sascha into more convulsed laughter. He straightened and wiped his eyes. "So Darian ended up with a witch version of Meryn."

Darian looked at her. "Witch?"

Amelia thought about it for a second. "Sort of."

Darian sighed and walked around Aiden to pluck her from his back. "How can you 'sort of' be a witch?" He set her down between them.

Amelia beamed up at him. "See, I knew you wouldn't hurt me."

He glared down at her, his expression unchanged.

She stuck her tongue out at him and crossed her eyes. He blinked in surprise. Smiling she answered. "I'm half a witch, my mother is human."

Aiden turned to her. "But Caiden, Kyran, and Tristan are full blooded witches."

Amelia nodded. "Our father evidently didn't want to wait to meet his mate before having children. He wanted to secure his bloodline, so he and another powerful witch got together and had my brothers. It worked out for the both of them to produce three strong male witches. Then about thirty-seven years ago, my father met my mother, they mated, and I was born."

Ryuu cleared his throat. "Since we're past the imminent attempted murder, maybe we should adjourn to the dining room for dinner?"

"Tacos! Tacos! Tacos!" Meryn high-fived a smaller blond man and another young man in a wheelchair.

Ryuu looked at Meryn with a hint of a smile. "I don't know why you're acting so surprised; you all but threatened my life this morning if I didn't make them."

Meryn rolled her eyes. "I didn't want tacos. Meryn two-point-oh wanted tacos."

Ryuu nodded, his expression serious. "Of course, that's a completely different story then."

Sascha pushed away from the wall. "I'll head out. Gamma is off duty tonight so Beta will be patrolling around the estate."

Aiden clapped a hand on Sascha's back and walked him to the door. "Thanks."

Sascha sniffed the air. "Tacos," he pouted, mournfully.

Aiden opened the door. "You'll live."

Sascha sighed dramatically and walked through the door. Aiden closed it behind him. He pinched the bridge of his nose. "Toddlers, every single one of them, toddlers."

Elizabeth stepped forward. "I don't know about all of you, but I'm starving. Come on, Amelia, you're in for a treat. Ryuu doesn't know how to make a bad meal." She turned and had only taken a few steps toward the dining room when she suddenly tripped and fell face first on the unforgiving marble.

"Beth!" The dark-haired man yelled and was at her side before Amelia could blink. Rheia moved away from her blond mate and helped the frantic man get Elizabeth upright.

"Sugar! I hate this damn floor!" Elizabeth exclaimed.

Rheia knelt in front of Elizabeth. Wincing, she sat back on her heels. "It's broken." Rheia reached up and placed her thumbs on either side of the bridge of Elizabeth's nose. "On three. One... two..." With a quick jerk, she snapped Elizabeth's nose back in place. A darling little girl next to Rheia winced in sympathy.

Gavriel handed her a handkerchief to stem the bleeding. Elizabeth held it to her nose. "I thought you said three!" Her voice was muffled and sounded nasal.

Rheia shrugged as her mate helped her to stand. "You should be used to this by now, Beth. I've had to snap your nose back in place three times since moving in. Thank God you're a shifter; otherwise, you'd be falling apart by now." She took the little girl's hand.

The dark-haired man scooped Elizabeth up, his face a mask of worry. She patted at his chest. "I'm fine now."

He shook his head. "I'm taking you upstairs to lie down."

"Like hell! It's taco night. Dining room, please." Elizabeth pointed down the hall.

Amelia looked up at Darian. "So, this happens often?"

Darian grimaced. "Unfortunately. Beth has a tendency to almost die every week. She keeps us on our toes." He looked down, laughing for a moment. Then it was as if he remembered he had to keep his distance. He stepped away from her and walked toward the dining room.

Amelia watched him as he walked away. Knowing what he felt didn't change anything. How could she convince him that they were meant to be together?

An arm looped around her elbow. She looked to her left, Meryn stood beside her. "Come on, Bubbles, no matter what is wrong with the world, it's nothing taco night can't fix."

Amelia couldn't help but smile. Meryn might be prickly and skittish, but she had a good heart. Even though she wasn't comfortable being around new people, Meryn did what she could to make her feel better.

"Thanks Meryn, I think I needed that," Amelia admitted as they started walking.

"Any time, Bubbles," Meryn replied before turning to her. "So, what do you know about explosives?"

"Meryn!" Aiden growled behind them.

Amelia couldn't help it; she began to giggle. Meryn was too cute!

CHAPTER THREE

As luck would have it, Ryuu had left an empty seat for her next to Darian. Keelan sat on her other side and gave her winks of encouragement.

Rheia turned to her. "Amelia, this is my mate, Colton Albright, and this is my daughter, Penny Carmichael." The tiny child waved at her, a bright smile on her face. She waved back. Rheia continued. "Elizabeth's mate is Gavriel Ambrosios, and the auburn-haired man to your right is Keelan Ashwood. Across from you are Jaxon Darrow and Noah Caraway; they are studying computer science with Meryn to better support the different units."

"Who's the sprite?" Amelia asked pointing to Meryn's shoulder.

Rheia turned to her. "You can see him?"

Everyone turned to Meryn. The tiny sprite on her shoulder waved to her and turned the pendant on his necklace.

"Hey, Felix," Colton said.

Amelia turned to Colton. "You can see him now?"

"Yes. We gave him that pendant so he could make himself visible to us, although most of the time, he likes to stay invisible. He's really bonded with Meryn, so much so, he left his colony at the fae elder's estate," he explained.

Felix waved at everyone and turned to her. "My name is Felix Skysong. Pleased to meet you." When he went to reach for the pendant again, Elizabeth held up a hand.

"Felix, actually, could you answer a question for me?"

Felix nodded shyly.

Beth smiled. "When Penny and the Carmichaels were attacked, you were able to create a shield to protect them, but when Meryn told me about her attack, she said you left to go get help. Why didn't you create a shield then?"

Felix pointed to his wrist.

"Time?" Elizabeth asked.

He nodded.

"What about time?" She asked looking confused.

Felix kept edging into Meryn's hair. He didn't look like he wanted to be the center of attention.

Amelia spoke up. "I think I get it. At home, the sprites can do their versions of spells, but since they are so small, there is a limit to what they can do. In Penny's attack, was help nearby or on the way?"

"Yes, the Gamma Unit was assigned to the house. They arrived in under a minute," Aiden explained.

"In Meryn's case, was anyone nearby that could help?" Amelia looked around the table. Everyone was shaking their heads. "There's your answer; he could have shielded Meryn for a couple minutes, but then what? He would have ended up exhausted, and the attacker would have still been there. Leaving to go get assistance was the only way he could help."

Beth smiled gently at Felix. "Thank you for answering, I was just curious since I don't know much about your people. I know you did everything you could to help. You're an amazing member of this family."

Felix turned ten shades of red before he activated his pendant and hid in Meryn's hair.

"Have you always been able to see sprites?" Rheia asked.

Amelia nodded. "When I realized my mate was over seven feet tall and blond, I put two and two together and figured out he was fae. I would visit the fae council member at Storm Keep regularly. He said my ability to see sprites made sense considering I was going to be mated to a fae." Amelia stared at the side of Darian's head. He still ignored her. She stuck out her tongue at him and Keelan laughed.

Elizabeth continued the introductions. "I am creating a census program for the council so we can better track our citizens. Rheia is a doctor and works with Aiden's brother, Adam, in what started off as the warrior clinic but has grown to support all of Lycaonia. Meryn is working on integrating updated technology throughout the city, not only to help the citizens but also to provide surveillance to help keep the city secure."

Amelia was about to reply when Ryuu walked out of the kitchen rolling a mobile taco station. Her mouth began to water as the smell of tacos and refried beans hit her nose. "Gods! That smells incredible!"

Rheia kissed Penny on the forehead. "Okay pumpkin, bedtime."

Penny hugged and kissed everyone at the table. When she got to Amelia, she mimicked what Rheia had done to her and kissed her on the forehead.

"Thank you, Penny." Amelia said giving the child a hug.

Penny gave her a thumbs up and walked out of the dining room.

Amelia turned to Rheia. "She puts herself to bed?"

Rheia nodded with pride in her eyes. "She said she had to hurry up and be a big girl so she can help me when her baby brother or sister is born. She's taking her role as big sister very seriously. Besides, she knows we give her a kiss every night when we go to bed, so she's happy."

"When does she eat?"

"Since we don't eat dinner until eight p.m. she eats earlier so it doesn't affect her bedtime. Colton and I will grab a snack and sit down with her in the kitchen while she eats her dinner. She loves getting our undivided attention. We're trying to indulge her as much as possible before the baby arrives," Rheia explained.

"You're pregnant, too! Congratulations!"

"Thank you. I have to say, it happened quicker than I thought," Rheia admitted.

"We had a lot of practice," Colton teased. Rheia turned pink as everyone laughed.

Meryn was served first and she immediately began to inhale her food. When Ryuu started to place something different on her plate, she swallowed, quickly frowning. "Ryuu, what the hell are these?" Meryn asked pointing to the newest addition as Ryuu continued to place dark green crispy leaves on her plate.

"Kale chips *denka*, they are high in iron."

"I hate kale." She pushed the chips to the far side of her plate.

"Try them, I made them special." He winked at her.

Meryn chose the smallest one, and with her nose scrunched up, she popped it into her mouth and began to chew. A delighted expression crossed her face. "They're good! More please!" She held up her plate.

Amelia watched in wonder as Ryuu filled half of Meryn's plate with kale. "Okay, I have to ask. Are they really good?"

Meryn nodded. "They taste like salt and vinegar. They're perfect!"

"That sounds heavenly. I love salt and vinegar."

"Me too!" Meryn agreed.

Ryuu smiled. "I hear you also have the same taste in ice cream."

Amelia turned to him. "Yes, it's really cool to have found someone else who likes bubble gum ice cream."

Ryuu nodded his agreement and made his way around the table. As Amelia waited to be served, she thought of something. "Does Alpha unit have a squire because y'all are Alpha?" she asked.

Aiden shook his head. "No, Ryuu serves Meryn. He was a gift from my mother for the day that Meryn will take over as Lady McKenzie."

"Lady McKenzie, huh? Doesn't seem to fit." She eyed Meryn.

Elizabeth sighed. "We're working on it."

"Elizabeth, are you doing a census for just Lycaonia or all of the pillar cities?"

"All of the pillar cities and please, call me Beth, Elizabeth is so formal."

"I call her Bunny." Meryn said between bites of her taco.

Beth turned to Amelia, a pained expression on her face. "Once you get a nickname, you have it for life."

"So, I guess I'm Bubbles then." Amelia smiled around the table.

Keelan laughed. "It suits your personality."

Meryn frowned. "The guys call me Menace."

Keelan nodded. "And that suits your personality."

Beth and Rheia laughed. Meryn scowled.

Gavriel ruffled Meryn's hair. "Admit it, it fits."

Meryn ducked away from his hand smiling. "Only a little bit."

Jaxon took a sip of his water and turned to her. "So Amelia, what do you do?"

"I'm a cosmetologist," she announced proudly.

The men looked around confused expressions on their faces.

"She does hair and makeup." Rheia explained.

Beth clapped her hands together excitedly. "I could do with a makeover! I've been wearing the same look for decades."

Meryn bounced in her chair. "Could you show me how to look sexy? I'm tired of everyone saying how cute I look. I want to be a femme fatale."

Aiden rolled his eyes. "You're already a femme fatale."

Meryn shook her head. "No, I'm not."

Gavriel cleared his throat. "By definition, a femme fatale is a beautiful woman who ultimately brings disaster to the man she is involved with. I think you qualify."

Meryn pouted and pushed her kale chips around her plate. "Y'all know what I meant."

Amelia jumped to her defense. "Don't worry Meryn. I have just the makeup tutorial for you. It will show you how to get the perfect smokey eye," she promised.

Meryn looked up, excitement back on her face. "Really?"

"Yup! We can break out my makeup case tomorrow. You can try any look you want."

Meryn turned to Aiden. "Ha ha! Be prepared to be wowed by my sexiness."

Aiden's face softened as he leaned over to kiss the tip of Meryn's nose. "You can wow me anytime, baby."

Amelia smiled at the teddy bear of a Unit Commander. If her brothers could see him now.

Ryuu stopped behind her. "How many and what type of taco for you *itoko-sama*?"

Amelia frowned up at him. What did he call her?

He held up the platter of tacos. Hurriedly, she looked over her choices. "One beef and one chicken please."

Carefully, he placed them on her plate. With a bow, he moved on to her mate. She opened up the shells and added cheese, sour cream and jalapeños. When she saw that someone had put a jar of banana peppers on the table she helped herself.

"Gods, they are alike," Aiden said looking worried.

Meryn was giving her a thumbs up and pointed to her own tacos.

Amelia looked around the table; everyone was staring at her choices. "Don't judge. They go perfectly together."

Rheia elbowed Colton. "You have no room to talk, sandwich master."

"So, is Storm Keep like Hogwarts?" Meryn asked.

Beside her, Keelan began to choke on his taco. Laughing, she pounded on his back. She turned back to Meryn. "Actually, kinda. The city of Storm Keep is named for the castle that was built by the only royal family we witches have ever had, the Stormharts. The different units live in estates like this one outside of city limits and maintain a perimeter around the city. There is a tall outer wall that surrounds the city proper, which is connected by four stone towers located at each directional point. The poorer section of the city is located close to the castle walls; it's the cheapest place to live since they are closest to danger. If we were ever attacked, that section of the city would be the first to fall. After that, in the event of an attack, everyone falls back behind the Inner City wall. The Inner city is where the middle class and merchants live. They have the best eateries and shops on the west coast. The different types of magic you can buy there is nothing short of awe-inspiring. Moving toward the center of the city, you reach Storm Keep itself. The castle is huge and is home to the ruling houses, our council members, and the Academy of Magic."

"Hogwarts," Meryn whispered, entranced.

Keelan shook his head smiling. "My brother, Kendrick, works in the archives located in the lower levels of Storm Keep."

Amelia turned in her chair to face him. "You look just like your brother, only he's... older and grouchier."

Keelan laughed out loud. "He is a bit grouchy. He always said it was because he was forced to work with idiots all day." He smiled at her. "I was surprised you knew my brother. He never mentioned becoming an *Athair.*"

Amelia frowned. "When was the last time you were home?"

He shrugged. "Maybe forty years ago, every once in a while we talk on the phone."

"Keelan!" Meryn exclaimed.

He blushed. "My brother and I had a disagreement before I left, so I haven't really felt in a hurry to visit. He can be very domineering."

Amelia shook her head. "The only time I ever saw him smile was when he said your name. You should visit."

Keelan looked pleasantly surprised. "Really?"

"Of course," Aiden interjected. "No matter how mad I get at Ben, he's still my baby brother."

"I can't wait to tease him tomorrow." Colton rubbed his hands together. The men laughed.

As everyone continued eating dinner, Amelia thought about the man beside her. Darian hadn't said a word throughout the meal. He ate with a cardboard smile on his face. She desperately wanted what she observed with the other couples. Someone to laugh with, to comfort, a lover and a friend.

"*Itoko-sama?*" Ryuu said, getting her attention.

"Yes?" She looked up at the squire.

"I just wanted to let you know that I have taken the liberty of carrying your luggage to the guest suite upstairs." Ryuu bowed.

"Thank you, Ryuu."

Darian turned to her. "You can't stay here," he said harshly.

Aiden stood, drawing all eyes to him. "Darian, I need to know. Is she or isn't she?"

Darian turned his head away from her to stare at the opposite wall.

"Well?" Aiden demanded.

"Yes," Darian said, clenching his jaw.

"Then you need to take care of your mate." Aiden crossed his arms.

"That's what I'm trying to do!" Darian bellowed, shocking everyone.

Aiden's eyes narrowed. "Is there something you want to tell me?"

Darian stood, knocking his chair back. He squared his shoulders, facing his commander. "I don't need a mate."

Aiden raised an eyebrow and jerked his head toward Meryn. "I remember thinking the exact same thing. Sometimes you have to accept the gifts Fate gives to you."

Keelan glared at Darian before turning to her. "I'll show you up to your room, it's right next to Darian."

Darian stared blank faced at Keelan. "Leave it be, Keelan," he warned.

Keelan smiled wide. "No, don't wanna," he said in a singsong child-like manner.

Darian looked down at her. "Do what you want." He turned away from the table and walked out the door.

"Will he be okay?" Amelia asked nervously.

Gavriel nodded. "We all went through something similar upon finding our mates. We will talk to him later. This is your home now."

His words sank in. "Good Gods! I live here now. How will I get my makeup orders?" She tried to keep the conversation light. She hated it when everyone worried or got upset. Living her life as an empath made her a human barometer for emotion, the happier people were around her the less anxious she was.

Meryn waved a taco at her. "Don't worry about deliveries. All the mail for Lycaonia goes to an outside post office box. Assigned teams go and collect the mail every day and bring it into the city where it is sorted into post office boxes here. Ryuu gets ours for us. It's how I get the Nerd Block subscription boxes Aiden got me for Christmas."

Amelia heaved a huge sigh of relief. "Thank the Gods; I was close to calling this whole mating thing off if I couldn't get my makeup."

Meryn nodded. "I could see that impacting life. I'd die without my geek stuff, especially since I'm trying to decorate the nursery with cool gear instead of typical baby stuff. Do you know how much baby boy stuff is decorated with bears? It would just be weird."

"You mean like giving little girls human like dolls?" Rheia asked sardonically.

Meryn paused and laughed. "I guess that's kinda the same, I never thought of it like that."

"What are you decorating in?" Amelia asked.

"It's going to be a *Star Wars*, *Doctor Who* mashup."

"That sounds cool."

"What if you have a girl?" Rheia asked.

Meryn frowned. "It would be a *Star Wars / Doctor Who* mashup, why?"

Beth carefully bit into a taco, careful not to get anything on her fingers. "Don't try to make sense of it, Rheia, it's Meryn."

"Girls can like *Star Wars* and *Doctor Who*," Amelia argued.

Beth nodded. "Of course they can, but I don't think a two-month-old will be able to operate the interactive Death Star she ordered."

Amelia laughed. "That is awesome."

"Don't encourage her," Beth laughed.

Meryn popped another kale chip into her mouth. "Are you okay? I mean about Darian."

Amelia dug into her dinner. "He won't be able to say no forever. I'm just as stubborn as he is."

"Maybe we should meet tomorrow and come up with a plan of attack," Meryn suggested.

Amelia nodded. "Good idea."

The men exchanged concerned looks.

Beth buried her face in her hands. "Two of them; there's two."

Gavriel rubbed her back. "There, there dear."

Amelia looked over at Meryn and winked, and Meryn winked back.

"Gods help us all," Aiden muttered biting into his ninth taco.

"Here you go," Keelan said, indicating the room next to Darian's. Now that she was up here, it hurt knowing that they would be in separate rooms, without saying so much as 'goodnight' to each other. Keelan opened the door and showed her around the two-room suite.

"Did you need help with the suitcases?" he asked, pointing to the large, silver rolling case.

Amelia laughed. "That's my makeup."

Keelan blinked. "And?"

"Just makeup."

"Wow. You promised Meryn and Beth makeovers tomorrow; would you like me to float this down for you and put it in Aiden's office?"

"Why Aiden's office?" she asked confused.

Keelan laughed. "It's actually Meryn and Beth's office, but Aiden would be in a foul mood for hours whenever we called it that, so we just call it Aiden's office to keep everyone happy."

"That would be great. I've never really mastered floating."

"What is your gift?" Keelan asked, sitting on the bed.

"Well, besides the generic stuff like candle lighting and fire balls, I'm an empath. I can use earth magic, though I haven't used that since I was a kid. I almost triggered a major earthquake when I was two. Caiden had to bind my powers since we lived close to a fault line." She sat next to him on the bed.

"Two powers, that's impressive. I have two as well. Premonition and air magic. I can float things or harden the air to create a shield. My brother, Kendrick, has four," he said proudly.

"You have the same powers as my eldest brother, Caiden. I knew Kendrick was powerful, but had no idea he had mastered four. I don't think anyone back home does either." Amelia was shocked. Even the elders usually had only mastered three.

"The guys here know and now you. He's very secretive about his powers. He said all he wants to do is record our history and read the archives."

"We need more men like your brother. Council politics are obnoxious. To use Meryn's Hogwarts analogy, it's like all the elders do is stand around whipping out their wands, trying to see who's the most powerful." Amelia had seen politics at work back home every time Caiden tried to get something for the unit warriors. Their first question was always how many prestigious bloodlines served in the units.

"So that hasn't changed, huh? The politics was one of the reasons I left Storm Keep. I couldn't live there anymore and keep my mouth shut. Kendrick is fine. He can just bury his head in some dusty manuscripts from a thousand years ago about the disadvantages of using water magic in an arid climate, but when it comes to people living in the here and now, he just doesn't care."

"You said you got into a disagreement with Kendrick before you left, what was it about?"

Amelia turned and sat crossed-legged in front of him.

Keelan leaned back on his hands. "He didn't want me to join Alpha."

"You mean he didn't want you to be a unit warrior?"

He shook his head. "No, he didn't want me to join Alpha. He said he had a dream and that I would die as an Alpha Unit warrior, but here I am nearly two hundred years later, alive and kicking."

Amelia nodded enthusiastically. "Tell me about it! My brother Caiden practically ordered me to come back to Storm Keep because he saw me quote fall into darkness unquote."

Keelan laughed. "Premonitions are so vague, they might as well be useless. Well, for the most part they're vague." His voice got quiet and his expression became serious.

"What is it, Keelan?"

"I'll have to remember to thank Fate later for bringing you here, not just for Darian who has been like a brother, but for me as well."

Amelia raised a brow.

He smiled softly. "No, not like that. You're a witch who isn't a unit warrior. You've lived in Storm Keep and know how it can be there. Hell, you even know my brother. You'd understand..."

"Understand what?"

"The frustration our magic can cause."

"I take it your frustration is around premonitions?" She leaned forward and rested her elbows on her knees.

Keelan nodded, and his eyes became unfocused. "I've been having the same nightmare every night, and every night, I try to change what happens in different ways, but nothing helps. I just wish that whatever or whoever is trying to send me a message would just come out and say it."

"You mean instead of 'fall into darkness', 'avoid assholes running stop signs'?" she asked.

Keelan laughed, his eyes coming back into focus. "Exactly! I knew you'd understand."

"All we can do is what we can, when we can. We'll face whatever it is to come, and if we get stuck, we can always call our brothers." She winked at him.

Keelan stood and stretched. "You know what? You're right." He turned to leave and paused. He turned back to her. "Darian really does care, you know?"

"I do know. Empath, remember?" She tapped her temple.

He winced. "Gods, that has to be awful. Remind me to kick his ass later."

"It wouldn't be so bad if we'd just met, but I've been dreaming of him my whole life. What if he just doesn't want me?" That was her biggest fear, that she wouldn't be enough to make him want to live, that her shortcomings would destroy his soul.

"Don't think like that. When I first moved in, I thought he was the noblest man I had ever met. You think Gavriel is courtly? Darian outshone him the way the sun outshines the moon. But over the years, it's like he just got tired. Nevertheless, I refuse to believe that who he is at his very core has changed. In his own way, he is protecting you. It's so ingrained in him to keep you safe that he won't risk you, not in any way, not even to save himself."

"I won't lose him, Keelan."

"We won't. I'll do anything I can to help. It's my hope that we can be friends as well."

She got up off the bed and gave him a hug. "I think we already are."

Blushing, he smiled. "Get some rest. I have a feeling tomorrow is going to be a long day."

"Premonition?" she joked as he walked toward the door.

He turned around and winced. "Darian is denying his mate, Meryn has vowed to help and I have a feeling you'd encourage her antics. Tomorrow is going to be a long day," he repeated. He walked over, grabbed her makeup case by the handle, and wheeled it toward the door. He turned and gave a wave.

Amelia laughed as he walked out of the room, shutting the door behind him. She looked at her one lone suitcase and wrangled it up into the chair. Unzipping it, she pulled out her toiletry bag and her nightshirt and headed to the bathroom. She got undressed, breathing a sigh of relief when she removed her bra. She slipped on her nightshirt and pulled her long brown curls back in a hair tie. Reaching into her toiletry bag for her face wash and moisturizer, she started her nightly routine.

When she was done, she folded up her jeans and shirt and walked back into the bedroom. She opened her suitcase and dropped her clothes inside. Staring at her wardrobe, she sighed. All her tops were either black or white. Her bottoms were either black slacks or jeans. Normally, she didn't mind her monochromatic look, thinking it was edgy, but she didn't want her new friends to think she was wearing the same thing over and over again. She definitely needed to go shopping soon. She looked around the room and found her tote bag on the dresser. She fished around the large bag until she found her phone.

She got comfortable on the bed and leaned back on a stack of fluffy pillows. She knew the conversation she was about to have would be hard, but it had to be done. She opened the phone and pressed the speed dial number for Caiden. He answered on the first ring.

"What's happened? Are you hurt? Are you dead?" he demanded.

"Dead? Yes, I'm calling on my ghostly iPhone, you idiot." She rolled her eyes.

"Don't roll your eyes at me, young lady. You never call this late, what's happened?"

How does he always know when I do that?

"Well, you know how I said I would be leaving first thing in the morning?"

"Yes?"

"Yeah, that's not happening."

"Why? Do you have a flat? Is it car trouble? Are you being held hostage?"

"How do you go from flat tire to hostage situation?"

"Well?" he demanded, ignoring her perfectly logical question.

"I found my mate! Isn't that exciting?" She held her breath and mentally counted down.

Three...two...one...

"What!? That sonofabitch! Waiting until we weren't around to swoop in and steal my baby girl!" He called out to their brothers, "Kyran! Tristan! Get Packed! We're going to Lycaonia to beat some fae bastard's ass and take back our baby girl!"

"What!?" she heard Kyran shout.

"Motherfucker!" Tristan yelled.

Amelia stared up at the ceiling. Yeah, they wouldn't complicate matters at all.

"Freeze!" she barked into the phone. A second later, there was silence. "Listen, I'm a grown woman; please don't interfere."

"You're barely grown and only because you're half human. I thought we agreed you wouldn't mate until you were two hundred," Caiden argued.

"No! *You* told me I couldn't mate until I was two hundred. I have met him. He's my mate. Get over it."

"Shifty, blond bastard. I bet he makes shoes or something," Caiden grumbled.

Amelia pinched the bridge of her nose. "Caiden!"

"Yes?"

"Where am I?"

"Lycaonia."

"And..." She waited to see if he would put two and two together.

"Oh Gods! You're moving!" he practically wailed.

"Can she do that?" Kyran demanded.

Fuck my life right now!

"Lycaonia is the city of..."

"Shifters," Tristan answered.

"Exactly!" she exclaimed. "What type of fae live in a shifter city?"

Silence.

Silence.

"Do you have the roster?" she heard Caiden ask.

"Right here," Tristan shouted. "Okay, so her fae bastard mate could be Larik Li'Mileren from Beta, Barak Ri'Anvial from Delta, Alanis Vi'Kilernan from Epsilon, Sulis Ri'Orthames from Zeta, Gods, if that is her mate, then he isn't getting the two hundred bucks I owe him."

"Tristan!" Caiden barked.

"Right. All that's left are the brothers Darian Vi'Alina or Oron Vi'Eirson."

Amelia sat up straight. "Wait, how can they be brothers if they have different last names?"

"Gods, it's one of those two surly assholes," Kyran groaned.

"Which one is it, baby girl?" Caiden asked.

"How are they brothers?" she repeated.

"From what I've heard, they were raised by the same foster parents. Now, which one?"

"Darian."

She heard them swearing softly.

"Is he treating you right?" Caiden finally asked.

She felt her eyes fill with tears. She wanted to cry and tell him it wasn't fair, that all her life she had wanted her mate and now he was denying her. She wanted her big brother to fix it, like he always did, but she knew he couldn't fix this. She smiled through her tears.

"He's been so unpredictable. He looks exactly like I dreamt him." Technically her words weren't a lie, but her heart still felt heavy.

"Okay, baby girl, we'll stay out of it. We don't really want to be around when you're freshly mated; that would be weird. But if you need us for anything—and I do mean anything—you call, day or night."

"I promise." She tried to keep her voice upbeat and cheery.

"Also, don't hesitate to go to Aiden. He's a good guy. He'll help you any way we would," Caiden said.

"If the need arises, I will. Now, if you'll excuse me, I'm heading to bed. Remember, I'm three hours ahead of you now."

"We'll visit soon," Kyran called out.

"Miss you guys already." This time she couldn't keep the tears from falling down her cheeks.

"We miss you, too, baby girl. Now get some sleep and give that mate of yours hell," he said gruffly. She knew he was fighting his own emotions.

"Night, night, CaiKryTri," she said, using the abbreviated nickname she had for the three of them.

"Night, night, doodlebutt," Tristan said, making her smile.

She ended the call, curled up on her side, and hugged the phone to her chest. After a few minutes of sniffling, she realized the room had gotten cold so she decided to turn out the light and get under the covers. Before she knew it, she was asleep.

CHAPTER FOUR

In her dreams, Darian was no longer her prince. She stared at his back as he walked away from her. She chased him down a long, narrow corridor. Menacing, bony arms reached out from the walls to grab her. She had to get to him before he went through the door at the end of the hallway. Once he went through that door, she knew she would never see him again, but no matter how fast she ran, she couldn't catch up. She felt a new wave of panic overtake her when he reached the door and turned the handle. When the door swung open, there was nothing but an unending, black abyss. He spread his arms wide and jumped, plunging into darkness where there was no light to save either of them. She ran to the open doorway and looked down; he was quickly falling away from her. When she jumped after him, he welcomed her with open arms, an evil grin on his lips.

Amelia woke with a start; Darian's sinister smile was burned into her mind. She prayed that what she saw wasn't a warning for something horrible to come. The image of the long hallway hit a little too close to home when it came to her mate's current mental state. She turned over and stared at the ceiling for a moment before reaching for her phone. It was after noon! She had slept the morning away, and despite the extra hours of sleep, her head felt like it was packed with cotton. Groaning, she got out of bed and headed to the bathroom. Compared to Darian's atrium, her room felt empty and dead. It had the warmth of a hotel room, despite the quality of the furniture and linens. She wondered what it felt like to go to sleep listening to the magic of the wind blowing through the trees and the birds singing you to sleep each night. She shook her head. What she needed was a nice, hot shower. She turned the water on to the hottest setting then backed it off a fraction. In no time, the room was filling with steam. She pulled off her nightshirt and stepped into the shower. Her travel size shampoo only served as a reminder that, for all intents and purposes, she was in limbo. Without being claimed, could she really call this place home?

She finished washing and stepped out. She dried off as fast as she could and wrapped her hair up in a towel. She would wait until it was almost dry before working a sculpting cream through her hair. Even during the coldest winters, she never blow-dried her curls; if she did, the natural curls she inherited from her mother would end up in a pouffy mess. More than once, when she was growing up she had longed for straight hair like her brothers.

Standing at the bathroom counter, she opened her everyday makeup bag. She went through her familiar routine of applying her favorite foundations and eyeshadows. Each action brought order to the chaos she was

feeling. When she was done, she was happy
with the soft, feminine look she had created. She
unwrapped her hair from the towel and worked
her favorite hair cream through her long curls.
She bent over and shook out her hair at the roots
to give it volume. Standing, she blew a kiss to
herself in the mirror. She hung up the towel and
stepped into the room. Coming from a heated,
steamy bathroom, her bedroom felt cold.
Goosebumps covered her from head to toe as
she raced naked over to her suitcase and pulled
out a haphazard outfit. Black knee high socks,
skinny jeans, black tank top, and a zippered
black hoodie sweater completed her outfit.
Smiling, she picked out her favorite ruby red bra
and panty set. Surprisingly, her underthings
were as colorful as the rainbow. Only her outer
clothes seemed to stay black and white.

Once dressed, she tucked her phone into her
back pocket, grabbed her coat from the chair,
and went downstairs. She walked through the
foyer and down the hallway to the empty dining
room. Without everyone around the table, the
room seemed much bigger than the night before.
She heard sounds from the kitchen and followed
the voices. She found Rheia and Ryuu at the
kitchen table sipping on tea.

Ryuu stood, smiling. "I'm happy to see that
not everyone in this house rises with the sun.
Please, join us." He pointed to an empty kitchen
chair.

Amelia hung her coat on the back of the
chair and sat down. Ryuu glided over to the
cabinet and pulled down another cup and saucer.
He placed them in front of her and sat down

again. Rheia poured her a cup of what looked and smelled like jasmine green tea.

"The aroma is lovely." Amelia added five teaspoons of sugar and stirred lightly.

"I don't know how you or Meryn have any teeth left. You both drink your sugar with a bit of tea." Rheia shook her head.

"I need the sugar this morning. I usually rise with the sun, as Ryuu put it, but woke up this morning after a nightmare feeling completely out of sorts," she confessed.

"Is there anything we can do to help?" Ryuu asked.

Amelia shook her head. "It's something I need to work out. The tea is helping, I feel calmer already."

Smiling, Ryuu and Rheia shared a look.

Amelia frowned. "What?"

Rheia apologized quickly. "I'm sorry. Let me explain. This is my mother's tea service. Whenever I needed a pick-me-up, she would use this set, and it seemed like my worries would just float away."

"Is it okay for me to use?" Amelia asked, worried she had blundered in where she didn't belong.

Rheia laughed. "Of course, it's okay. In fact, maybe my mother is looking out for the both of us this morning."

"Why do you need its calming effects?" Amelia asked.

"I'm worried about having this baby; it's my first. Like Meryn, I'm human having a shifter baby. I have heard that sometimes human women can have issues delivering." Rheia sat back in her chair.

Amelia frowned. She was confused. She could have sworn she met Rheia's daughter the night before. "But Penny..."

"Penny is my adopted daughter. Even though I didn't give birth to her, she couldn't be more like me if we tried. So, even though I'm already a mother, I've never actually experienced giving birth. I bet it's much different being the one pushing than telling someone to push."

"I think you'll be fine, at least you know what to expect. You're not going into it wide eyed with expectations of a twenty minute delivery before holding your perfect baby, hair and makeup still looking great."

"You're right, but I think it's a double-edged sword. I also know everything that can go wrong." Rheia stared into her cup, a frown pulling her eyebrows together in worry.

Amelia knew no matter what she said, Rheia would continue to fret until her baby was safe in her arms, so she decided to change the subject to something happier.

"So are you decorating in *Star Wars* and *Doctor Who*, too?" Amelia joked.

Rheia's face brightened and she laughed. "God, no. Colton and I decided on a baby wolf theme. Evidently, it's very popular here in Lycaonia at the moment due to a suggestion Meryn made to another pregnant woman a couple months ago. A lot of shops in the city started creating different shifter-themed items. We chose wolf, not only because my baby will be half wolf shifter, but we're also including Penny in the decorations. The baby's nursery will have a mural of Colton and Penny in their shifted forms painted on one of the walls."

"That sounds perfect! My brothers are the ones that raised me, so they did the decorating when it came to my own nursery. Since they couldn't decide on a single theme, they decided that they would each decorate one wall, leaving the wall with the door blank to keep things even." She took a sip of her tea and continued. "Caiden chose dragons since he had mastered the element of air, but they weren't cute cartoon dragons; they were realistic ones with long fangs and bodies."

"Oh no!" Rheia covered mouth to hide her smile.

Amelia held up her hand. "It gets better. Kyran had mastered water so he had sharks painted on his wall. Finally, Tristan chose an erupting volcano for his wall, since he had mastered fire."

By this time, Rheia had given in to her giggles, and even Ryuu was smiling.

"I wasn't able to redecorate that room until I was thirteen! But on the bright side, not much scares me as an adult." She shrugged.

"Where were your parents?" Ryuu asked.

"After I was born, my mother realized she wasn't the maternal type. She wanted to be a free spirit, untethered by earthly shackles." Amelia made air quotes around free spirit and earthly shackles.

"Then why have a child?" Rheia asked.

"Because my father wanted another one. When I was born, he handed me off to Caiden, and he and my mother left on a free love adventure. My nature loving, bell bottoms-wearing mother turned my high-born, ruling-house father into a nomadic hippie, although I think he fakes it because he loves her. He still makes them stay in five star hotels after their 'sojourns' into the woods."

"So Lady Ironwood is a free spirit?" Ryuu asked, rotating his mug.

Amelia shook her head. "My mother is also quite the feminist, she kept her maiden name much to the utter shock and dismay of my father, so it's not Lady Ironwood; it's Lady Camden."

"She sounds fascinating." Rheia said, setting her cup down.

"Indeed," Ryuu murmured.

"She's something else, I'll tell you that. I don't know how many times I thanked the Goddess that my brothers raised me, nightmare walls and all. During one of her visits, my mother took me on a nature hike. She made me sit crossed-legged in the woods for hours, trying to hear the voices of the spirits. I couldn't have been more than four or five at the time. When Caiden found us, I was hungry, crying, and covered in mosquito bites." Amelia shuddered thinking of how her life might have been if her parents had stayed home all the time to raise her.

"It sounds like you're very close to your brothers," Rheia commented, a knowing look in her eye.

"You have brothers, too?"

"Yes, but like Penny, not by birth. We chose each other, kinda like the family we have now."

Amelia looked around, remembering the empty dining room. It was eerily quiet considering how many people lived there. "Where is everyone?"

Rheia stood and stretched. "Penny is in the front room being homeschooled by her grandmother. Beth is with Meryn, Jaxon, and Noah in Aiden's office, and the boys are doing drills as usual, though after Meryn's comment last night about explosives, I heard Aiden wants to do an inventory of the armory."

Amelia brightened. "We have an armory?"

Rheia shook her head. "No. Just...no."

"Do they have grenades?"

Ryuu nodded. "Oh, yes; according to *denka,* they explode when you pull the pin, not when they land after you throw them."

Amelia nodded. "Good to know."

"Okay, on that note, I'm heading back to the clinic. Be good and stay away from the armory." Rheia wagged a finger at her, waved goodbye and left.

Amelia quickly drained her cup before standing. She pulled on her coat. "I'm going to go see what Darian is doing."

Ryuu stood, his face serious. "Be careful *itoko-sama*; his light is all but faded."

"I know; it's why I'm trying so hard."

Ryuu walked over to the counter and picked up something small and metallic. "This is from Meryn, for your stalking efforts, and this is from me for breakfast." He handed her a pair of binoculars and a sandwich wrapped in paper towels.

"Thank you for the food. Tell Meryn she rocks socks!" Amelia accepted the binoculars.

"I will tell her you were most thankful." Amelia laughed at his paraphrasing and waved goodbye.

She walked out the front door and looked over to the open field where the men had been training yesterday. Sure enough, they were at it again. Acting as if she had every right to be there, Amelia sat down on the stacked crates next to Aiden. He grinned at her, and kept counting, making notes on a piece of paper on his clipboard. Rheia hadn't been kidding when she said Aiden would do an inventory.

She placed her sandwich in her lap and unwrapped the paper towels. Ryuu had made her a ham and cheese sandwich, one of her favorites. Smiling, she began to eat as she swung her feet happily. When she had finished her breakfast, she stuffed the paper towels in her pocket and pulled out her binoculars to look for her mate. She found him dangling from a rope attached to one of the drill towers. When he began to do pull-ups on the rope he was hanging from, she sighed. When he turned his body upside down and began lowering himself up and down in an inverted pull up, she had to check for drool. When her hand came up to check her chin, she heard the men start laughing. She gave them the bird, making them laugh even harder. With each repetition, his arms bulged, and she felt her heart beat a little more out of control. She had a death grip on the binoculars that were giving her the up close and personal view of her gorgeous mate.

When her mate suddenly flipped off the rope and walked over to Sascha, she wondered what he was up to until Sascha pointed in her direction. With the binoculars still at her eyes, she raised her hand and waved. With a face like a thundercloud, he stalked over. When she could no longer look through the binoculars to see him, she lowered them to find he was standing right in front of her.

Grabbing her chest, she took deep breaths. How fast had he been walking? "You scared the crap outta me!"

He frowned down at her. "You are an odd little half human."

"My brother says I'm a 'limited edition', thank you very much."

"What are you doing?"

"Stalking you."

His mouth dropped. "Out in the open?"

She shrugged. "Why hide?"

He stared at her, clearly at a loss for words.

"Miss me this morning?" she asked brightly.

"No, in fact I was wondering when you were leaving."

"I'm not."

"I can make you go," he threatened.

Growling, Amelia stood up on the crate in front of him. "Here are *your* choices, princess." She poked him in the chest. "One: You mate with me, and we live happily ever after." She poked him again. "Two: You kill me. Which one will it be?" She folded her arms across her chest.

"Those choices are unacceptable."

"Too bad."

"If you won't leave, I will." When he turned to walk away, she felt a moment of panic. He was right; he could leave the city, and she would never see him again. He could lose his soul and become feral, or he could simply wait for her to die. Since she wasn't a full-blooded witch, she only had another forty to sixty years to live, tops. To him, that would be the blink of an eye. Desperate to stop him, she reached out to grab him. Unfortunately, she had not accounted for the loose slate in the crate she was standing on. She twisted her ankle and started to fall; she braced for the impact that never came.

Out of the corner of his eye, he saw her reaching for him. On instinct, he turned toward her. When she lost her footing, his body moved without conscious thought. He lifted his arms and caught her easily, bringing her to rest snugly against his chest. Everything in him was screaming that this is where she belonged.

Taking a deep ragged breath, he placed her on her feet. "Are you okay?"

"I think my leg is broken," she said, pointing to her right leg.

Panic took over. "What!" he bellowed. "We need to get you to the clinic!" The men began to gather around to help.

"Just kidding." She stood and did an abbreviated tap dance before lifting an imaginary top hat in his direction. "I'm fine."

Darian dropped his head back and began to mentally count to ten.

One, two, three...

"Four, five, six..." Amelia continued.

Shocked, he opened his eyes. "Can you read minds?"

She shook her head. "No, but I was raised by three brothers; I know that look well."

"This can't be baby Amelia that Caiden is always talking about, can it?" Quinn asked.

"That would be me, and you are...?"

"Quinn Foxglove, and this monster is Graham Armstrong," he said, pointing to the extremely large warrior beside him. Graham smiled at his mate. Darian mentally corrected himself; she was not his mate. She was a random strange woman.

Amelia squealed and launched herself into Graham's arms. Graham laughed until he looked in his direction. Grinding his teeth, Darian forced himself to breathe slowly. Graham gently extricated himself from Amelia's enthusiastic hug.

Darian fought back waves of jealously. Why should he care what this random woman did? Wait, wasn't Graham holding her just a bit too long?

"Not that I don't appreciate the hug, but what was that for?" Graham asked.

"Your mother taught me growing up. I heard about you all the time." She bounced up and down while holding his hand.

Graham's mouth dropped open before he broke out in a huge grin. He laughed out loud and swept her up in another bear hug. "You're Amy!" Still grinning like an idiot, he put her down. "There wasn't a single time that my mother called when she didn't tell me about your latest exploits. My brother, Hunter, serves under Caiden in the Nu Unit. Is it true you hold the speed record for the Storm Keep obstacle course?"

Amelia nodded and let go of his hand to blow on her fingers before rubbing them on her chest. "No one has broken it yet."

"Are you two quite finished?" Darian asked coldly. At least she had stopped touching him.

Graham stepped back. "Now that we know she's okay, we'll get back to drills. Nice meeting you, Amy."

Amelia shook her head. "The only person on this planet who can call me Amy is your mother, and we both know you don't tell her no."

Graham nodded. "That's the Gods' honest truth. Welcome to Lycaonia!" He and Quinn waved goodbye and went back to their exercises.

"Maybe you and Amelia should walk around the property, just to make sure she's okay." Keelan suggested.

"Good idea, Keelan," Aiden agreed.

"Subtle," Darian said, eyeing the two men.

Aiden shrugged. "It's either us, or Meryn gets involved, and you know subtle is her middle name," Aiden joked. Darian remembered Aiden's hard lesson about ignoring his mate and shuddered. Would Amelia set his car on fire? He looked over to see her smiling up at him. He wouldn't put anything past her.

Darian realized there was no way to ignore the suggestion and, without saying a word, began walking toward the front of the house. Amelia jogged to catch up.

"Wait for me, princess."

"Stop calling me that."

"You can only order me to do that as your mate; otherwise, it's just a request, and one I will continue to ignore."

When they reached the back of the house, he slowed down then stopped. He turned around to face her. "Why are you trying to hard?"

She looked surprised at his question. "Because you're my mate. As much as your instincts are telling you to stay away to keep me safe, mine are just as loud—and probably more obnoxious—and they are telling me to save you."

Darian felt his mouth twitch. Something about her got to him. He turned and began walking again, slower this time. "If I knew for certain that I wouldn't drag you down with me..." He shook his head; he might not risk it even then.

"Maybe that is my destined future. Maybe we're meant to fall together."

He stopped suddenly. His head snapped back to face her. "That is unacceptable."

She scrunched up her nose. "You say that a lot."

He resumed walking. "Only around you."

He felt her grab the back of his shirt. When he turned around, he saw tears in her eyes. "Please," she whispered.

Unable to stop himself, he leaned down toward her. When their lips touched, he felt as if he had finally come home. He wrapped his arms around her and pulled her close to his body, enjoying the feel of her soft curves pressed against him. When he felt the tiny flicker that was the remainder of his soul trying to merge with hers, he broke off their kiss and stepped away. His breathing was ragged and labored. There was no way he could deny that she was his mate now. She had to have felt the merge begin.

He walked over to the large oak tree at the edge of the property and placed a hand on the trunk. He felt a modicum of control return.

"Damn that spell," he whispered.

"I dreamt of you before the spell remember? We were always meant to be. Almost from the moment of my birth, I belonged to you," she said softly.

He took a deep breath and straightened his shoulders. He turned to face her. He owed her that at least. "I'll walk you back."

They walked in silence until they stood at the front door.

"I'll see you at dinner," he said, stepping off the porch.

"Is that a date?"

He felt himself smile and dared not turn around. "Don't read anything into it."

"I'm wearing you down, princess."

"You need to find someone from your own planet," he called after her. She laughed and reached for the doorknob.

He waited until her heard the door open and shut before he walked back over to the men.

"I take it she's okay?" Aiden asked.

"Yes, she's fine." Darian stretched, looking around the workout yard.

Keelan walked up beside him. "She's getting to you."

"I can't afford to let her get any closer. If you were my friend, you would help me save her."

Keelan looked away. Pain shined behind his eyes. "It's because I *am* your friend that I am trying to save you. Did you ever stop to think that maybe it's not up to you? Trust that Fate knows what she is doing."

"If I..." Darian hesitated looking around.

Keelan stepped close. "I will protect her with my life, Darian. I'd take care of you myself," he promised.

Darian ruffled his young friend's hair. He hadn't felt brotherly affection for his friend in nearly forty years. "As if you could take me," he joked, enjoying the ability to do so. Every time he was around Amelia, it was as if his emotions were restored with her smile.

Keelan's eyes danced with relief at his playful attitude. "My kung-fu is strong."

"Come on, princess, we don't have all day!" Sascha yelled across the training grounds sending the men into peals of laughter.

Darian heard Keelan whispering under his breath and smiled. Crossing his arms over his chest, he waited.

Seconds later, Sascha's curses rang out over the men's laugher.

"Dammit, Keelan, undo the spell right now!" he ordered, banging on an invisible wall. Keelan had hardened the air all around the Gamma Unit leader.

Colton was pointing and laughing, which fueled Sascha's anger to new heights.

"Poor tiger wiger!" Colton teased.

"Leave him there, Keelan. We have actual work to do," Darian said, walking back over to the ropes where he had been working out. "I want to see the progress you made increasing the strength in your upper body."

"Sure thing," Keelan said, joining him at the ropes.

"Bastards! Let me out of here!"

Everyone went back to their workout.

"Guys?" Sascha called.

Darian held the rope while Keelan climbed.

"Guys, come on, I have to piss!" Sascha yelled.

"Go ahead, Sascha, I mean it's not like the women are watching," Colton cajoled.

"Although, Amelia did get those binoculars from somewhere," Gavriel interjected, sending Colton into fresh fits of laughter.

All around him, the men laughed and teased the Gamma Unit leader until Aiden couldn't stand seeing Sascha squirm anymore and ordered Keelan to take down the wall. Darian felt lighter than he had in years.

Maybe I have a chance after all.

CHAPTER FIVE

Amelia walked into the house and shut the door. Darian's kiss had changed something in her. In her mind, she had always known he was her mate, but after his kiss, she suddenly felt empty without him. She keenly felt the separation from him, and it scared her. Desperately needing a distraction to take her mind off her still tingling body, she headed toward the kitchen.

When she entered, Ryuu looked up from the stove. "Is there something I can do for you, *itoko-sama*?" he asked.

She frowned. "What does that mean anyway?"

He gave a noncommittal shrug. "It is a mode of address in my language. I find that the English language lacks proper terms to covey certain meanings," he said, not explaining anything at all.

"It sounds pretty."

Ryuu smiled and gave a half bow.

"Could you show me where Aiden's office is? Keelan brought my makeup case down last night so I could do makeovers for Beth and Meryn."

"Of course, one moment." Ryuu untied the starched, white apron and set it to one side. He walked her out of the kitchen to the foyer and down a second hallway on the other side of the staircase. He paused at a closed door before knocking.

"Come in!" she heard Meryn yell.

Smiling, Ryuu opened the door for her, and she walked in.

"Thank you, Ryuu."

"You're very welcome." He bowed again and left.

"Are you here to do makeovers?" Meryn squealed.

"Yup, my case should be around here somewhere." She looked around.

"If you mean the silver, toolbox-looking thing, it's against the wall," Jaxon said, pointing it out.

"That would be it." She wheeled the case to the small seating area where Beth and Meryn now sat.

"Is it okay if I join in, too?" Noah asked shyly.

"Of course!" Amelia pointed to the empty seat next to Meryn on the small love seat.

Meryn turned to Noah. "I'm going to get sexy."

Noah blushed furiously. "I want to look pretty."

Beth laughed. "Noah, you are pretty."

"I wish I had your eyelashes," Amelia sighed. "Women pay a lot money for false mink lashes to look half as good."

Meryn's eyes lit up. "I want to try those."

Amelia started pulling different palettes and brushes from her case. "So, will the order be Beth, then Meryn, then Noah?" she asked.

Meryn and Noah looked at each other. "Can we try it ourselves?" Meryn asked.

Amelia looked between the two of them. "You know what? Let's use my laptop. I'll fire up a makeup tutorial on YouTube, and you two can try it out. How's that?"

"Perfect! I can't wait to shock Aiden." Meryn grinned evilly.

Amelia pulled out her laptop from the back of the case and logged in. "What type of look did you want?"

Meryn pulled the laptop between her and Noah. "We got this, you do Beth."

"Are you sure?"

"Absolutely." Meryn started typing. "We just have to find a video we want."

"Okay, if you have any questions or need help, let me know." Amelia slid a tray of assorted makeup and beauty supplies over to them and turned to Beth. "So what's your normal look?"

"Pretty natural, I tend to go for neutral colors like cream, pink, and light brown."

She assessed Beth's gorgeous blonde hair and blue eyes. "How do you feel about bold colors?"

Beth flinched. "How bold?"

"Trust me." Amelia grinned and started pulling out the makeup she knew she wanted for Beth's new look.

"So, Amelia, do you know The Doctor?" Meryn asked, her eyes still glued to the laptop. Noah pointed to one video and she nodded.

"*Doctor Who*?" Amelia winked at Beth.

Meryn laughed. "Exactly!" Then she paused. "Wait, did you actually mean to ask doctor who, as in the question?"

Amelia just raised an eyebrow at her, and Meryn rolled her eyes.

"What are the odds that most of the mates watch *Doctor Who*?" Beth asked, lining up the pencils by length.

Amelia shrugged. "Maybe the Doctor is gathering all of his supporters into one place so that, when the time comes, we can help him save the Earth?"

Meryn looked up, her eyes wide and her face filled with wonder.

Beth groaned. "Don't encourage her nutty conspiracy theories."

Meryn glared at Beth. "Some of my theories are true, thank you very much."

Beth shook her head. "It worries me that you even think of those crazy ideas to begin with."

Meryn shrugged. "Aiden snores; it's what I think of when I'm trying to get to sleep."

"Ahh, sleep deprivation. I knew there had to be an explanation."

Amelia pulled out her pack of makeup remover wipes. "Before we get started, is anyone wearing makeup?" All three shook their heads. "Ideally, I would have you exfoliate and moisturize before we get started, but I think we can skip it today. Remind me to establish skin care programs for you later." She put the wipes on the table.

"This one?" Meryn pointed to the screen. Noah nodded. Meryn started their video as Amelia picked up a tube of primer. As she was smoothing it over Beth's skin, she heard a masculine voice from her laptop. "And you if don't like it, don't fucking watch it; you know the drill."

Amelia and Beth turned to Meryn and Noah at the same time. "What are you watching?" Beth asked.

"Manny Mua. So far, he rocks!" Meryn's eyes were glued to the monitor.

"Mua?" Amelia laughed. "Meryn, that's Manny M-U-A, as in makeup artist, not his last name."

"That makes more sense," Meryn said.

"He's gorgeous," Noah sighed, watching the video with a dreamy expression on his face.

"He must be pretty," Jaxon quipped, without looking up from his work.

"He is," Meryn and Noah replied in unison.

Amelia turned back to Beth. "I'll have to check him out later." She held up one bottle of foundation then another. Beth was so fair she knew she would probably have to mix foundations to get the correct shade. She chose two of the lightest shades she had and ran test strips down her neck. While they were drying, she lightly filled in her brows with a brow pencil. Since she was blonde, she didn't want to go too dark.

"No, he said a two-twenty-four brush, where is that one?" Meryn asked.

"Found it." Noah held up the black handled brush.

Amelia lucked out in that Beth was a match with a foundation she had. With a flat-topped brush, she buffed the foundation into Beth's skin. She used her favorite concealer not only to highlight under her eyes but to prime her eyelids as well. Next, she set the foundation and concealer with a translucent powder.

"My fucking eye is twitching," Manny complained from her laptop. Meryn giggled at the video. "I love him!"

Beth chuckled at Meryn's giggles. "She would find a kindred spirit via YouTube somehow."

"Meryn, I don't think that's right," Noah commented nervously.

Amelia dug through her case, looking for her palest pink blush. She wanted just a hint of color in Beth's cheeks. "Found it!" She opened the compact and picked up her fluffiest brush.

Beth leaned back, looking skeptical. "I don't usually use blush."

"Trust me, I know what I want to do with your eyes." Amelia ignored Beth's nervous expression and added a flush of color. She finished Beth's face by adding a shimmery highlight to emphasize her high cheekbones.

"Why do they say, 'I'm going in with'? Going in where? It sounds like it's going in your eyeball." Meryn asked.

"Meryn, I think that may be too much," Noah said, his voice sounding strange.

Amelia shrugged and closed the highlighter compact. "It's just what they say." She beamed at Beth. "Now my favorite part, the eyes." Amelia went straight to her custom palette and began layering and blending colors.

"You really like this don't you?" Beth asked.

"I do. I love colors and bright, sparkly things. I like fun music and cute stuffed animals. I don't like when people are upset, so I always try to make things fun and lively."

"It's why I call her Bubbles," Meryn added.

Beth giggled. "You are bubbly."

Amelia laughed. "I like that nickname. I just hope my brothers never hear it; I'll never hear my own name again."

Beth rolled her eyes. "Tell me about it! My uncle, to my knowledge, has never called me Elizabeth. I always get Bethy."

"The guys call me Menace. I don't think that's entirely accurate," Meryn protested. Behind them, they heard Jaxon laugh and cover it quickly with a cough. Beth winked at Amelia. Something told her that Menace fit Meryn to a T.

Amelia tilted her head and stared at Beth. She was mostly done, having chosen bronzes and browns for her lids. She was debating how Beth would handle a pop of color. She decided, to throw caution to the wind, and added a gorgeous teal color to her lower lash line. Between the bronze and the teal, Beth's eyes popped. The result was exactly what she was going for.

"Well, what do we have here?" a male voice asked from behind them.

Amelia turned and saw the men and Rheia standing just inside the doorway looking in with smiles on their faces—except Aiden.

"What's wrong with Meryn?" he asked, frowning.

Amelia and Beth turned to Meryn and Noah, and Amelia's mouth dropped. How had things gotten so bad, so fast?

Meryn blinked one eye repeatedly. "It's my sexy, smokey eye."

The men shook their heads in unison. Aiden broke the silence. "No baby. You look like a sad little panda."

"A drunk, psychotic, panda," Colton added.

Rheia swatted at his shoulder, a fierce frown on her face. Colton instantly looked contrite.

"What about Noah?" Meryn asked, pointing to the blond who ducked his face in embarrassment.

Colton nodded. "Looks good." He gave Noah a thumbs up.

Noah flushed with the praise. Amelia knew he must have been nervous facing a group of warriors with makeup on.

Meryn looked at Noah with one eye, and her bottom lip started to tremble. "But we both watched Manny. Why does he look good and I don't?"

Aiden walked across the room and scooped her up. "Come on sexy, let's go take a shower."

Meryn looked up into her mate's face her one eye wide. "I'm sexy?"

Aiden nuzzled her neck. "I can barely contain myself."

Meryn smiled and kissed him all over the face. "I did it for you."

"I know."

As he walked past the men to head upstairs, Keelan tilted his head. "Why do you keep winking at us?" he asked.

Meryn sighed. "I'm not winking. I think I glued my fucking eye shut with the lash glue."

Aiden turned to Amelia a panicked look on his face.

"Olive oil," she said, answering his unasked question.

He nodded. "We'll get some from Ryuu. Thanks Amelia." He carried Meryn out, telling her again how sexy she was.

Rheia and Beth sighed. "He's so sweet," Beth said, smiling softly.

Rheia looked over at Beth. "You look like a model. Standing next to you, I look like a pumpkin."

Colton quickly pulled Rheia into his arms and dipped her back low. "You'll always be a goddess to me."

Rheia laughed. "Do we have time for a shower?"

Colton growled low and righted her. "Challenge accepted." Rheia squealed as he chased her out of the room, grabbing at her butt.

"Pup." Gavriel shook his head at Colton's antics before he walked up to Beth's chair and lifted her hand in his. He bowed over it before kissing it gently. "You have taken my breath away. I desire your company upstairs where I can look my fill a bit longer." When he gave her a heated look from beneath his dark brows, even Amelia almost swooned. Beth's hand in his began to tremble, and she nodded shyly. Gavriel helped her to stand and laid her hand on his forearm before escorting her out of the room.

"Wow," Noah breathed, fanning himself.

"No kidding. I'll be in the shower, too, though it's not as much fun when you do it alone," Keelan grumbled and left.

Noah blinked. "Did he say what I think he just said?"

Jaxon laughed. "Probably. Come on Noah, I bet if we look pitiful enough, Ryuu will serve us dinner early, then we can log in to beat Lennox's ass in Call of Duty," he said, wheeling toward the door.

Noah jumped up excitedly. "Good idea, I'm starved." He turned to Amelia. "Thank you for letting me use your makeup."

"Any time and I mean that. Colton was right; you nailed that smokey eye." Amelia could clearly see that Noah had an interest in cosmetics.

"Thanks, maybe you can show me different styles later?"

"Sure," Amelia said sincerely. Not many people shared her passion for creating new looks.

Once they had left, she noticed that Darian alone stood by the door.

"Aren't you going to shower, too?" She started cleaning her brushes and putting her stuff away.

He pushed away from the wall. "In a moment." He walked into the room and sat down on the love seat. He didn't say anything, just watched her as she lovingly put things back where they belonged.

"This comforts you, doesn't it?" he asked when she was done.

"Yes. The ritual of it, the bright colors and soft fragrances, it makes me happy. I like making things beautiful." She snapped her case closed.

He stood and walked over to her, his face unreadable. "I'd like to see you do your own makeup, your ritual."

She swallowed hard, her throat suddenly dry. "Come to my room after your shower, I'll let you watch."

She watched as his eyes darkened.

"I'll be there." He easily lifted her heavy case and walked out of the room.

Amelia took a deep breath. She would seduce him with the sultriest look she knew. Feeling her confidence rising with her excitement, she hurried up the stairs.

When she got to her room, she immediately grabbed the case Darian had left in the hallway and hurried to get everything set up. She set up her case in the middle of the room, using it as her portable vanity. She dragged the heavy wingback chair over to create a place for Darian. Satisfied with her room set-up, she ran into the bathroom to clean and moisturize her skin. Using bobby pins, she carefully arranged her hair away from her face, giving her a pin-up look. She ripped her suitcase apart looking for her favorite dusty rose silk robe she'd bought on a whim at Victoria's Secret years ago. Knowing that she had a mate out in the world somewhere made dating impossible, so the sexy robe was more for her than anyone else; now she was grateful she had it.

She looked down and almost screamed in panic. It looked like her suitcase had exploded. She had just finished throwing everything back in when there was a knock at the door. Without bothering to zip it, she shoved it under the bench at the foot of the bed.

"Come in," she said, trying to slow her breathing. Nothing said sexy like puffing for breath because you were so out of shape you couldn't dig through your own suitcase.

When Darian walked in, she couldn't catch her breath for another reason. Instead of his normal elegant slacks and sweater, he was wearing the traditional long fae robes that were so well known throughout their world. Unlike her dream, this robe wasn't golden with jewel-tone leaf embroidery. Instead, it was a deep black; the cuffs of his sleeves and collar were accented in sharp, ruby-red geometric designs. It had a high collar that gave the robe a formal look and the dark hues only emphasized his fair skin and blond hair. The contrast was almost ethereal. He held two glasses of red wine.

He smiled at her, and she was shocked at her reaction to it. At first, she was filled with a gleeful joy, and for a moment, her fears for the future faded, until she saw his eyes. They were no longer their normal lavender; instead, they were a dark amethyst, almost black. She was losing him.

He glided across the room and sat down in the chair she had set up for him. Nervously, she sat down at her impromptu vanity, and he handed her the glass of wine. She took a sip to calm her nerves. As she expected, it was a very good wine. She carefully set the glass down in the top open compartment of her case.

"Did you change your mind about claiming me?" she asked playfully, indicating his attire and the wine.

He shook his head. "I stopped fighting. The idea of seeing you like this, this intimacy, I couldn't stay away. Like a moth to a flame, except I want to be burned. If these are to be my final days, I want your touch to act as the brand that will set me on fire. I don't mind bathing myself in your blazing light, knowing that my cremation will set you free."

She turned her head away to hide her tears. He had given up completely, and she didn't know how to save him. How did you give someone the will to live? She slowly reached for her wine and took another sip. If he was so ready to set her free, then she would have to show him something worth living for.

She tossed the idea of her sultry look; he was bathed in enough darkness. She picked up her rose-scented powder and lightly dusted her chest and neck sending its soothing fragrance throughout the room. "I think you're being terribly unfair; I think I should have a say considering this is my mating, too."

He lifted the glass to his mouth, a slight smirk on his lips. "You're too young to appreciate the unfairness in life."

She shrugged and pulled out the bottom drawer where she kept her oils. She never used them on clients, but found that, even if the spelled oils weren't directly applied to whomever she was working on, the aromas alone helped. She reached for her two most powerful oils. One was a present from her brothers, the other one she had made herself. Brotherly Love was a mixture of frankincense, myrrh, sandalwood, and lilac, essences associated with protection. All three of her brothers had poured their love and energy into this oil, so much so, that simply touching the bottle made her long for home. Midsummer's Night was a mixture of gardenia, jasmine, rose, geranium, and vanilla, it had been inspired by her dream of Darian as a child, when they walked together in the fae gardens. She hoped that the properties of love and fertility with the protection properties of Brotherly Love would help guide and protect her mating.

She dabbed a few drops of each oil on the inside of her wrists and brought them up to rub lightly behind her ear and down her neck. She peeked over and was satisfied to see that Darian had visibly relaxed and was smiling softly. She turned back to her task at hand.

"I like using a light powder in the evenings, something with a bit of luminosity. This one is called, Hope of Light." She used a brush to powder her face. "A lot of people think you have to go with a darker look when you go out at night, the smokey eye that Meryn was attempting for example, but that's not true. Lighter colors have their place when the sun goes down." She picked up an eye shadow palette. "This color is called Heart's Desire; it has a gorgeous champagne gold color." She used a small, fluffy brush to apply the color all over her lid. "This one is called, Shimmering Love." A pearlescent cream color, she used it to highlight her brow bone, her inner eye, and the center of her lip. One by one, she chose bright colors named for hope, love, and light. When she was done, she turned to him. His empty wine glass sat on the floor beside his chair, forgotten. He no longer smiled but desperately gripped both arms of the chair, as if he was fighting an unseen enemy to stay seated.

"You don't like it?" She turned and looked in the mirror. She looked fresh-faced and golden. She had worn the look many times in the past when she wanted to feel closer to him.

She reached up and slowly removed the bobby pins, letting her curls fall where they would, and his hands on the chair arms cracked the wood. She put the bobby pins aside and folded her hands in her lap. "You do like it."

He took a ragged breath. "You look like an innocent angel. Everything you did was pure magic." He released the chair arms and stood.

"You keep using terms like young, innocent, and angel to describe me, but that's not right. I have seen so much darkness, I feel like my soul is stained with it. If there is anyone on this earth that can help you fight back your demons, it's me, yet you won't even let me try to help you." She stood to face him.

His features became a hard mask; gone was his easy smile. "Who has shown you darkness? Why didn't your brothers protect you?"

"Don't blame them. It was my choice; every single time, it was my choice." She hugged herself tightly. If he knew, would she still be his innocent angel? Would he give up completely? She turned her back to him.

"Tell me," he demanded.

She shook her head. "You haven't earned the right to ask that of me. You deny me at every turn and expect the privilege of my trust. It doesn't work like that, Darian."

"If someone has hurt you..." His voice was sharp and ice cold.

She turned and slowly made her way over to him. When she stood directly in front of him, she reached up and laid her hand over his heart. "What would you do, my prince? What if I told you that, without your love, I would spend the rest of my life trapped in a hell of my own making? That not even losing my soul could compare to the nightmare I would endure every day without you, lost in an inescapable cycle of torment and abuse? If you're not willing to live for me, are you willing to fight for me?"

He swallowed hard, repeatedly. "You ask too much."

"I only ask for what I was promised so long ago."

He reached up and removed her hand from his chest. "There is nothing left in me that could save you." He walked past her and out of the room.

She stood there, unable to move. She kept her breathing even. She wouldn't cry. How many times had the thought of ruining her makeup acted as a suit of armor? Her mate thought he had nothing left to give her, but she knew that wasn't true. If he couldn't see the light of his own soul, then she would become a mirror and reflect his own light back to him. If his light was too dim, then she would ignite the flames of his heart. She would never give up, not until he was safe.

Goddess, help me.

CHAPTER SIX

Alone, Amelia walked downstairs to the dining room. She had changed into a simple white dress and slipped her phone into her pocket. She decided to leave her hair down; Darian had liked it better this way. When she stepped into the dining room, she noticed she was the last one to come down. The men stood and sat again when she did.

"Sorry I took so long," she said quietly.

"It's no problem, Aiden and I just came down ourselves," Meryn said as she pulled a steaming roll apart.

"We just got here, too. We had to tuck Penny in," Rheia admitted, smiling at her.

Meryn took a huge bite of her roll. "You two are like a matched set of black and white. You look great. I'll never be able to get my makeup to look like that," she sighed.

Amelia looked between herself and Darian and realized that Meryn was right; they complemented each other perfectly. She forced a smile. "You'll get it, it just takes practice. Did you get all the glue off?" She unfolded her napkin and laid it in her lap.

"Yup. Aiden gave me incentive to keep my eyes closed in the shower." Meryn leered up at her now blushing mate.

"Meryn! How many times do I have to tell you, no sex talk at the table!" Aiden exclaimed.

Meryn's face became a mask of innocence. "I didn't say anything about sex, you did."

Colton choked on his water, and Rheia beat him on the back.

Aiden growled at his friend. "Shut up, mutt."

"Too bad Jaxon and Noah ate earlier. I am sure those youngsters would appreciate the pointers," Gavriel commented.

Aiden shot him a dirty look. "*Et tu?*"

"Aiden, they know we have sex. I didn't get this way by immaculate conception." Meryn pointed to her rounded belly.

"No, you got that way on your hands and knees, if I remember correctly," Aiden commented smugly, reaching for his water.

"Aiden!" Meryn screeched, turning bright red.

This time, it was Colton who lightly pounded Rheia on the back as she tried to laugh and swallow her roll at the same time.

"Touché." Gavriel raised his wine glass to the commander who winked at the vampire.

"I can't believe you said that!" Meryn said, her eyes wide. She stared for a second and then began to giggle. "That was awesome." She held up a fist to her mate.

Aiden's huge fist dwarfed Meryn's little one, but he tapped her knuckles gently before leaning in to kiss her nose.

"There is something to be said for doggy style, if you know what I mean." Colton wagged his eyebrows looking self-satisfied until Rheia cuffed him upside the head.

"You mean puppy style?" she quipped.

Colton's mouth dropped open. Next to her, Keelan had fallen over to his right and lay across the seat of the chair next to him, laughing so hard he wasn't making any sounds. Darian covered his mouth, but Amelia was willing to bet he was hiding a smile. Everyone at the table was having a hard time breathing for the laughter.

"Puppy? Puppy!? I'll show you puppy later," Colton murmured under his breath.

Rheia leaned in close to him. "Challenge accepted."

Colton growled and bit a roll in half.

Meryn wiped her eyes with her napkin and looked over at Darian. "You look more relaxed than I've seen you in months. Did you enjoy shower time, too?"

He simply shook his head.

Amelia played with her roll. "He watched me get ready for dinner. A lot of husbands will sit in on their wives' makeovers. I've been told by many of them that they found it soothing."

"There is nothing soothing about trying to peel glue off your mate's eyelids," Aiden grumbled.

Amelia chuckled at the image of Meryn with one eye closed. "I think you encountered an extreme case."

"I enjoy watching Beth brush her hair at night. I agree, it is very calming," Gavriel admitted.

Aiden glanced down at Meryn's pixie and sighed. He looked around the table. "I got a phone call from my father. The council is returning the original necklace from our gooey corpse and the necklace from Penny's father to us. They want us to go over them again."

The men groaned. "Why? What in the hell do they think we'll find? We've been over those things a thousand times," Colton complained.

"I happen to agree with you; however, at the moment, they are our only lead regarding our rogue ferals. So we'll go over them again." Aiden sat back looking as frustrated as the rest of his unit.

Amelia frowned.

Rogue ferals?

She spoke up. "I'm sorry, but what do you mean by rogue ferals?"

Aiden exchanged surprised looks with Gavriel and Colton. "Your brothers didn't tell you?" he asked.

She shook her head. "They tend not to tell me the grittier stuff. Caiden did mention a lot of kidnappings going on in this area, which is why he wanted me to come home right away."

"When was the last time you were home?" Gavriel asked.

"Last year. I moved back to Storm Keep after having lived in Atlanta for a few years, but I couldn't sit still. So I packed a bag and my makeup case and decided to visit each of the other pillar cities. I traveled around the country for a while, this was my first city to visit."

"Fate hard at work again," Beth said.

Amelia turned to her. "What do you mean?"

Beth smiled. "The same thing happened to Meryn and me."

Meryn laughed. "In my case, I threw a dart at a map."

"So I was brought here?" She stared up at Darian who didn't say anything.

"We're all being brought here. The spell was cast, so the warriors get mates. I, for one, am grateful." Beth looked over at Gavriel. He raised their joined hands and kissed her knuckles.

Amelia wanted more information on the ferals. She reached beside her and tugged on Darian's shirt. He looked down at her, surprised. She could tell he hadn't expected her to touch him.

"What is going on with the ferals?" She couldn't keep the tremor from her voice. Growing up, she had had nightmares about the vacant-eyed monsters her brothers fought.

His reaction to her fear was immediate and without thought. He reached to his side, pulled her hand away from his shirt, and clasped it in his. "You fear them?"

She nodded. "More than most, I think. All I had growing up were my brothers, and all three of them are unit warriors. If there was anything that could take them away from me, it was ferals. I hated and feared them as a child."

Darian looked over at Aiden who nodded. "She needs to know, now more than ever, especially since she's your mate. She could end up a target like Beth or Rheia."

"Target?" she squeaked.

Darian took a deep breath. "Last year, we noticed that ferals started behaving strangely. They were attacking in groups with visible leaders, taking orders, and had higher brain functions than normal. Some wore necklaces that we now know allows them to somehow retain the abilities they should have lost when they turned feral; it gives them abilities they should never have, like becoming invisible. When Meryn arrived, she started compiling information and saw patterns that we had missed. She discovered that shifter couples were suddenly going missing, especially couples expecting babies. When she widened the search, we saw that the disappearances weren't limited to just the counties around Lycaonia but were occurring all around the country.

"Thanks to Rheia, we were recently able to figure out that the necklace not only gave them new abilities but also halted the decay of their bodies. They no longer smelled like a feral and could for pass as a normal paranormal."

Amelia felt herself begin to shake. "How come our people don't know this? They have a right to know."

Darian squeezed her hand. "Because they would panic, and because there's nowhere safe they can go."

"Darian," Aiden chastised.

Darian shook his head. "It's true, and you know it. The women have been attacked here twice, Rheia at the clinic twice. With those necklaces, they can come and go undetected. I'll say what we've all been thinking for months: We are strictly on the defensive, and not doing a good job at that either. We have to wait for them to strike because we cannot take the fight to them." Darian dropped her hand and ran his fingers through his hair in frustration.

Amelia looked around, incredulous. "Why haven't you created a detection spell?"

Keelan shook his head. "Elder Airgead has tried and says that it is impossible. What would the spell detect? Blood from a blood spell? We all have blood in us."

"Not even Elder Airgead could find a way?" she asked, feeling shaken.

"No. The witches in the units here in Lycaonia have been casting everything we know at those damn necklaces to get them to reveal their secrets to us so we can figure out how they are made, a clue, anything!" Keelan banged a fist on the table.

Amelia turned to Darian. "How can you fight them? How can we possibly win?"

"I'll tell you how," Meryn declared, jumping to her feet. "We find out where these murdering bastards are and then we launch a nuke straight up their—"

"Dinner is ready." Ryuu interrupted from the kitchen doorway. He looked over at Meryn who had a fist raised in the air. "*Denka,* you know it is not good for the baby for you to get so excited before a meal."

"Uh, Meryn, you keep talking about explosives. They're just figures of speech, right baby?" Aiden asked.

Ignoring him, Meryn pouted and sat down, crossing her arms over her chest. "You ruined my moment, Ryuu."

"How will I ever live with myself? Mashed potatoes?" he asked blandly, holding a spoon over his cart.

Meryn brightened. "Yes, please and lots of them. Oh! Can you also mix the peas in with mine?"

"Baby?" Aiden prodded.

"Give up, Commander, lost cause," Colton advised.

Aiden reached for his wine glass.

"Of course." Ryuu dished out a large portion of potatoes and mixed in a spoonful of peas. Without asking, he added two large slices of meatloaf.

"Might as well add a third." Meryn said, watching his every move.

Ryuu's eyes widened. "Your food consumption cannot be normal." He turned to Rheia. "Please check her for a tapeworm."

"Hey! I do have a parasite, but it's a half human, half bear shifter and future Time Lord, thank you very much. So please Ryuu, Meryn two-point-oh would like another slice of meatloaf and some tuna."

Ryuu's eyes widened. "Tuna and meat loaf?"

Amelia's fear over the terrifying feral development evaporated as she watched Meryn bicker with her squire. Meryn was completely unfazed by the alarming changes in the ferals because, having only been here for a few short months, that was all she had ever known.

Around the table, everyone was smiling at the tiny human, and Amelia realized that maybe the mates truly had been brought here for a reason. Meryn's attitude and fresh perspective were needed to keep them from becoming too overwhelmed. It gave her hope because there was no way Fate would bring her all this way after giving her dreams of her mate for over thirty years just to take him away.

"Tuna sounds good to me, too," Amelia agreed feeling as if a huge weight had been lifted from her shoulders.

"Actually, me too, Ryuu. Sorry." Rheia blushed.

Ryuu pinched the bridge of his nose. "Anyone else?" Everyone else shook their heads. Ryuu frowned at Rheia then at Meryn, but when his gaze turned to her, he looked confused. "I know why the two of them have odd cravings, but you're not with child."

Amelia shrugged. "I'll try anything once. I live in the moment. Life is too short not to eat meatloaf with tuna."

Ryuu shook his head. "Two, there's two."

Beth nodded her head. "I know Ryuu, it'll be okay," she said in a soothing manner.

Ryuu straightened his back. "Ladies if you will but give me a moment to serve the rest of the table, I will return with your additional side dish."

Meryn grinned evilly. "But it's not going on the side; I'm putting it on top."

Ryuu sighed and continued to serve the table. "Yes *denka,* of course."

Gavriel leaned back in his chair. "Amelia, may I ask, how old are you?"

"Thirty-six, why?"

"Just curious. Ryuu and Beth are right, you and Meryn both have a very optimistic and simple view of the world," Gavriel explained.

"Dammit! You're older than me. Except for Penny, I'm still the youngest. Even Jaxon and Noah are older." Meryn growled.

Aiden kissed his mate's neck causing her to laugh. "Meryn, you know, as a human you are treated according to how humans age, not paranormals."

"Exactly," Amelia agreed. "To a paranormal, age is just a number, unless you have brothers."

"Amen," Rheia said.

"Or fathers," Beth agreed.

"Yeah, unless you have testosterone-driven male relatives, ages don't really mean anything, just like expiration dates on food," Amelia added.

Everyone stared at her except Meryn who just nodded and ate a huge bite of her peas and mashed potatoes.

"What?" Amelia asked, looking around.

Keelan sat forward. "Do you mean that ages and expiration dates are the same because they are both numbers?"

"No, I meant that they are both pointless numbers. Ages are a pointless unit of measure for races that can live thousands of years and expiration dates are pointless because they are just for show."

Meryn nodded again. "True."

Aiden turned to her, looking horrified. "No, baby, they are *not* just for show."

Meryn scrunched up her face and turned to Amelia. "Really?" Amelia shrugged.

Aiden nodded vigorously. "Yes!"

Meryn thought about it for a moment. "What about pickles? Pickles don't expire, do they, Ryuu?"

"Not the ones packaged by NASA for deep space exploration, *denka*. Did you want the tuna plain or mixed with mayonnaise as if it were going on a sandwich?" he asked as he finished serving Aiden before refilling his wine glass. Keelan snickered.

Meryn looked at her and Rheia. "With mayonnaise?" Amelia and Rheia nodded.

Ryuu gave a half bow. "I will be back in a moment with your tuna."

Meryn turned to Rheia. "What about medicines? Do they really go bad?"

Rheia nodded. "Yes, sometimes they lose potency, and sometimes they develop dangerous side effects."

"Ryuu!" Aiden bellowed.

"I'll check everything," Ryuu replied from the kitchen.

Aiden picked up his wine glass again.

The rest of dinner went by at a leisurely pace as everyone discussed the events of their day. When the meal was over, Meryn stretched. "Come along, Pond, it's time for movie night."

"Why did you call her Pond?" Colton asked.

Rheia patted his arm. "It's a *Doctor Who* thing."

"I haven't caught up to Penny yet."

Rheia laughed. "You will. You're her favorite *Doctor Who* watching partner after Meryn."

Keelan quickly agreed to movie night. "Great idea, Meryn. I think we should watch something fun, uplifting, and lighthearted." He winked at Amelia. She felt her heart melt a bit. Keelan was trying so hard to help his friend.

"Cool, how about *Bedazzled*?" Meryn suggested.

"I've never heard of that one; what's it about?" Keelan leaned forward.

"A guy sells his soul to the devil for seven wishes," Meryn replied.

Keelan stared at her his eyes wide. "How is that happy and uplifting?"

"It's funny," she protested.

Amelia tried hard to keep a straight face. "I'll have to pass. I'm turning in early so I can have breakfast with you all tomorrow."

Meryn clapped her hands. "Good! We're going to visit Adelaide tomorrow. I can introduce you."

"Who's Adelaide?"

"She's Aiden's mom. Her squire, Marius, makes the best cake I have ever eaten." Meryn patted her belly.

Gavriel sat forward. "You're driving?"

Beth shook her head. "We were going to walk."

He paled. "But, it is a thirty-minute walk. There are animals and branches, and exposed roots." Gavriel's eyes looked a bit wild.

Beth placed a comforting hand on his arm. "I'll be fine."

"Yeah, if they get into trouble, Meryn can always come back here to tell us Beth has fallen down the well," Colton joked.

"What the fuck am I? Lassie? You're the dog," Meryn shot back.

"I'm not a dog!" Colton protested.

Gavriel turned to Aiden. "Are there wells?"

Laughing, Beth shook her head. "Fine, we'll drive."

Meryn shrugged. "Whatever works." She stood. "Okay, let's go watch a movie."

Amelia watched as Beth shared a look with Ryuu. Both looked at Meryn and then at her. "Meryn, before we go, I'd like to check on something," Beth said, pointing to Meryn's chair.

Meryn frowned and sat down. "If this is about the chocolate cupcakes, I didn't know they were yours," she said nervously.

Beth shook her head. "No, this isn't about cupcakes." She waited until Ryuu was standing behind Meryn. Now Amelia was starting to get nervous.

Beth took a deep breath. "It's just that I couldn't help noticing the similarities between you and Amelia, so I approached Ryuu to see if he had any suspicions. When he agreed with my hypothesis, I started to do some digging."

Meryn held up a hand. "Whoa, hold up, Bunny. Suspicions about what?" She looked behind her and glared up at her squire. "What did you agree with?"

"Meryn, what was your mother's maiden name?" Beth asked.

Everyone turned to stare at Meryn. "Camden, why?"

Amelia felt her stomach drop as she gasped. "That's impossible."

"What?" Meryn asked again.

Beth turned to Amelia. "I checked the birth records. In 1952, Lily Camden was born to Estelle and William Camden. Ten years later, in 1961, Violet Camden was born."

Amelia stood. "That's impossible! If my Aunt Violet had had a child, my mother would have told me I had a cousin!" she insisted.

"What the fuck is going on?" Meryn shouted, jumping out of her chair.

Ryuu placed a hand on the back of her neck, and instantly, Meryn's face became serene; she sat back down in her chair. "Easy *denka*, you need to stay calm."

Meryn shook her head back and forth slowly and leaned forward, effectively removing his hand from her neck. "Stop with the sneaky ninja shit."

Ryuu's eyes danced, though he didn't smile. "Of course, *denka,* I will keep my stealthy ninja skills to a minimum."

Amelia refused to believe what she was being told. Her mother might not be perfect, but she would have told her she had a cousin her own age. She pulled out her phone and called her brother. As usual, he answered on the first ring. She felt a warm hand on her lower back. When she looked down, she was surprised to see Darian supporting her gently, glaring around the table.

"Why are you upset?" Caiden asked immediately. He had always had the uncanny ability to know when she needed him.

"Do you know anything about my mother's family?"

"I know that you had an aunt who was about ten years younger than Mother, and that she and her husband died in the early eighties."

"Did they have any children?"

"No."

Amelia turned to the room to face Beth. "You must be wrong."

"Amelia, what's going on out there?" Caiden demanded.

"They're saying that Meryn's mother is my aunt," she explained.

"What!" Meryn exploded finally putting the pieces together.

"Hold on, it just so happens our parents are visiting right now, let me get Mother on the phone." They all heard loud footsteps on stone a muffled conversation, and then her mother, Lily, was on the phone.

"Amelia, are you there baby?"

"I'm here."

"What does Meryn look like?"

Amelia turned to Meryn and really looked at her. Why hadn't she noticed it before? She evaluated people's faces for a living! She and Meryn had the same bone structure, the same nose and lips. When she looked closely, she could easily see that they could be related. The only difference was the eyes and the hair. Meryn had bright green eyes, whereas Amelia had the same grey-silver eyes of her brothers and father.

"When your hair is long, what does it look like?" Amelia asked, barely getting the words out. Meryn couldn't answer. She just let her tears fall. Amelia knew then that they shared the same brown curls.

"She looks like me, only she has a short pixie cut and no curls, and bright green eyes like..."

"Like me," her mother said, sniffling. "Can Meryn hear me?" she asked.

"Yes, you're on speaker."

"Meryn, sweetheart, who raised you?"

"My grandmother. I hated her, just so you know." Meryn crossed her arms over her chest looking defensive.

Lily sobbed. "Oh Violet, I failed you."

"Lily, Lily, darling what's the matter? Who is this?" Amelia heard her father demand.

"Father, it's me."

"Amelia? What in the world is going on?"

"Give me the phone, Marshall." Seconds later, her mother was back. "Meryn, sweetheart, I am so sorry! If I had known, I would have moved heaven and Earth to bring you to Storm Keep. The last time I saw Violet was two years before she died. She hadn't been pregnant then. When I heard about her death, I called Mother, and she told me that I wasn't welcome to come home. The funeral was over, and she never wanted to see me again. She never once said anything about caring for Violet's child because, she knew if she had, I would have come and gotten you."

"Why?" Amelia asked.

"Because my mother wasn't a very nice person. She believed that I was one step up from the devil because I thought differently than she did. I practically raised Violet after she was born. She was only thing that kept me in that house. I refused to leave Violet alone.

"When Violet was thirteen, Mother and I had an argument. She disowned me and kicked me out of the house. I swore to Violet that I would come back when she was eighteen and take her out of there.

"It was the seventies, so I drifted, hitching rides and camping with friends. Eventually I met your father. Two years after mating with him, when Violet was seventeen, I kept my promise. Your father and I went back home to check on Violet and make preparations for her to move out on her eighteenth birthday. But to my surprise, she had already married and moved out with her husband.

"When we were saying goodbye, she made me promise that if anything happened to her and she had children, I would take care of them. I swore to her that I would, and no child of my baby sister's would ever live in that house." The venom in her mother's voice scared her; she had never heard her sound like that.

Aiden looked ill as he faced Meryn who'd buried her face in her hands. "Baby?"

Meryn didn't look up; she just continued to shake her head behind her hands. "It's just when I imagine how my life could have been different if I had been raised in Storm Keep, I get so angry. If Amelia's mom had known about me, I could have had a sister and brothers, a family that loved me. I wouldn't have gone hungry or worried that my one pair of shoes wouldn't last the winter. I would have been wanted." Meryn choked out the words between sobs. Aiden pulled Meryn into his lap and wrapped his large arms around her as if to protect her from her own memories. Ryuu ran a gentle hand over her hair in an effort to comfort her.

Amelia saw the shocked expressions around the table and realized that Meryn had never told anyone exactly how bad her childhood had been. She felt her own tears trickle down her cheeks.

"That's it! Marshall, I don't care about your magic rules! We're going to dig up my mother and you're going to bring her back to life so I can beat the everloving shit out of her!" Lily yelled.

Amelia felt her eyes widen. What her mother was talking about was black magic.

"Lily, honey, calm down. You know we can't do that." Even over the phone, she could feel her father's shock.

"Kyran! Tristan! Don't just stand there; get our bags from our room and take them back down to the car. Thank God, we haven't unpacked yet."

"Lily..." Her father was trying to get her mother's attention.

"Today boys! My niece is crying, and my baby is crying! We're going to Lycaonia after we make my mother a broken corpse!"

"Lily..."

"Marshall, don't just stand there, help the boys with the bags."

"Yes, love." After a few quiet moments, she heard her mother take a deep breath. In all her life, she had never once heard her mother raise her voice. She was normally very laid back, and went with the flow, always smiling. Amelia liked this new side of her mother.

"Girls, listen to me. There's so much I want to tell you, but I can't right now. Just know that you were brought together for a reason. Stay close to each other. We'll be there soon."

Meryn sniffled. "Are you really going to beat Estelle up?"

"I know that we can't use black magic to bring her back, but I will be getting in touch with the city back home to make arrangements to move her grave to our estate. That way we can desecrate it whenever we like," Lily promised.

Meryn smiled weakly. "I'd like that."

"Mother, maybe you should take this opportunity to change before Father brings the bags down," they heard Caiden suggest. "You spent the entire day in those clothes traveling already."

"You're such a good boy, Caiden. I think I'll do just that. See you soon, girls."

"Remind me to never piss that woman off," Caiden muttered.

"Well, we knew Meryn got her crazy from somewhere. Evidently, it's hereditary," Colton said, winking at Meryn, making her smile.

Amelia sat down in her chair with a plop. "I have a baby sister-cousin."

Meryn brightened. "I have another sister!"

"Commander, if you ever need tips on how to handle those two, let me know. I have over thirty years' experience raising Amelia," Caiden offered.

Aiden cleared his throat. "Actually, is there a way to know if they're lying?"

Caiden laughed. "Ask her a question."

Aiden turned Meryn in his lap until she was looking up at him. "Baby, are you playing with explosives?"

Meryn looked up at the ceiling in an exaggerated eye roll. "Where am I supposed to get explosives to play with?" Aiden smiled and relaxed.

"Sir, did she make eye contact?" Caiden asked.

"No." Aiden answered frowning.

"She didn't make eye contact and answered with a question," Caiden confirmed.

Aiden swallowed hard. "What does that mean?"

Caiden laughed. "It means you're fucked. She's building a bomb."

"Hey!" Meryn protested.

Amelia smiled. She didn't feel like such an oddball now; someone else thought like her. "What kind of bomb?" she asked.

Meryn just turned to her and grinned.

"Yea, though I walk through the valley of the shadow of death..." Colton intoned dramatically.

Darian wrapped a supportive arm around her shoulders. Not wanting to waste a single moment of his affection, she leaned into his body and was rewarded when he pulled her closer. She didn't know what had changed with him, but she would take what she could get.

"I'm going to let you guys go. Father looked a little shell-shocked earlier. Kyran, Tristan, and I will help him adjust. We raised Amelia so we weren't really all that shocked at Mother's ideas, but I don't think Father has ever seen her so angry."

Amelia snorted. "I never threatened to raise the dead to pummel it."

"Yes, you did. Technically, you threatened to beat Morgan Fiero to the point of death and then beat him again while he was recovering, basically the same thing," Caiden reminded her.

She laughed out loud. She hadn't heard the name Morgan Fiero in years.

Beside her, Darian stiffened. "What did he do to her?"

"He kept snapping her bra, trying to get it to come off. Kyran was about to step in when Amelia turned and completely unloaded fourteen years of techniques she learned watching us train on him. It took Kyran and another unit warrior to pull her off him. From the time Amelia was eleven until she was eighteen, we hid every weapon in the house."

"I wasn't that bad," she countered.

"Keep telling yourself that, baby girl. There's a reason why grown men are afraid of you." Caiden teased.

"But she's so bubbly," Beth said, using Meryn's expression.

"Yeah, and that's what makes her so scary. She never stopped smiling her pleasant smile when she damn near beat little Morgan Fiero to a pulp. I swear she should have been born a redhead. It's like a universal warning label that the person you're talking to could lose their shit at a moment's notice," Caiden sighed.

"Two, there's two of them," Keelan whispered.

"About to be three. Her mother is on her way for a visit. Two generations of wackiness." Caiden laughed out loud. "Kyran, Tristan, and I were planning a visit to Lycaonia to threaten Darian about how to treat our baby girl, but having Lily head out there is a thousand times better."

"Almost three generations!" Meryn said brightly pointing to her belly.

"Sir, can I request a transfer to Storm Keep?" Colton looked worried.

"Denied," Aiden grumbled.

"On that note, have a great visit." Caiden laughed again and hung up.

"Sonofabitch!" Aiden growled. "He's enjoying this."

Meryn practically bounced in his lap. "I get to meet my aunt and uncle. I have family!"

Amelia looked at her and shared a wide grin. Even though she had brothers, Meryn was different—she was like her. She watched *Doctor*

Who and ate expired pickles. Suddenly, she didn't feel alone or homesick, not when she had a baby sister-cousin who was just like her!

"Meryn, let's skip the movie and go to bed. You've had a lot thrown at you tonight," Aiden suggested.

Meryn immediately looked alarmed. "But..." She looked at Amelia.

Amelia smiled. "I'm not going anywhere, especially now that I have found my mate and my baby sister-cousin."

Colton frowned. "That's not a real term."

Amelia and Meryn turned at the same time to glare at him. He immediately capitulated and held his hands up in surrender. "I will write Webster myself to get it added to the dictionary."

Meryn's laughter was cut short by a yawn. Ryuu lifted her off Aiden's lap and placed her on her feet. "Come along, *denka*. Let your mate go upstairs to warm your side of the bed while I prepare a nice cup of heated milk for you."

Amelia realized that Ryuu only called her and Meryn by a Japanese term. "Ryuu, you call Meryn *denka* and me *itoko-sama*, why do we get special names?"

Ryuu's smile was mysterious. "I am bound to serve Meryn's house for as long as I live, this includes anyone who shares the bonds of blood, as you do. *Denka* is the title that Meryn was comfortable with me calling her, it means, Lady. *Itoko-sama* is a very formal and polite way of saying cousin."

Amelia's mouth dropped. "That means you knew almost from the beginning."

Ryuu nodded. "I would be a poor squire indeed if I could not identify the members of my charge's family. The bond I share with *denka* allows me to monitor her health and moods, but it also tells me when someone of her bloodline is nearby."

Meryn scowled at her squire. "We still need to work on your communication skills."

He bowed. "I think it was timed perfectly." He held out his arm. She sighed and placed her hand on his forearm, and let him lead her toward the kitchen. They were almost to the doors when she stopped suddenly and turned. "You won't forget about getting up early tomorrow, will you? I can't wait to introduce you to Adelaide. It will be the first time in my whole life I'll introduce family."

The joy on Meryn's face brought tears to Amelia's eyes. "I wouldn't miss it for anything," she promised.

"Yes!" Meryn threw a fist in the air and walked into the kitchen with Ryuu.

"This evening has been most enlightening," Gavriel remarked.

Darian stood and held out his arm to Amelia. "Will you allow me to escort you upstairs?"

She placed her hand on his arm and stood. "Yes, please."

"Thank the Gods for no movie night." Keelan exhaled and stood.

"We'll take our leave first." Darian said and led them toward the doorway.

"Goodnight, you two. Congratulations, Amelia on finding new family," Colton called after them.

"Thanks!" she yelled back.

She was still thinking of Meryn when they
reached her room. When Darian opened the
door and walked in with her, she realized where
they were. He shut the door behind them, and
her eyes widened. What on earth was her mate
up to?

CHAPTER SEVEN

"Darian?" She looked at him questioningly. He hadn't said much during dinner, but he'd reached out to comfort her when she needed him during the startling revelations. The action spoke volumes to her, but she had to make sure they meant the same to him.

"You know how close I am?" he asked, leaning against the door.

"Yes, in fact, I'm shocked that you haven't turned yet. Your strength of will must be immeasurable."

"Hardly, I've just surrounded myself with things that help."

"Like your atrium? I noticed earlier today in the woods, your aura lightened when you touched the tree."

"You can see auras?"

"Not in the same way that the fae do. You can only see the auras and soul light of your mates. I can see different colors tied to emotions. It's tied into my empathy."

He nodded. "Interesting. To answer your question if my oasis helps, yes it does. I am fae, a child of the earth. Plants help bring us light."

She stepped forward. "Then why don't you go back to the fae garden, the one from my dream. That place has to have enough light to help."

His eyebrows came together in a frown. "You keep mentioning a dream from when you were a child, that we were evidently in the fae gardens, but I don't remember that dream. The only dreams I can remember having of you are the ones that happened recently. In them, you are an adult, and you're always laughing."

"I've had those, too, but the one that keeps coming back to me is the first one. I was six, and we were in a garden. You promised you wouldn't forget me." She stared at the floor. All her life, she had feared he would forget her. Maybe in her own way, she had known this would happen.

Darian moved away from the door and pulled her into his arms. "I would never hurt you intentionally. If I made such a promise, I am sorry more than you know that I don't remember such a beautiful dream." He kissed the top of her head.

"I thought you didn't want anything to do with me? That you wanted me to 'find someone from my own planet'." She tilted her head back to stare into his beautiful face. He looked so conflicted.

"If I were half the man I used to be, I'd send you away. I would do anything to keep you safe, but I find myself drawn to you. The more I am with you, the more I want to live, to fight this insidious darkness in my heart. I just don't see how this is going to end well for either of us."

He rested his forehead against hers, and she wrapped her arms around his waist.

"If being with me pushes back the darkness, then never leave my side. If you need a reason to live, do it for me, do it for our future children. Please don't assume I would be better off without you, not now.

"You fear that if we're tied together, you turning feral would drag my soul down with yours, but what you don't realize is that I would happily jump into the depths of hell to be with you. If I lost you, I wouldn't be able to live in this world alone. I would take my own life to be with you."

His arms pulled her closer, squeezing her tight. "Don't say such things," he said, his voice breaking.

She pulled back and raised her hands up to cup his face. "There is no other for me and no life without you, so make the decision. Are we to live or die?"

She saw a flash of fear in his eyes before it was replaced by resolve. "You're not going to ever back down are you?"

"Nope." She popped her lips on the letter 'p'.

He smiled gently. "Then I guess all I can do is stay by your side for eternity."

"It's good to have life goals." She was smiling so much her cheeks hurt.

Shaking his head, he swept her up in his arms. "I can't, in good conscience, claim you yet, I want to see if being around my mate is enough to pull me from the edge."

"Then make love to me." She laughed at his shocked expression. "If being around me helps, just think of what making love to me could do?"

He laughed out loud and her heart soared. When he looked down at her, he wore the same roguish expression she had fallen in love with as a child. "I came in here tonight to tell you to stay away, but I can't fight temptation anymore. I cannot refuse your offer of paradise; I'm not strong enough." He laid her down gently on the bed.

"I've been waiting my whole life for you," she said sitting up. She reached around and unzipped her dress. When she looked up, he was staring down at her, his eyes wide.

"What do you mean you waited? You can't be a..."

"A what? A virgin? Let me break it down for you: I have three extremely overprotective older brothers and three extremely overprotective half-brothers. Their moral compasses tend to break if they are pissed enough. I have six units of warriors who would happily destroy any guy I dated who made the mistake of hurting me. To top everything off, I have been dreaming of you since I was six. Dating has never really been an option for me.

"So yes, I am a virgin, but that doesn't mean I haven't been taking care of business myself, if you know what I mean."

Darian's mouth opened and closed, then open and closed again. He blinked once before a sexy smile appeared. "Does that mean you have toys?"

Amelia kicked her shoes off and dropped them over the side of the bed. "Maybe." She shimmied out of her dress and threw it on the floor. When she was down to her bra and panties, she lay back on her elbows and crossed her legs at her ankles, getting comfortable. "You going to keep me waiting much longer, princess?"

With a low growl, Darian slowly began to unbutton his dress robe. "Lie back and close your eyes."

Amelia relaxed, lay flat on her back, and closed her eyes. She waited and listened carefully, trying to figure out what he was doing. She heard the rustle of fabric and assumed he had removed his robe. She wanted to open her eyes.

"Keep them closed." His deep voice came from her right. He'd walked around to that side of the bed. She shivered at his tone.

After a couple minutes, her mind had worked itself into a hectic mess. Where was he? What was he doing?

"Are you thinking about me?" His words now came from the foot of the bed.

"Darian, I don't understand, what are you doing?" She wanted to open her eyes and manhandle him onto the bed. Her body was coiled in anticipation of his touch, knowing that she was about to make love to her mate.

"Being with a lover is very different than 'taking care of business' on your own. The fact that I am the one to teach you the difference humbles me. I am going to take my time and introduce you to lovemaking."

She felt his fingers at her ankle. Casually, lazily he began to run his fingers up her leg to her knee and back down again. She felt completely out of control even though all he was doing was touching her leg.

"Darian..." Even to her own ears, her voice sounded strained.

"I bet you never took the time to explore every inch of your own body. How could you? Did you ever stop to appreciate the way your body changes as it prepares itself for loving?"

She shook her head. Her insides were shaking. All she wanted was for him to drive into her as fast and as hard as he could. She needed him desperately. She squirmed, squeezing her legs together.

"Are you imagining what I will do to you? You saw my cock when I was getting dressed. Are you wondering what it looks like hard and dripping for you?" His voice came from her left. He was circling the bed.

She swallowed hard, her throat dry. "Yes."

With the lightest of touches, she felt his fingers at her hips as he pulled down her panties.

"You wanted to give me a reason to live, and now I have one. Fate has given me my own piece of heaven, and I will guard it ferociously." He spread her legs and she nearly came unglued when she felt his tongue slip between her folds and nibble her gently.

"You taste like the sweetest of nectars. If we could stop time, would you let me stay right here? I could feast on you for hours and never get enough." He began deliberate strokes over her clit, pushing her climb toward madness.

"Darian! Please! Don't tease me anymore," she begged.

She felt his body move between her legs as his hands slipped under her body to release the clasp on her bra. He pulled it from her body, exposing her breasts.

"How can one woman be so perfect?" His voice was louder now that he was closer.

His hot mouth wrapped around her nipple, and he tugged and twisted mercilessly. When his hand reached between their bodies to circle her clit, she cried out and bucked against him wanting more, needing more.

"Open your eyes, my love," he whispered.

Her eyes flew open to see him leaning over her, his lavender eyes bright.

"My love?"

"How could I not love the crazy female who kneed me to prove that I wouldn't hurt her? How could I not love the woman who is willing to descend into hell rather than lose me? I have so very little to offer you, not even a certain future, and you give to me at every turn—your trust, your faith, your body. How could I not love you?" He buried his face between her neck and her shoulder.

"I've loved you for so long," she sobbed. It felt like a dream having him here with her. She wrapped her arms around his head and her legs around his waist. She would never let him go.

He pulled back to look down at her. "I wish I could give you more."

She sniffed and let her tears fall over her temples. "All I have ever wanted was you."

"I don't deserve you."

She began to protest, and he kissed her lightly on the lips. "I don't. I know this. But Goddess willing, I will have enough time on this Earth to make up for the sadness I have caused you."

"I wish I had found you a month ago," she whispered.

When he realized she was referring to her conception cycle, his eyes filled with tears. "I can do no less than try to hold on for the next year. Nothing could honor me more than for you to have my child."

"I'll hold you to that, princess." She smiled.

His eyes danced, and he leaned down to nip her collarbone, making her laugh. "We need to talk about this nickname you've given me."

"I like it." She grinned.

"You need a nickname, too, then," he said, kissing her neck.

She sighed. "I have one."

He pulled back and looked down at her. "What is it?"

She shook her head. "Nope, I'm never telling you. I'll never hear the end of it."

His smile was wicked. "I'll find out." He reached down, and seconds later, she felt him begin to push inside of her. She lifted her hips to end his slow impalement. He kept eye contact and chuckled. "None of that. You've been in control all your life; it's my turn."

Inch by inch, as he stretched her, she realized two things: One: Sex toys couldn't compare to the heated flesh that she felt. Two: She should have been using larger toys. She was just about to tell him to stop when her body stretched again, accommodating his size. She breathed out a sigh of relief.

His eyes were filled with concern. "Are you well? Should I stop?"

"You stop and I'll kill you. Just give me a second to adjust."

His eyes crinkled when he smiled, and he kissed the tip of her nose. "Trust me?"

She nodded. He took her at her word. He leaned down and bit her neck as he plunged deep into her. The pain from the bite turned the burning sensation from his stretching her into pleasure, and her body short-circuited between the pain and pleasure.

"Gods! Yes! More, Gods, more!"

With a deliberate rhythm, he worked his body in and out of hers, each thrust causing them both to cry out. She had never felt so strung out like this. The time he spent not touching her had built up her desire to unimaginable proportions. Each time he didn't touch her intensified a hundred fold the times he did.

When he began to increase his pace, she knew he was close. He reached between them and placed a finger on either side of her clit. Every time his hips surged forward, he stroked her with his movements. When he threw back his head and roared his release, she easily followed him.

For a few seconds, they enjoyed the feeling of being intertwined before he pulled out of her. Grinning like a schoolboy, he stared down at her. Breathing heavily, she flipped him off. Laughing, he headed toward the bathroom and came back with a washcloth.

He cleaned her gently, kissing her belly and using his finger to tickle her opening. When she clutched down involuntarily, she groaned. She would be feeling this tomorrow. He disposed of the washcloth in the bathroom, returned to bed, and pulled her into the curve of his body.

"It's so quiet," he murmured.

"I thought so, too, after visiting your room." She yawned and snuggled into his chest.

"You'll move to my room tomorrow."

"Oh, I will, huh?" She poked at his side, making him laugh.

He pulled back so he could look her in the eye. "Would you do me the honor of moving into my quarters?"

"Yes, my prince." She yawned again and got comfortable. For the first time since meeting him, she fell asleep hopeful of the future.

Amelia woke the next morning to soft kisses on her face. When she opened her eyes, Darian was smiling down at her. "Morning, sleepyhead."

"What time is it?" She sat up and saw that he was already dressed in his black fatigues.

"Not even seven. Breakfast is at eight. I thought you'd like time to get ready." The difference in him was amazing. There was life in his eyes, and he hadn't stopped smiling.

"You look..."

He laughed. "I hardly recognize myself. I woke up this morning and the darkness was nearly gone. I haven't felt this good in years."

"So it's still there?"

He nodded. "Maybe it will always be there, which means you will have to help me keep it at bay." He grinned at her and tugged at the sheet covering her body.

"Darian! Horndog! What have I created?" She jumped from the bed and ran into the bathroom.

"Need help?" he offered.

"No, thank you. If you come in here, I won't get anything done."

His masculine laughter was cut short when she shut the door.

Men!

She replayed the events from the night before. Squeezing her legs together, she shook her head. She turned on the shower and quickly went through the motions of getting ready. She put on her makeup and smiled at her fresh-faced appearance. She loved her job, but didn't feel like doing a complete look every day. Wrapped in her towel, she walked into the room and pulled out her suitcase. Darian watched her get ready.

"What happened to your suitcase?"

"I was in a rush trying to get ready for you last night."

"So your suitcase exploded?"

She nodded. "Pretty much."

She dug her way through her clothes and pulled out her favorite jeans and a cream sweater. She was debating between her green boy-cut panty set and the blue when she heard Darian clear his throat behind her.

"Blue."

She turned. He was staring at the navy blue lace set as if it were the rarest treasure on the planet.

"Blue it is." She stood and let the towel drop, quickly pulled on her bra and panties, and could have sworn she heard her mate whimper.

Bending over, she shimmied her breasts into place. She grabbed a pair of socks, put those on, and then slid on her jeans. Finally, she pulled on her sweater.

"Warmth!" She snuggled her face into the neckline.

"Come on, love, I can smell breakfast from here." Darian stood and held out his arm.

She had imagined how life with him would be. He'd never know how happy it made her for him to escort her down to breakfast.

Amelia hummed happily as they walked into the dining room. The men stood, nodded at her, and sat when she did.

"She's alive!" Beth declared with a smile.

Amelia blinked, thinking that Beth was referring to the amazing night she had shared with Darian. Her confusion must have shown because Meryn elaborated.

"You're up before noon." Meryn yawned.

Ryuu was already passing out cups of steaming beverages. He turned to her. "*Itoko-sama* what would you like before breakfast?"

"Before breakfast?"

Darian chuckled at her side. "We have learned to appease the beast before we start eating." He pointed to a bleary-eyed Meryn who was blowing on her mug.

"The beast, huh?" She turned to Ryuu. "I'll just have a cup of coffee."

Ryuu nodded and picked up a carafe. "Cream? Sugar?" He turned over her cup. As he poured, the rich smell of coffee filled the air. "Yes please, both, and lots of each."

Ryuu poured milk into a tiny creamer on his serving cart. He set the creamer and a sugar bowl on a small silver tray and set them beside her coffee cup.

"Thank you, this smells amazing." She lifted the cup and inhaled deeply.

Ryuu nodded, his expression intent. "We take our coffee very seriously around here."

"Thank the Gods we do! Ryuu, can I get what you normally serve Rheia? The coffee with the espresso?" Keelan collapsed into his chair. Ryuu immediately headed for the kitchen.

"What's the matter buddy? Sandman kick your ass?" Colton laughed.

Keelan looked up with a murderous glare. "Why in the fuck are you so happy?" he growled.

Colton jerked back as if he had been electrocuted. Everyone around the table stared. To Amelia Keelan just seemed more like Kendrick than usual.

Colton stood, his eyes wild, and looked down at his mate. "Fix him! He caught a case of Meryn!"

Rheia rolled her eyes and pulled her mate back down into his chair. Penny giggled at her father's actions.

Meryn growled. "I am not contagious, asshole."

Ryuu swept in from the kitchen, a tall mug in hand. "I made it extra strong." He set it down in front of the witch and stepped back.

Eyes half closed, Keelan took his first sip and grimaced but kept drinking. His eyes opened slowly, and he blinked, looking around the table. "What's for breakfast?"

"We have an assortment of bagels and pastries," Ryuu answered turning to head back into the kitchen.

Keelan nodded and yawned. "Sounds good."

Aiden stared at him. "Everything okay?" he asked in a very neutral voice.

"Yeah, I'm just working through some stuff. Oh! Here, I finished it last night when I couldn't sleep." He stood and walked to the other side of the table, stopping in front of Meryn. He handed her something, and she stared at it for a second, looked up at him and then back down, and squealed. She popped out of her chair and threw herself at Keelan, hugging him tight.

Amelia exchanged looks with Darian who shrugged. Amelia turned back to Meryn. "Meryn, what is it?"

Meryn was hopping up and down, trying to kiss Keelan's face. Aiden scooped her up and set her back down in her chair. She was so excited she was practically shaking. Keelan made his way back to his chair and sat down.

"He made me a sonic screwdriver!" Meryn waved the cylindrical metal object around.

Beth turned to Keelan. "I didn't know you knew that much about science."

Keelan shrugged and took another sip of coffee. "Who needs science when you have magic?"

Meryn turned it over in her hands. "What does it do?"

"I recorded the sound that the sonic screwdriver makes from the show; it plays that when you press the button," he explained.

Meryn looked crestfallen. "Is that all?"

Keelan shook his head. "No, it plays that sound when you press the green button and launches a stun spell when you press the white button. Each spell is set to knock out a full-grown vampire, the paranormal race least susceptible to electric shock. I think it has a hundred charges stored. When you run out, Ryuu should be able to charge it for you."

Meryn covertly began eyeing her mate, her finger twitching over the button.

"No," Aiden said.

"But..."

"No, Meryn, you cannot test it on me." Aiden gave her a stern look and kissed her forehead.

Amelia could tell that her baby sister-cousin was dying to see it in action.

Meryn turned and stared at Colton.

"No," Rheia said.

"Y'all are no fun." Meryn set her screwdriver down next to her plate, but kept looking at it longingly.

"Breakfast is served," Ryuu announced as he wheeled the cart in. One by one, everyone picked what they wanted. Amelia was stuck. She wanted a bagel but also wanted something sweet.

Darian leaned in. "Get both."

She kissed his cheek and did as he advised. She selected an asiago cheese bagel and a raspberry and cream cheese danish.

"Look who is all kissy-face this morning," Meryn teased.

Amelia looked up and Meryn winked. She grinned back and gave Meryn a thumbs up. The men chuckled.

Darian turned to her. "Speaking of last night, you said you had three brothers and three half-brothers. As far as I know Caiden, Kyran and Tristan are the only Ironwoods I know."

"Well, technically, Caiden, Kyran, and Tristan are my half-brothers. Thane, Justice, and Law aren't related to me at all; they are Caiden, Kyran, and Tristan's half-brothers. But growing up, we never made the distinctions, and they all looked after me."

She heard a fork drop and looked over at Colton who was staring at her.

"What?"

"You can't mean Thane, Justice, and Law Ashleigh?" he choked out.

"Yeah, why?" she looked around in confusion; even Darian looked impressed.

"Because they are like ghosts. They work completely outside the system and don't report to anyone. Frankly, they are fucking badass." Colton's voice was full of reverence.

Meryn glared at Aiden. "More people you forgot to mention?"

Aiden shook his head. "Baby, no one tells them what to do. Even the council can't order them to do anything; they live by their own code. Every fifty years or so, I extend the offer for them to join a unit, but they always decline."

"So how are they related to your brothers?" Gavriel asked.

Amelia spread cream cheese on her bagel. "The Ironwood brothers and the Ashleigh brothers have the same mother. The Ashleigh brothers were born about fifteen hundred years before Caiden, but unlike the Ironwood brothers, the Ashleigh brothers are triplets."

"Rumors are true then," Gavriel said, rubbing his chin.

"It explains their strength," Aiden added.

"How is that special?" Meryn asked. Rheia was the only other one who looked confused.

Amelia realized that they didn't know because they were human. "Meryn, multiple births are really rare amongst paranormals. The essence of what we are tends to demand all of the mother's resources in the womb. Shifters have their animal, vampires their strength, fae their light and witches their magic. Usually, in instances of multiple births, one baby becomes dominant and tragically kills their sibling by taking all the nutrients. Twins are rare and triplets are considered divine gifts."

"We have a set of twins serving in the units don't we?" Meryn asked.

Aiden nodded. "Yes, Nigel and Neil Morninglory, they are twin witches from Storm Keep."

"What was it like growing up with legends for older brothers?" Colton asked, his face alight with hero worship.

Amelia laughed out loud. "Difficult. I used to call Thane all the time to complain that Caiden hated me and didn't want me to have any fun. Thane would let me cry and vent then explain how much Caiden loved me because he wouldn't let me jump from the castle battlements like the boys did. Even though we're not related by blood, they spoiled me terribly."

"Do you think they'll like me?" Meryn asked in an unusually quiet voice.

Amelia stared and then she remembered Meryn was now family. She had forgotten such an important fact after being with Darian. "They are going to freaking love you! Especially Thane. He's like you and Kendrick; they don't like people either."

Aiden choked on his danish. "Oh Gods! She is related to them now."

"Ha ha! Wait until I tell them you locked me in your trunk." Meryn grinned.

Aiden turned milk-white. "Now, baby..."

Amelia heard a roaring in her ears, and it felt like ice covered her heart. "You did what?" she asked through clenched teeth. It felt like the floor had shifted under their feet.

One moment she was glaring at Aiden, the next, Darian turned her and took full possession of her lips. His tongue teased hers, and she felt her anger drain away. When he pulled back, the concern on his face was clear to see. "Are you okay?"

"Yes, thank you for the help." Amelia couldn't believe what she had almost done.

"What just happened?" Beth asked, gripping the table.

Embarrassed, Amelia covered her face. She had almost lost control of her magic like an untrained child. "I'm so sorry! I haven't lost control like that in a while. I normally don't get angry like that. It's just the idea of poor Meryn locked away..."

Colton laughed. She removed her hands and glared at him. He held up his hands in surrender. "You didn't get the full story. Aiden put her in his trunk after she knocked him out with the back of his toilet and used his head as a kickboxing bag. She ended up denting the shit out of his trunk."

Amelia blinked and slowly began to smile. "Ryuu did mention that bear shifters were susceptible to toilet decks."

Aiden growled. "Anyone would be. Those things are heavy!"

"Again!" Penny yelled, her face glowing with excitement.

Rheia shook her head. "No pumpkin dumpling, the ground shaking isn't good for the house." Penny frowned looking disappointed.

Aiden winked at the small child. "How about we give your grandmother a couple hours off this afternoon, and you can help me train the men again?"

Penny brightened and rewarded Aiden with a smile. " 'Kay!"

Aiden looked like he would swagger in his chair if he could. He was that proud of himself for making the small child smile.

Amelia felt Penny's excitement and could relate. The days she got to 'play' with her brother's units were some of her best memories growing up. She'd have to give Penny pointers before they left.

Meryn clapped her hands together. "Okay, if we don't have any more revelations or earthquakes about to happen, let's head over to Adelaide's. If we time this right, we can get a second breakfast from Marius."

Ryuu stared at his charge. "You can't be hungry."

Amelia giggled. "I don't think he knows about second breakfast," she said in an exaggerated accent causing Meryn to laugh.

Ryuu turned to Rheia. "Are you sure she doesn't have a tapeworm?"

Rheia shook her head. "Afraid not." She turned and kissed Penny on her forehead. "Let's get you settled in the front room before I head to the clinic."

"You're not coming with us?" Beth asked.

Rheia shook her head. "I wish. We're getting one of the two necklaces back from the council. We'll be running tests on live cultures to see what happens. Fun times."

Colton looked over at Aiden, and Aiden nodded. "I've already assigned Delta and Zeta to guard the clinic. Epsilon and Beta have patrol, and Gamma will be joining us for training. I've sent the trainees back to Adair for the rest of the week to help him get the newer cadets trained up. They will be assisting in drills." Colton looked relieved.

Meryn grinned evilly. "Gamma is coming over?"

Aiden nodded. "They should be here any moment."

Meryn stood. "Let's go."

Everyone walked toward the front door. Ryuu handed coats to Beth, Meryn, Rheia, and her.

Darian grabbed her hand and let the others pass them in the hallway. He cupped her face.

"Are you sure you're okay?"

She turned her face and kissed the center of his palm. "Yes, I'm fine. Have fun with the boys."

"Thanks to you, I will. I haven't enjoyed the company of my friends in so long, thank you."

"No charge," she quipped.

Hand-in-hand, they entered the foyer. Colton was saying goodbye to Rheia and Penny. When he walked to the door, she let go of Darian's hand, approached the little girl, and knelt in front of her. "Hey, Penny."

"Hello," Penny replied in an adorably sweet voice.

"I was raised by my brothers, and they used to have me help train, too. Want some tips?"

Penny nodded enthusiastically.

Amelia leaned in close making sure none of the men were listening. "They are used to being the tallest people around; if you need to go around them, go vertically. They hardly ever look up." Penny nodded. "Also, if it's a matter of speed and it looks like they're about to get the upper hand, make it look like you're about to fall. They will instinctively slow down and try to catch you." Amelia winked at the small child. Penny gave her a thumbs up and raised her hand. Amelia slapped her a high five.

Rheia watched her as she stood. "Should I be concerned?"

Amelia shook her head. "Nah, if I lived through it, so can she. Shifters are sturdier than witches."

"Fair enough." Rheia turned to her daughter. "Be a good girl."

" 'Kay!"

Darian walked up behind her and wrapped his arms around her. "Be a good girl," he whispered in her ear. She shivered and turned in his arms. "Only for you."

"Okay break it up you two, virgin eyes over here!"

Amelia and Darian turned to see Sascha leaning against the doorway. Amelia was about to tell him what he could do when Meryn walked passed her toward the door. Without pausing, she extended her sonic screwdriver and stunned the unit leader. He dropped to the floor with a loud thud.

Meryn jumped, throwing her fist in the air. "Yes! This shit is awesome!"

Aiden sighed, but the grin tugging at his mouth showed that he really wasn't too mad. "Meryn, no stunning the men. We need them able to protect you," he chided gently.

She shrugged. "It was worth it." She stepped over Sascha's body and tilted her head back for a kiss. Aiden chuckled and gave her one.

Keelan stepped past Sascha's body, looking smug. "It worked better than I hoped."

Aiden turned to Colton. "Drag him to the training course."

Colton grabbed Sascha's ankle. "I'm not even going to complain about dragging his heavy ass. It was worth it to see him go down." He turned and was about to take his first step when Rheia's voice stopped him short. "Do *not* let his head bump with each step. I don't have time to tend to him this morning."

Colton sniffed. "You just ruined my morning."

Rheia gave him a sly smile. "I'll make it up to you later."

He immediately brightened and dropped Sascha's ankle and grabbed the Gamma unit member by the back of his jacket. "Come on, old man, time to train."

Darian leaned in close. "And you were upset about a tiny tremor. This is everyday life at the Alpha estate."

Amelia smiled. "I love it!"

Ryuu walked past them with the car keys. "Ladies, whenever you're ready." He bowed.

"Hey, Penny, Felix is staying with you today. Keep him warm," Meryn called. Amelia watched as the tiny sprite flew over to Penny and sat on her shoulder.

" 'Kay!" Penny said snuggling the sprite close.

Meryn turned to Amelia and Beth. "Let's blow this popsicle stand!"

Darian kissed her gently and accompanied her to the door.

She had a new baby sister-cousin and was closer to claiming her mate. Things were definitely looking up.

CHAPTER EIGHT

Amelia sat with Meryn in the back of the car, and Beth sat up front with Ryuu. Amelia pulled out her phone. "What's your name on Facebook? I'll send a friend request."

Meryn scrunched up her face. "I'm not on Facebook."

"What?" Amelia and Beth asked at the same time.

Meryn shrugged. "Besides y'all, I don't have any friends, and I live with y'all, so I never saw the point."

"But you're a computer genius, you've used Facebook in tracking down potential shifter couples," Beth said sounding shocked.

"I used Aiden's Facebook profile," Meryn explained.

Amelia turned to her. "You're not on social media at all?"

"Nope, never needed it. I email Adair and text Aiden and my minions, that's about it."

Amelia frowned. "Minions?"

Beth spoke up. "She means Noah and Jaxon."

"Where were they anyway? They weren't at breakfast." Amelia asked.

"They are working on their first solo project, building the database for Beth to use to keep track of census information. In fact, I should check on them." Meryn pulled out her phone. Her small fingers moved quickly as she sent her text. Seconds later, she began to giggle.

Beth turned in her seat with a suspicious look. "What?"

Meryn just grinned. When her phone buzzed again she looked down and started to crack up.

Amelia looked at Beth who shrugged.

"Spill it, Meryn," Beth ordered.

"I'm sexting Aiden." She continued to type.

Amelia frowned. "Why is that so funny?"

Beth groaned and sat back in her seat. "Leave Keelan alone. You know he's having a rough morning."

"Huh?" Amelia looked between Meryn and Beth.

Beth turned back to face her. "Aiden never reads his text messages. He always has Keelan do it because Aiden's fingers are too big to type."

Amelia turned to Meryn. "And you know this?"

Meryn grinned. "Yup. I always know it's Keelan because he downloaded an emoticon pack that has bears. He never says 'I love you' back, he just sends a bear and a heart. He's fun to play with."

"You're bad!" Amelia said laughing.

Meryn shrugged. "There's nothing else to do."

"You could be studying the history books I bought you," Beth reminded her.

Meryn looked up. "I finished those already, in fact I sent Noah to Mystic Tomes to buy more. I found something very interesting referenced in one of the articles. The potential for fun is limitless. Paranormal history is fascinating. I have decided to delete all memory of US history to make room for the paranormal volumes."

"What do you mean delete?" Beth asked.

Meryn tapped her temple. "In my brain. I got rid of all the useless information, like US history, statistics, and trigonometry."

"Meryn, US history is important," Beth countered.

Meryn shook her head. "No, it's not. It's all lies anyway. I've asked Gavriel to verify some of the stories I've read in the paranormal history books and he said they're right. I'll believe someone who was actually there rather than the stuff I learned as a kid."

Amelia turned to her. "Like what?" She was fascinated. She had learned paranormal history the same as every paranormal child, but Meryn had been raised human. She could have been told anything.

"For example, did you know that, in human history books, they fail to mention that George Washington made a deal with locals to fight against the British? And by locals, I mean unit warriors? Gavriel freaking knew Paul Revere!" Meryn ranted.

Beth looked surprised. "He did?"

Meryn nodded. "And Darian took time off from being in the Alpha Unit to be a pirate! How fucking cool is that?"

Amelia smiled. Maybe she could talk Darian into wearing a ruffled shirt and leather boots later.

Meryn's stomach growled. "I hope Marius has food."

"Are you sure you're not eating for five?" Beth teased.

Meryn stuck her tongue out her. "At least I'm not having a jackalope."

Beth bristled. "I will not have a jackalope. I thought we decided he or she would be a bunny with fangs?"

Amelia couldn't hold her giggles. "What about Rheia?" she asked.

Meryn grinned. "Wolfman."

Beth snorted then laughed. "I am so telling her you said that. What about Meryn's future baby?"

Amelia thought about it for a second. "She's having an Ewok!"

Beth lost all composure and began to giggle uncontrollably.

Meryn frowned for a second and then became thoughtful. "That's not too bad, but what if it's a boy?"

"Chewbacca," Amelia said wiping her eyes. Beth's giggles were contagious.

"Stop, I can't breathe!" Beth gasped.

"That's kick ass." Meryn nodded happily and looked over at Amelia. "What about your future baby?"

She patted her tummy. "I'll have a Legolas that gets into Gryffindor."

Meryn glared at her. "I kinda fucking hate you right now."

"Boo hoo," Amelia teased laughing.

"Okay, I'm done. Let's go back home," Beth was trying to catch her breath.

Meryn shook her head. "No way! We can't miss today at Adelaide's. It's sewing circle day."

Amelia swayed as the car swerved. Ryuu quickly regained control. "I'm sorry *denka*, what did you just say?"

"We have to go to today's sewing circle meeting," Meryn insisted.

Beth's eyes were wide. "Are you feeling okay?"

"Why are you asking if she's okay?" Amelia asked.

"Because she absolutely hates that sewing circle," Beth informed her.

"What? I can't have a change of heart?" Meryn tried to look innocent.

"No," Beth and Ryuu said together.

"Well, we're pulling up now so it's too late." Amelia pointed out the window.

"Gods help us," Beth whispered under her breath.

"He-he-he." Meryn rubbed her hands together.

Amelia fought the urge to cross herself, and she wasn't even Catholic.

Ryuu parked and got out to open the doors for them. He helped Meryn out of the car and they walked up to the front door. Before they could ring the bell, the door swung open to reveal an older gentleman in attire similar to Ryuu's.

"Marius! I've missed you!" Meryn hugged the man around the waist.

"And I have missed you, too, Little Miss. Come inside and get warm." Marius held the door open and everyone walked inside.

"Oh, good, you're here! Before we head to the salon, you girls come with me," A female voice called out.

Amelia looked and a beautiful blond woman was quickly approaching them. "Marius, if you could bring a pot of tea to Byron's office?"

"Of course." Marius bowed and headed to the back of the house.

"That's Marius Steward—he's the squire here—and this is Aiden's mom, Adelaide, or as everyone else calls her, Lady McKenzie." Meryn indicated to the beautiful woman. "Mom, this is Amelia Ironwood. You'll never guess what we found out..."

Adelaide placed a finger over Meryn's lips. "Let's head to the office, darling. You can tell me there." She winked at the three of them and led the way.

No one said anything until Adelaide closed the door and removed a brass key from its hook to hang it within a spell circle. "There, now the room is soundproofed. I got the idea from the perimeter Keelan did for the Alpha estate. With so much going on, Byron needed a place he could have private conversations."

Ryuu gathered their coats and left to go hang them up.

Beth got comfortable in one of the wingback chairs. "And why do we need to have a private conversation?"

Adelaide pointed to the other chairs and Amelia and Meryn got comfortable. "Now, before I get started, what were you going to tell me dear?" She sat close to Meryn.

Meryn bounced up and down in her chair. "We found out that Amelia is my cousin, my actual, real cousin! Our mothers were sisters."

Adelaide paled. Beth clucked her tongue. "Trust me, I know."

Amelia turned to Meryn who looked as confused as she felt.

"What?" Meryn demanded.

"Meryn, do you remember the reaction we got when I announced I had adopted you as my baby sister?" Beth asked.

"Yeah, everyone freaked out because I was tied to two major houses... Oh, now it's three." Meryn strummed her fingers on the arm of the chair.

"Four Meryn, remember? I have two sets of brothers, the Ironwoods and the Ashleighs." Amelia reminded her.

Adelaide gasped, her hand going to her throat. "How?"

Amelia turned to Lady McKenzie. "I am the half-sister to the Ironwoods. The Ironwoods are half-brothers to the Ashleighs. Both sets of brothers will be very protective of me and Meryn."

"Interesting isn't it?" Beth said, leaning back in her chair.

There was a knock at the door before Marius and Ryuu entered with a tea tray. Ryuu closed the door behind them and helped serve everyone a cup. Meryn pouted up at Marius who immediately set a basket of cookies on the table next to Meryn. She dived into the basket humming happily.

Beth took a sip. "But you didn't know when you brought us in here. What did you have to tell us that required a soundproof spell?"

"Oh, dear, I'm not quite sure how to tell you this." She took a deep breath and glanced at Meryn for a second before she turned to Amelia and Beth. "Do you girls follow the society column, *Dear Gentle Reader*?"

Amelia and Beth shook their heads.

Adelaide frowned. "That's what I thought. Over the past few weeks, the columns have been systematically belittling a certain group of women." She paused and looked down at her hands as they twisted together.

Beth's eyes narrowed. "Which group of women?"

Adelaide sighed. "You all. The mates of the Alpha Unit. Nothing overt, mind you. Everything is said in such vague language, but everyone knows who they are talking about."

"What are they saying?" Amelia asked. She might not keep up with the *Dear Gentle Reader* column, but she knew it was one of the oldest and most popular paranormal publications in the world. Whatever it was, it was being seen in all four of the pillar cities.

"I refuse to repeat any of that drivel. Here is last week's edition." Adelaide handed Beth a folded newspaper. It was the Lycaonian paper, *The Observer*. Beth's eyes quickly skimmed the paper. All color drained slowly from her face after which her cheeks flushed a dangerous red.

"How dare they!" Beth stood, nostrils flaring.

"What are they saying?" Amelia asked.

"What aren't they saying? One article is insinuating that the reason why ferals are attacking more is because the men of the Alpha Unit are mating with 'women of ill repute'."

"People still use that term?" Amelia frowned.

"They couldn't get any clearer had they used actual names. Anyone with half a brain can figure out that 'the human, whose initials are MM, mated to the bear shifter ' is Meryn! I won't let them get away with this! This is libelous!" Beth paced back and forth in front of the fireplace.

Adelaide shook her head. "I wish it were that simple. The identity of the person or persons writing this column has been the best kept secret in our world for centuries. Because their identity is hidden, they can say what they want with impunity, and people take what they print to be truth."

Beth turned her eyes flashing. "We all know that Daphne Bowers is behind this attack."

Adelaide nodded. "But there's no way to prove it. Daphne more than likely used her vast social network to flood the gossip mongers with these ridiculous, hate-filled 'stories' on the off chance that the writers of the column would pick one for publication."

Meryn stood and stretched. She grabbed one last cookie and popped it into her mouth. She chewed and swallowed, and smiled at everyone. "Let's get going. We don't want to keep the sewing circle waiting."

Adelaide jumped to her feet and placed a hand on Meryn's forehead. "Oh Gods, is she sick?"

Beth threw the paper down on her empty seat and paused to take a deep breath. "She said something similar in the car on the way over. I'm blaming Meryn two-point-oh.

Meryn grabbed Adelaide's hand and pulled her toward the door. "Come on!"

"Okay sweetheart, let's get this over with." Adelaide kissed Meryn on the cheek, and they all headed toward the front sitting room. Meryn waved happily at everyone and took the seat next to Adelaide. Beth sat behind Meryn to let Amelia sit next to her cousin.

Everyone said hello and started their projects. There were multiple baby blankets being made along with two sets of curtains and a few dresses. Amelia watched curiously as Meryn kept checking her phone. Was she waiting for a text back from Keelan?

After about a half an hour, Marius knocked on the door and entered, carrying a small silver tray.

"The paper, my lady." He held the tray as Adelaide picked up the paper with as much enthusiasm as she would if it had been a dead mouse.

"Thank you, Marius," Adelaide said weakly.

He bowed, set the tray down on the side table, and joined Ryuu to stand next to the door.

"We should read the *Dear Gentle Reader* column." Daphne suggested, smiling at everyone.

"Perhaps we should concentrate on our projects instead. We have so many baby blankets to finish," Adelaide countered.

"I think we should have Rosalind read it out loud for us. It will entertain those of us who aren't sewing," Meryn suggested.

Beth and Adelaide stared at Meryn in horror. Amelia sat back and waited. Now was the moment of truth; how much was Meryn like her? If her actions were any indication, shit was about to get real ugly, real fast.

Rosalind tittered and accepted the paper from Adelaide. "Oh, my, let's see what has been going on in the paranormal world this week." Her eyes skimmed the column, and every ounce of color drained from her face. She swayed slightly in her chair. "Maybe Lady McKenzie is right; we should just concentrate on our blankets." She was folding up the paper to tuck it in her chair beside her when Daphne laughed obnoxiously.

"Come on, dear, don't leave us in suspense. I'm dying to hear what has been reported this week." Daphne cooed in a sweet voice.

"I-I..." Rosalind stuttered.

"Go ahead, Rosalind, don't keep us waiting," Meryn prompted.

"Well... the main article is very scandalous! *Dear Gentle Reader* reports that a certain Lady DB was seen in a human plastic surgeon's office to undergo a procedure known as a vaginoplasty. The article goes on to explain that this is a type of surgery to tighten up lady parts that have been overused." Gasps filled the air, but Rosalind wasn't finished. "The article wraps up by saying that Lady DB may be under investigation for"—she swallowed hard—"suspicion of performing indecent acts with farm animals." Her voice seemed to echo throughout the room.

Amelia turned, Beth's eyes looked like they were about to pop out of her head. This was getting interesting.

"This is preposterous!" Daphne screeched, reaching for the paper. She ripped it out of Rosalind's hands and proceeded to shred it into tiny pieces, letting scraps of paper fly everywhere. Around the room, whispers and muffled laughter filled the air.

Daphne looked as though she had swelled in size as her wolf seemed to take over, and her eyes locked on Meryn. Growling, she stalked in their direction. In seconds, Adelaide and Ryuu were standing in front of them to head off Daphne's advance.

"Get out of my way! I know that little bitch is behind this!" Daphne hissed.

Meryn blinked, an innocent look on her face. "I have no idea what you're talking about. But since you're getting so upset, are you confirming you're 'DB'?" she asked innocently.

Daphne shrieked her rage and launched herself toward Meryn. Adelaide raised her hand and simply pushed her back with a shove to the chest. "Stay away from my daughter," she warned with a low growl.

Daphne sneered. "What are you going to do? You can't lay a finger on me or you risk your mate's Elder seat. The degenerate next to you posing as a squire can't touch me or risk being deported from Lycaonia." When she smiled, she revealed a set of fully extended canines.

Amelia felt the room begin to close in. The roaring that she'd heard during breakfast returned. Ice began to form around her heart and started to spread through her body. She stood as a rage so cold it burned expanded across her soul. She shouldered her way between Adelaide and Ryuu. When she smiled at Daphne, she was pleased when the older woman flinched.

Daphne made the mistake of looking in Meryn's direction. That was all it took to trigger Amelia's fury. Moving faster than she ever had in her life, her arm shot out and she gripped Daphne around the throat. Pulling strength from the earth, she easily lifted the woman off the ground keeping her at arm's length.

In the recesses of her mind, she heard Beth usher the other women out of the room. She didn't care who was there. All she wanted to do was destroy the woman in front of her. How dare she threaten her family! The darkness around her heart whispered to her, telling her that if she didn't kill Daphne, the woman would hurt her baby sister-cousin.

"Let me go!" Daphne gasped.

"Why should I? You're going to hurt my family," Amelia said in a monotone voice.

"What family? I don't even know you!" Daphne's lips had started to turn blue.

Amelia smiled. She thought that the color looked pretty.

A warm hand on her arm broke her train of thought. She turned her head slowly to look at Ryuu.

"*Itoko-sama*, think of how sad Meryn would be if you were exiled from Lycaonia." His voice was calm and even.

"She wants to hurt her," Amelia protested.

Ryuu shook his head. "I would never allow that to happen. You can let go." He squeezed his hand, and warmth ran from her wrist to her shoulder. She turned back to face Daphne.

"Gods! Her eyes are black! Help! Someone help me! She's feral!" Daphne babbled.

Slowly, Amelia lowered Daphne to the ground and released her. Daphne fell backward sobbing and clutching at her throat. "The council will hear of this!" she croaked and ran from the room.

Amelia collapsed back into her seat, appalled at what she had almost done. Ryuu's warmth began to slowly thaw the cold parts of her soul. Reality was catching up to her. She had nearly killed someone. She covered her face with both hands, unable to look at anyone.

"That kicked ass on every single level!" Meryn said excitedly.

"Meryn! Can't you see Amelia is upset?" Beth chastised.

Amelia looked out from behind her hands to see Meryn's confused expression. "Why is she upset?"

"Why?" Amelia's voice cracked. "I was going to kill her, really kill her," she whispered. The truth was almost too much to bear.

"Too bad you didn't. That bitch is going to stir up trouble later; I just know it. Better to kill her now," Meryn said as she rummaged through the cookie basket.

"Normally, I don't condone violence, but in this instance, my quirky daughter is right. That woman is better off dead," Adelaide looked weary.

Marius appeared at the door, his mouth twitching. "All the ladies have left. I think you will find it interesting that most of them offered to stand with Amelia if this goes to the Tribunal. They all confided in me that Daphne was out of line threatening a pregnant human who was in no way responsible for what was printed in *The Observer*."

Adelaide sat down abruptly on a sofa. "Thank the Gods for that."

Amelia scooted closer to Meryn and rested her head on her shoulder. Without looking, Meryn reached up and patted her on the head, her focus still on the cookie basket. Maybe what she did wasn't crazy after all. No one seemed particularly upset that she had almost killed someone.

Beth stood in front of Meryn, her arms crossed over her chest. "You little demon! How did you get that article in *The Observer*!?" Beth exclaimed before bursting out into laughter.

Meryn chuckled. "What do you mean?"

"Now Beth, you know there's no way that she could..." Adelaide stopped mid-sentence. She gasped and covered her mouth with both hands. "You wanted to attend the sewing circle this week."

Amelia yawned, emotionally spent. "And you kept checking your phone. I thought you were checking for text messages, but you were checking the time. You knew the paper would be delivered this afternoon."

Ryuu and Marius stared. Ryuu, in an uncharacteristic show of emotion, broke down laughing. He leaned against Marius whose grey mustache was twitching as he tried to hide his smile.

"Out with it, Menace!" Beth took the cookie basket from Meryn who glared up at her.

"Fine! Remember how I said I found something of interest in the history books? It was a reference to the *Dear Gentle Reader* column. After that, I subscribed to the paper and started reading all the columns. Once the nasty ones about us started, I went to the library in Lycaonia with Noah and looked at all the back issues of *The Observer*, and I noticed a trend that started about five years ago. A lot of the major articles were pulled from sources found on Facebook and online message boards run by paranormals. I had pulled all that content trying to find correlations with the missing persons so nearly all the articles looked familiar. Daphne may have flooded the city with gossip, but all I had to do was carefully place one or two reference documents online and the rest is history." Meryn grabbed the cookie basket back from Beth who stared down at her in shock.

"Even if you had placed something on a message board, they would have checked sources before printing that in the paper," Beth said.

Meryn nodded. "It wasn't that hard to create a business website for a plastic surgeon. I even hacked the Plastic Surgeons of America and added his name. For all intents and purposes, he is as real as you or I online. Hacking into the local police department was easy since I had already done it last year. It took two seconds to create a police report filed by a concerned local farmer."

Amelia sat up straight and hugged Meryn close. "You little genius!"

Meryn frowned, looking up at Beth. "She's doing it again."

Beth shrugged and grabbed a cookie. "She's family, she's allowed."

Meryn sighed. "True."

Amelia released her baby sister-cousin and sat back. Losing control had been terrifying. She couldn't help noticing that she had only started having these episodes after making love to Darian. It was as if some of his darkness had seeped into her. Never before had she felt such rage. If this was what her mate had faced alone, it was a miracle he hadn't turned yet.

Ryuu walked over and bowed low in front of Meryn. "Well played, *denka*, well played, indeed."

Adelaide tapped her chin. "But does this help us or hurt us?"

Amelia watched in amazement as Meryn huddled in on herself and began sniffling, wiping at her eyes like a child. "But Elder Vi'Ailean, I didn't do anything. She lurched at me and I was so s-s-scared! I'm only human; I was afraid for my baby!" Meryn broke down into tears. Seconds later, she sniffed once dramatically, dried her eyes and resumed eating her cookies. Amelia held up a hand silently. Meryn gave her a crumby high five and grinned.

"If anything, this should silence the faction that was feeding into the tripe about the Alpha Unit losing its effectiveness. Those who play the game will see this for the power play that it was. Excellent work, Meryn," Beth praised.

"Vaginoplasty," Meryn snorted.

That was all it took to send Amelia into uncontrollable laughter. Beth crumpled into a ball of giggles taking the seat on the other side of Meryn.

"Oh girls, you're good for my heart," Adelaide said.

Meryn stood and stretched, rubbing her lower back. "We better get back home. I kinda want to be there when Aiden hears what happened."

"So that he knows that you're okay?" Adelaide asked.

Meryn shook her head. "No, so I can watch him freak out."

"Oh dear." Adelaide shook her head and hugged Meryn tight.

Amelia and Beth were still grinning.

Meryn turned to Ryuu. "I'm hungry."

He sighed. "Of course, you are. You've only been eating nonstop all morning."

"I want a Colton sandwich, it seems to be the only thing that satisfies Meryn two-point-oh." Meryn said, a dreamy look on her face.

Amelia turned to Beth. "Colton sandwich?"

Beth shuddered. "A crazy sandwich Colton and Aiden created as a child. It has peanut butter, mayonnaise, pickles, cheese, and beef jerky."

Amelia licked her lips. "That actually sounds kinda good."

Ryuu looked from Meryn to Amelia. "I think I need hazard pay."

"Man up, squire, you have sammiches to make." Meryn grinned evilly at Ryuu.

"Of course, *denka.*"

"Ladies, your coats." Marius appeared in the doorway with their coats.

"The phone call to Byron should be interesting," Adelaide chuckled.

"Tell Dad I said hi." Meryn had one arm in the sleeve of her coat but kept turning in a circle trying to find the opening for the other sleeve. Ryuu stopped her spinning and held the coat open for her.

"You girls stay safe," Adelaide said as she walked them to the door.

"We will," They replied in unison and grinned at each other.

"Definitely need hazard pay," Ryuu murmured under his breath as they headed to the car.

Amelia kept smiling, but inside, she was worried. Just as she started to feel the darkness in her heart begin to lighten, she feared that whatever light Darian had carried would be turning back to darkness.

CHAPTER NINE

"Hold on, Darian, I'll help you with that," Oron called from across the training grounds. Darian looked up and nodded. He had been expecting his brother to say something sooner, but they had both decided to keep the fact that they were brothers low key to keep their queen safe.

Oron fell into step beside him as they lifted their weight equipment to carry back into the storage shed. Aiden wanted the course clear before Penny came out to play. Once inside the shed, Oron turned to him.

"Brother, your light..." he started.

"I know."

"Why don't you claim your mate? Merging your souls could keep you from turning." Oron sat down on one of the crates.

"It's too late, Brother," Darian said in a somber tone.

Oron punched the side of a stacked crate easily breaking the boards. "Don't say that. Let me go to Mother..."

"No." Darian shook his head.

"You're both so damn stubborn," Oron cursed under his breath.

"I promised Amelia that I would hold on as long as I could, but the light I received from her is already fading, and the darkness is returning." Darian sighed. He wanted so badly to be able to give Amelia a child, but in his heart he knew he wouldn't make it until the next winter solstice.

"When I..."

"Don't!" Oron stood and turned away from him.

"Brother, please..." Darian said quietly.

When Oron turned to face him, his jaw was clenched.

"When I turn, promise me that you will take Amelia to Éire Danu. She'll be safe there." Darian smiled at him. "Please."

With tears in his eyes, Oron nodded. "I swear on my honor she will be safe."

"Thank you, it helps knowing that she will be taken care of." Darian stood. "Come on, let's not keep the commander waiting."

Oron hesitated. "Are you sure nothing can be done?"

"The darkness is too great. Even if I were allowed to go back home, the portals would never accept me."

"We could try."

"When the time comes, don't hesitate to kill me. It will no longer be me. Already the darkness is leeching away everything that makes me who I am. Don't let it take my honor." Darian laid a hand on his brother's shoulder.

"Hold on," Oron begged.

"I will, as long as I can." He let his hand drop and walked toward the door. "Come on, old man, I still have enough life left in me to kick your ass." He turned and watched his brother swallow hard and force a smile.

"Old man? Just because I used to change your diapers..." Oron smiled.

Darian winced. "Don't let the guys hear you say that."

Oron's smile disappeared. "It should be me, I'm older. I shouldn't have to watch my little brother fade."

Darian looked out at the training grounds where the men laughed and tussled with each other. "Fate doesn't make mistakes. If this is my destiny, then it must be for a reason."

Oron fell into step beside him. "Doesn't mean I have to like it," he grumbled.

Darian shook his head. "I don't think she cares if you do."

They walked together in silence back to the training grounds. He was glad that he had had the chance to speak with his brother. Knowing Oron would look after Amelia took a great weight off his shoulders.

"All right men, gather 'round!" Aiden yelled. Beside him, Penny looked even smaller as she waved at the warriors circling them.

Aiden was about to speak when a buzzing sound caused them to look toward Keelan. He frowned and pulled a phone out of his pocket. "It's Meryn," he said, unlocking the screen.

Aiden waved at him. "Tell her I'll see her later." He turned back to the men. "We have a special helper today. Penny has agreed to help train you men by playing hide and seek."

Darian turned his attention from his commander back to Keelan. The young witch was blushing furiously and looking up at Aiden with a mixture of nervous fear and panic.

"Sir, maybe you should answer this," Keelan said holding up the phone.

Aiden shook his head. "Later."

Keelan looked down with a painful expression at the phone, which buzzed again. He quickly typed something and then buried the phone at the bottom of Aiden's gym bag.

Sascha groaned and stood from where he had been propped up against the climbing wall.

"Good morning, sunshine!" Aiden called cheerfully. "Perfect timing. We're about to train with Penny, so get your mangy ass up," Aiden ordered.

"Damn, Menace," Sascha grumbled, lurching forward on unsteady feet.

Around him, the men chuckled.

"Okay ladies, here are the rules. Don't hide in the house and no hiding in the armory; it's off limits to our girl here. Other than that, have fun." Aiden blew a whistle, and Sascha cringed. The men scattered while Penny hid her eyes.

Oron bumped fists with him and took off. Darian couldn't muster up the energy to be excited. He strolled toward the trees next to the obstacle course and got comfortable at the base of one of the maples.

It wasn't long before he heard rustling in front of him. He couldn't see Penny, but he could see Felix. In fact, he and Oron were the only two that could. The little minx was using the sprite to scout for her.

Felix was bundled head to toe in clothes and Penny had used a fabric wrapped hair tie to keep a small hand warmer held firmly against the sprite's waist. Felix looked like he was having the time of his life.

"That's cheating," he said quietly.

Seconds later, Penny shimmered into view, a guilty look on her face. He winked at her, and she brightened. "Don't worry about me, I won't tell. I'll wait until the game is almost concluded and head back to the course. I'll tell Aiden you found me. I just want to stay here a bit longer."

Penny grinned and gave him a thumbs up. Darian noticed that though she had started speaking more, she still reverted to hand signals for most interactions.

Penny turned and was about to keep searching when he stopped her. "Penny," he called quietly. She looked back at him. "Yes?" her voice was clear and sweet.

"Oron is like me, he can see sprites. When we were boys, he always used to hide in oak trees. Check for him there. Use Felix as a decoy and you'll catch him."

"Kickass!" Penny quipped throwing her fist in the air, just like her favorite adopted aunt.

Darian chuckled. "Don't let your Mom or Papa hear you say that."

Penny grinned and shimmered out of sight. He watched as Felix waved and trailed behind his friend. Darian had been faced with his imminent death for years now, but seeing Penny, it was truly beginning to sink in, he would never see her grow up. He would never know what kind of woman she would turn out to be.

For the first time he, was afraid. "I don't want to go," he whispered.

As promised, Darian exited the forest when he noticed most of the men had been found. He approached Aiden. "She find everyone?" he asked.

Aiden nodded looking proud. "Of course. The men are flabbergasted." Aiden laughed and turned to him. "Did she find you?"

Darian nodded. "She sure did."

"Last one to be found is Colton." Aiden pointed to where the rest of the men sat joking with one another.

They heard a squeal of laughter to their right, and Penny burst from the trees heading straight for Aiden. She ran up to him arms raised. Aiden swept her up and sat her on his arm. Seconds later, Colton emerged from the trees. He saw who was holding his daughter and scowled.

He walked over to them wagging a finger. "She cheated!" Colton accused.

Aiden raised a brow at Penny who shrugged. Aiden turned back to Colton. "What'd she do?"

Colton's scowl turned into a begrudging grin of admiration. "I could tell she didn't know exactly where I was, so she pretended to trip over a branch. When I left my hiding spot, she popped up like a jack-in-a-box, tagged me, and ran."

"She got you good, Colton!" Ben called out.

Colton laughed. "That she did." He took his daughter from Aiden. "Where did you learn how to do that?"

"Aunt Amelia," she answered. The men around them groaned.

"They are infecting the next generation," Sascha complained.

"Meryn seems more grounded than Amelia," Quinn said. He shot an apologetic look to Darian. "Sorry Darian, but your mate does seem a bit flakey."

"Yeah, well Meryn gets 'stabby' and doesn't think twice about stunning a perfectly innocent tiger," Sascha grumbled.

"Okay men, that's it for the day. Alpha Unit, head inside to my office for necklace review," Aiden ordered. "The council dropped it off while everyone was hiding."

Darian went back into the house with the others and watched as Colton dropped Penny off in the front room. He set her up with her coloring book before joining them in the hallway. Once in Aiden's office, they got comfortable in the chairs Meryn had ordered.

"Colton, can you get the necklace? I put it in the bottom right drawer," Aiden requested setting his bag down next to his chair.

"Sure thing, boss." Colton pulled the necklace out and twirled it around his finger. Darian watched as Colton's foot slipped on one of Penny's crayons, and he dropped the necklace on the hardwood.

"Is it broken?" Aiden asked. They all crowded around the necklace, staring down at the floor.

"There was no green light, so I think it's okay," Colton speculated, exhaling in relief. He picked it up and gently carried it over to the sitting area.

"Well?" Aiden asked.

"It's still a necklace," Colton replied.

"Smart ass." Aiden cuffed Colton.

Gavriel leaned back. "I agree with Colton in this case, Aiden. The necklace hasn't changed a bit since the day we found it. Adam's poured every chemical in the clinic over it, and every witch in the units has tried every spell they know to figure this thing out. I don't know what the council expects us to do."

Aiden picked up the necklace from the coffee table. "As frustrating as reality is, this is all we have to go by gentlemen. Darian was right earlier. We're constantly on the defensive, and one of these days, they will catch us off guard. Five months ago, that wasn't an issue, but we have women and children here now, *our* women and children. We can't afford for even one of those bastards to win. So, rack your brains, what else can we do?"

Darian tried to think of something, anything they could do. He looked around and each man wore a similar serious expression. The problem was how to look for something you're not sure is there to begin with?

"Sascha is being so touchy," Meryn observed.

"You did electrocute him," Beth reminded her as Ryuu took their coats.

"Big baby. Come on, he said they were in Aiden's office." Meryn turned down the long hallway.

Amelia followed Meryn beside Beth to Aiden's office. She was unsure how she was going to tell Darian she might have accidentally started a political mess by assaulting a shifter founding family's matriarch.

Before they reached the door, she heard a buzzing in her ears. When Meryn opened the door, Amelia had to take a step back. Screams, she heard screams. Pushing past Meryn, she threw herself into the room first to protect her baby sister-cousin from whatever threat was causing those screams.

The men jumped to their feet and reached for their sidearms, their eyes darting around the room. "What?" Aiden demanded.

Amelia looked around. The room was empty except for the men, yet screams still filled the air. Covering her ears did nothing to alleviate the noise. Darian was at her side before she realized she was falling. He held her up, and she started shaking her head.

"Make it stop!" she yelled trying to be heard over the cacophony of endless shrieks.

Darian, looking terrified, held her face between his hands. "Make what stop?"

"The screams! They're just screaming and screaming and screaming!" She wept as waves of helplessness, hopelessness, and fear swept her away.

"No one is screaming, my love." Darian smoothed a hand over her hair. He turned to Aiden. "Help me!"

The men looked at each other helplessly. "Move her to the couch," Gavriel suggested.

Darian picked her up and started to carry her toward the couch. The screams got louder. "Stop!" she sobbed. She squeezed her eyes shut and prayed. He took another step forward and she screamed as her head exploded in pain.

"For Gods' sake stop! She's bleeding!" Meryn cried.

In the background, she could hear the sound of a terrified child crying.

Darian took a step backward, then another. The screams were there, but less intense. Slowly, one step at a time, the screams got more and more muffled. Soon, they were a dim clamor, and then nothing. She opened her eyes. When she looked around, she realized Darian had carried her out into the foyer. Colton was on the floor holding a frightened Penny against his chest rocking her back and forth.

"It got better when I left the room didn't it?" Darian asked.

Amelia nodded. "What in the hell is in that room?"

She heard sniffles to her left and saw Meryn crying with Aiden at her side. "I'm okay." Amelia said, her throat raw from her own screaming.

"You started to bleed from your eyes, ears, and nose. You're not fucking okay!" Meryn yelled.

Amelia blinked in astonishment. "Really?" She touched her hand to her face and it came away bloody. "That's new."

"I called the clinic, Rheia is on her way. She'll want to examine Amelia and, of course, check on Penny. We gave her quite a fright." Beth looked pale. Gavriel had an arm wrapped around her.

Keelan walked over to Colton and started to make Penny's dolls dance. Penny had wiped her eyes, but her head never left Colton's chest. She watched the dolls perform and started to calm down.

Amelia rested against Darian's broad chest. She felt like a wet noodle. "I'm sorry for scaring you, Penny, it wasn't intentional." She motioned for Darian to set her down. He did, but stayed close.

Amelia knelt on the floor where Colton sat with Penny in his lap. "You know how you're a shifter?" Penny nodded.

"Well, I'm a witch. One of my gifts is empathy, which means sometimes I can hear and feel things that others can't. It's not a cool gift like Keelan's." Amelia pointed to her dancing dolls. "But I learned how to make the most of my gift by helping people. Sometimes—it doesn't happen often—but sometimes, what someone is feeling can overwhelm me, and I get scared. Can you forgive me for yelling?"

Penny wiggled out of Colton's arms and wrapped herself around Amelia. She patted the top of her head. " 'S okay. 'S okay."

Amelia hugged Penny close, being careful not to get any blood on the small child. A wet cloth appeared to her left. She looked up and nodded at Ryuu. "Thank you." She pulled back and started to clean herself up. She wiggled her nose and looked down at the red and pink cloth. "Ewwww." She wiggled her lips making Penny giggle.

The door opened, and Rheia walked in. She took in everyone's expressions and Amelia's bloody cloth. "Having fun without me?"

"Momma!" Penny launched herself at Rheia who swept her up on her hip.

"Hey, pumpkin dumpling, I heard you had a scare."

"I'm okay now, but Aunt Amelia got hurt. Fix her." Penny pointed to Amelia.

"I'm here to do just that." She looked around. "Maybe we should go to the office?"

"No!" Everyone answered at once.

Rheia blinked. "Or not." She looked down at Colton. Amelia felt sorry for him, he looked like she felt. It couldn't have been easy comforting a hysterical child.

"Penny, you can hang out with us. We can watch *How to Train Your Dragon* again." Jaxon offered. Noah stood very close to his friend. From their perspective, it must have sounded like someone was getting murdered in Aiden's office.

Penny nodded and wiggled to get down. "Fix Auntie," she ordered her mother, hands on her hips.

"Yes, ma'am." Rheia smiled and kissed her daughter's forehead.

"Might I suggest you all adjourn to the front room? I'll bring in some calming tea," Ryuu suggested.

Everyone nodded and headed into the front family room. Amelia stood feeling a bit wobbly and Darian wrapped an arm around her waist to steady her.

"Come on, Colton." Rheia said.

"Leave me here, I can't move." Colton said from the floor.

"If the person who was bleeding can walk in, you sure as hell can." She nudged her mate with her foot.

Groaning, Colton stood and pulled Rheia into his arms. "I never, ever want to hear our daughter scream like that again."

Rheia's face softened. "My poor mate. Let's help Amelia and then we can go lay down," she promised.

When everyone was seated and each held a cup of tea, Aiden stood. "I think it's safe to say that Amelia was responding to the necklace."

"Agreed. The closer I got to it, the more she screamed. When I moved farther away, she quieted down," Darian said, holding her hand.

"Why has only Amelia had a reaction?" Colton asked.

"Is she the only empath to be near the necklace?" Meryn asked.

Aiden shook his head. "Tobias Laurel from Delta is also an empath. He had no reaction."

Rheia shined a penlight into Amelia's eyes, and she blinked. Rheia frowned. "You ever have this type of reaction before?"

"In my previous job, I got overwhelmed, but it was mostly depression. I didn't have a physical reaction." She sipped her tea.

"Previous job doing makeup?" Beth asked.

Amelia shook her head. "No. Before I became a cosmetologist, I was a psychologist. I used my gift of empathy to lessen the trauma of rape victims. I specialized in children's cases. The side effect of using my gift like that is that I take on their trauma for a short time. It got to be too much. I had to quit to stay sane."

"Oh, my God." Rheia looked ill. "The things you must have lived through."

Amelia shrugged. "They were not my memories. The children had the real scars. They showed me every day what true strength is by choosing to live."

Darian squeezed her hand. "That's what you meant, isn't it? When you said you had your own darkness."

Amelia nodded. "I wasn't strong enough to keep going. After my brothers came and got me, I surrounded myself with bright, colorful things, it helped me recover."

"So, whatever the necklace is, it's worse than the memories you got from those poor children?" Beth asked.

Amelia swallowed hard. She hadn't even thought of it like that. "Yes. Whatever that necklace is, it's a thousand times worse than anything I have ever felt before."

"Well, fuck a duck," Meryn remarked flatly.

Keelan excused himself. "Be right back,"

"So what do we do?" Beth asked. No one responded.

Seconds later, Keelan appeared in the doorway. "It's cracked! When Colton dropped it, the necklace must have cracked, which would explain why Tobias didn't have a reaction."

"Good work, Keelan!" Aiden said. He turned to her. "I hate to ask this, but can you try to go back in there?"

"No way, Aiden. You're asking too much!" Darian protested.

Amelia steeled herself. "I have to try. I'm prepared now. It won't hit me unexpectedly. I'll go in a little at a time."

Darian's eyes were hard. She knew he was angrier at the situation than he was at his Unit Commander. "Are you sure?" He cupped her cheek with one hand.

She rubbed her cheek against his hand. "I'm sure."

Aiden and the men stood. "Ladies, wait here."

"Yeah, right."

"No way!"

"Keep dreaming." Meryn, Beth, and Rheia replied.

Aiden pinched the bridge of his nose. "Fine. Let's *all* go."

Amelia waited until everyone had left for the office. She turned to Darian. "Hold my hand?"

"You don't even have to ask." He took her hand and kissed it gently.

"We're ready!" Aiden yelled.

"Let's do this." Amelia stood and Darian walked with her.

When they got close to the office, she felt the first wave of nausea. She breathed through her nose and kept walking. By the time she was at the doorway, she could hear the screams but they weren't overpowering.

Using her gift, she reached out to them. She pushed past the terror and tried to listen to the words being yelled.

Brian! Penny! My poor baby!

Amelia jerked back, she kept walking backwards until her back hit the wall of the hallway.

"Well?" Aiden yelled.

"It's a woman's voice I hear, one of them anyway. She's crying out for Brian and Penny," she answered.

She heard a low cry before Rheia appeared at the door wild eyed. "What did you say?"

"This woman is terrified. She keeps calling for Brian and Penny and saying, 'My poor baby'." Amelia watched Rheia's reaction carefully. Rheia began to shake, Colton appeared behind her.

"She means your Penny doesn't she?" Amelia asked gently.

Rheia nodded. "I think that's Penny's mother, her mate was named Brian. They were murdered almost two years ago." She turned to Colton. "That could explain why she could see her father when he was invisible, maybe she could feel her mother?"

Colton nodded. "It makes sense."

Amelia's heart stuttered. It was impossible, but there was no other explanation. Pushing past Rheia, she ran into the room, heedless of the searing pain ripping her mind apart. She staggered forward and grabbed the necklace. She swung it up and shattered it against the coffee table. The silence that followed was deafening. Green light flared, and the screams were gone.

Her knees buckled at the full weight of the truth behind the necklace. One moment she was standing over the coffee table, the next she was flat on her back with Rheia bent over her on one side and Darian on the other.

"You need to lower your heart rate Amelia." Rheia said holding her wrist.

"Where's Aiden?" she yelled.

"I'm here."

She looked past Darian to see Aiden standing close by. She began to sob, she couldn't get the words out; it was too terrible to say.

"It's okay, my love, just rest." Darian rubbed her back soothingly.

She shook her head over and over again. It would never be okay again. How had such abominations crept into this world with no one the wiser? She curled into a ball and wept.

"Take her upstairs, Darian; whatever she has to say can wait," she heard Aiden say.

"No! It can't wait." She turned her head and looked up at the Unit Commander. "They were souls, actual souls. They were trapped in the terrifying moment of their murder. Each bead in that necklace was a person!" she cried.

The sound of soft weeping filled the room. The men did everything they could to comfort their mates. Keelan, the only one without a crying mate, by default was the one to call Byron and explain what they had learned.

Amelia lay passively on the floor in Darian's arms. She wanted to cry. She wanted to rail against Fate for allowing such a thing to happen, but she was out of tears. She looked up. "My head hurts," she whispered.

"Rheia?" Darian called.

Rheia looked down and gave Amelia a weak smile. Rheia's eyes and nose were red from crying. "On a scale of one to ten, how bad is it?"

"Thirty. It's a migraine starting." Amelia kept her eyes closed against the light.

"Shit. I don't have anything for migraines at the clinic; paranormals don't get them. I can write a prescription if someone can pick it up," Rheia offered.

Darian kissed Amelia's forehead. "I'll go. If I remember correctly, the Duck In has a large medical counter."

Amelia smiled slightly. "Pharmacies. They're called pharmacies."

"If you're going to the store, can you pick up some chocolate?" Beth asked in a small voice.

"And jalapeño Cheetos?" Meryn asked sniffling.

"Let's put the women to bed and head out," Aiden said, standing with Meryn in his arms.

Keelan joined them. "I'd actually rather go to that wretched human store than answer any more council questions. René Evreux is a world class dick."

"Then it's settled. We meet in the foyer in ten minutes." Aiden left the room with Meryn.

Darian stood, scooping Amelia up, and followed his commander up the stairs. He opened the door to his room, and the smell of the night flowers immediately began to ease some of the pain. He gently tucked her into bed.

"Is there anything else that you need?" he asked, smoothing her hair away from her face.

"Chocolate, please. For when I feel better" She peeled her eyes open and smiled at him.

"Of course. I have heard about the magic of human chocolate. I will return with a selection for you," he promised.

"Hurry back."

"Always."

When the door shut behind him, Amelia closed her eyes and stopped fighting to stay awake. She was too tired to face their new reality with Darian gone.

CHAPTER TEN

Darian and the men sat in the SUV for a few minutes letting the new information sink in. After a few minutes, Aiden started the car and pulled out of their driveway.

"What's a migraine?" Colton asked, turning to him.

"It has to be bad, Amelia rated it a thirty on a pain scale of one to ten," Darian replied. He hated leaving her when she was in so much pain, but the only place that had her medicine was the human store.

"Keelan," Aiden barked.

Keelan sighed and pulled out his phone. He tapped his screen several times. "It says here that exact causes are unknown, but migraine headaches can cause severe pain, sensitivity to light and sound, eye pain, nausea, and vomiting." Keelan swallowed. "They sound awful. Amelia may be half witch, but she's also half human and susceptible to these things. It says here stress is a contributing factor."

Darian felt ill. His poor mate! How could she survive such a thing?

"Aiden..."

Aiden nodded and looked at him in the rear view mirror. "We'll be there soon. I know you're anxious to get back. I felt the same way when I knew Meryn was having her cycle. It killed me knowing she was lying at home alone with her womb turning inside out, but like before, we have to get what Amelia needs to overcome this."

Colton shook his head. "I can't believe your mate is a psychologist. I thought she was a bubbly, air-headed version of Meryn. I don't think I could do what she did. She's kinda amazing."

Pride for his mate welled up in him. "She is, isn't she?" Darian found himself once again realizing that his mate deserved so much more than what he had to offer. Nevertheless, he would keep his promise to her and try to stay in the light for as long as he could. It was the least he could do for such a selfless creature.

None too soon they were pulling into the parking lot of the Duck In.

"Weapons?" Keelan asked.

Aiden nodded. "But keep them small. Bart told me that we make the other humans nervous when we're visibly armed."

Gavriel smiled. "It makes sense, we are already much larger than the average human. Even without weapons, I believe we are intimidating."

They got out of the car and checked their sidearms before heading into the store.

"Aiden m'boy! What has you gentlemen out today?" Bart called from behind he counter.

They walked up to the older man. Darian stepped forward. "I have need of your medical counter. My mate is having migraines and our doctor gave me this to get her medicine." He held up the prescription that Rheia had given him.

Bart lowered his glasses onto his nose and took the piece of paper. "Real sorry to hear about your woman. Come with me boys. I'll show you where the pharmacy is." Bart stepped out from behind his counter and slowly made his way to the back of the store.

"Bill! Bill! I got a pre-scrip-shun for ya." Bart yelled over the high counter.

A man not much younger than Bart peered out over the counter. "Well, give it here!" Bill reached out his hand and Bart gave him the piece of paper.

Bill looked it over. "Hmmm. Hmmm. Sumatriptan huh? Someone must have a migraine." He looked out over the men. "Who's this for?"

Darian stepped closer. "My mate."

"Hmmm. Give me fifteen minutes," Bill said shortly, before disappearing behind his tall counter.

"You boys behave. No shenanigans like last time," Bart warned shaking a finger at them.

"No, sir," Aiden affirmed, nodding at the older man.

"Good." Bart walked back up to the front.

The men stood in front of the counter for a few minutes before they began to wander around. Colton made Keelan squirm by showing him different condom boxes, and Gavriel discovered the aisle that had imported chocolate. Feeling like they had discovered lost treasure, they loaded up with the brightly colored paper wrapped bars and made their way to the front. They placed the assortment of chocolate and the bag of jalapeño Cheetos for Meryn on the counter, smiling at each other triumphantly. Bart looked at their selections and shook his head. Once they were checked out they headed back to the pharmacy.

"I wonder what this is?" Colton asked, pointing to a strange looking chair.

They all gathered around it. Gavriel stepped closer to read the text on the machine. "It says here you place your arm through this cuff and it will tell you what your blood pressure is."

Everyone looked at each other before turning to stare at Keelan. Keelan started to back away slowly. "No way!"

Darian and Colton looked at each other and each grabbed an arm. "Don't be like that, Kee. Let's see what happens," Colton said with a devilish grin.

They manhandled him into the chair and slid his arm into the cuff before stepping back.

Aiden frowned. "Nothing is happening."

"Prescription for Amelia Ironwood," Bill announced.

Reluctantly, Darian walked back over to the counter.

Bill handed him a small paper bag with multiple pieces of paper stapled to it.

"You can pay back here," Bill said.

Darian got his wallet out and handed him the credit card. While he was waiting for the slip to sign, he started to read the paper attached to the medicine.

Be careful when using if you are pregnant, planning to become pregnant, are breast-feeding, or post menopausal.

May cause mental or mood changes, hallucinations, fast heartbeat, fever, loss of coordination, muscle spasms, increased sweating, nausea, vomiting, or diarrhea.

What the fuck!

"Sir! Sir! This package says that no woman who is pregnant, planning to become pregnant should be taking this medication." Darian waved the bag at him.

"Is she pregnant?"

Darian shook his head. "No."

"Then you don't have to worry. Sign here." Bill passed him the slip. Grinding his teeth, Darian scrawled his name.

"Ha! You have to push the button," he heard Colton say.

"I don't like this," Keelan said in a small voice.

"Have a nice night." Bill gave a stiff smile and disappeared behind his counter.

Darian pulled out his phone and called Rheia. She answered on the second ring.

"Hello?"

"Rheia, I'm concerned. The instructions on this medicine state that it could cause certain side effects."

"She'll be fine, Darian. Just bring it home. If you're that worried, I'll check on her throughout the night," she promised.

"Rheia, it said it could cause hallucinations!" Darian clutched the bag in his hand.

"I know, I know. Just bring it home, Darian. It's fine, I promise." Rheia hung up and Darian frowned at his phone.

Human medicine could kill you!

"Guys, my arm hurts." Keelan said, wiggling in the seat.

Darian walked over to see Keelan's hand was starting to turn a dark, purply-red color.

"Is it supposed to do that?" Darian asked Aiden who shrugged.

"Okay guys, this shit hurts, get it off!" Keelan said pulling on his arm trying to extricate it from the cuff.

"Just press the release button," Bill called out.

Colton looked around and pressed the button. He looked down at Keelan. "Well?"

"It's still squeezing!" Keelan yelled.

"I will go get Bart." Gavriel volunteered and headed to the front.

"Get it off me!" Keelan screamed hysterically.

"What do we have here?" Bart asked.

"We can't get his arm out of this contraption." Aiden pointed to Keelan.

"Did ya press the button?"

"Yes," Colton said pressing the button again.

Bart rubbed his chin. "Well, ain't this a pickle." He turned toward the pharmacy. "I told you this darn thing was broke," he yelled.

"I can't feel my fingers," Keelan whimpered.

Gavriel turned to Aiden. "We have a sword in the car."

Keelan's eyes widened and he began to struggle even harder to get free.

Bart turned to Gavriel. "A real sword?" His eyes were bright with curiosity making him seem more like a little boy than a grizzled old man.

Gavriel winked.

"You don't really need two arms, do you Kee?" Colton joked.

"Yes I do!" Keelan yelled back.

"We could try cutting the cuff off," Aiden suggested.

Keelan shook his head. "You'll cut my arm off!"

"Don't be silly Keelan. If we cut your arm off, blood will get everywhere." Aiden chastised.

Keelan had just started to hyperventilate when Darian had an idea. He stepped forward and leaned in close to his friend. "You're a witch who has mastered air; can you deflate the cuff," he asked.

Seconds later, Keelan yanked his arm out of the blue cuff and slid off the small bench to sit on the floor.

"I hate going to the store. I hate going to the store. I hate going to the store..." Keelan repeated over and over.

"Hey, blondie!" A cantankerous voice called. Darian turned to see Bill waving him over. "Give this to him. It will calm him down. If you tell anyone I gave it to you, I'll deny it. I normally wouldn't do this, but it is my fault for not getting that thing fixed." Bill dropped a small pill in his hand.

"Will this cause hallucinations, nausea, vomiting, fever...?"

Bill rolled his eyes. "Just give it to him." He turned and disappeared again.

Darian looked around. He spotted a display of bottled water and grabbed one. He walked over to Keelan and knelt down. "Here you go Keelan. This will help." He handed him the small pill and the opened bottle of water. Keelan didn't even question what it was; he just downed it.

"How's the arm?" Aiden asked.

Keelan looked up, his eyes a little less wild. "I can move it." He extended his arm and rotated it.

Aiden turned to Darian. "Did you get Amelia's medicine?"

"Yes, though I have concerns about giving it to her." Darian frowned.

"Trust Rheia, she wouldn't give her anything that would be harmful," Colton said.

"I say, is the boy all right?" Bart said pointing to Keelan who had slumped over on one side, mouth open and drooling.

"Keelan!" Colton knelt down and checked for a pulse.

Bart turned to the pharmacy counter. "What'd ya give the boy?" he demanded.

"Just a little something to calm his nerves, though it shouldn't have kicked in so soon, it usually takes between thirty and forty minutes to get that sort of reaction." Bill said peering over the counter.

"Pick up him, Colton. Let's get him home," Aiden said.

Colton pulled Keelan into a sitting position and wrapped the witch's arm around his neck. "Come on kiddo, let's go home."

"I try so hard, but nothing changes," Keelan murmured incoherently before passing out again.

"I know, I know." Colton nodded and stood. "We'll get you home and then you can go beddy-bye."

"He is out cold." Gavriel observed.

"The only thing that could contribute to this type of reaction is possible sleep deprivation. Has he been sleeping?" Bill asked.

Or it could be that it affects witches quicker than humans. Darian shook his head. Trust Keelan to find out the hard way.

The men looked at each other. "He did say at breakfast that he was having a hard time sleeping lately," Gavriel said.

"Then I'm glad he's getting some sleep now," Aiden said before turning to Bill. "You have my thanks."

Bill waved off Aiden's thanks. "He should be fine by morning."

Aiden nodded and they walked to the front of the store.

Colton lifted Keelan into the back of the SUV and shut the hatch.

"Colton, you couldn't put him in a seat?" Aiden asked frowning.

"He'll be fine, just drive carefully," Colton said hopping into the back.

Once they were on their way, silence filled the cab.

"You know he'll never go to the store with us again after this, right?" Darian asked.

That was all it took, first Gavriel then Aiden started laughing. Colton put his hands behind his head and chortled.

Darian shook his head and smiled.

There were worse ways to spend an evening.

Amelia opened her eyes when she heard Darian return. She had been dozing off and on since he left.

"Did I wake you?" he asked stopping in his tracks.

"No, I've been awake for a little while. Any problems picking up the prescription? I didn't give you any of my ID."

He shook his head. "No, I was able to get it with no issues." He set a bottle of water on the nightstand, opened the paper bag, and pulled out a small bottle. He broke the tamper proof seal and gently tapped out a pill for her. He handed her the medicine. She placed the pill under her tongue gratefully, willing it to dissolve and kick in as soon as possible. Prying one eye open she looked longingly at the water but knew it would have to wait until the nausea subsided to take a sip.

"I'll sleep in the guest room." He turned to leave.

"Please stay." All she could think about was Darian wrapping his arms around her and never leaving. She wanted the problems of the world to stop at their bedroom door and leave them alone.

Quietly, he stripped off his clothes and climbed in behind her. On any other occasion, she would have done anything she could to seduce her mate. Their one night of lovemaking had left her with a taste for more, but she could barely keep her eyes open.

"Sleep, my love. Tomorrow is a new day." He kissed her shoulder and pulled her close to his body.

When the medicine started to kick in, taking the edge off her migraine, she let out a sigh of relief; sleep wasn't far behind.

"How in the hell did you drug Keelan?" Rheia demanded checking Keelan's pupils the next morning at breakfast.

"I slept great," he said, yawning.

"You were completely non responsive, I thought you quit breathing at one point last night." Rheia glared at her mate who chuckled. Colton swallowed his laughter and turned his attention back to his omelette.

Amelia stretched. "I feel great, too. No trace of a headache now."

Rheia finished with Keelan by taking his pulse. "No more Valium for you."

"Yes ma'am." He grinned shyly.

Rheia sat down and pulled her medical bag into her lap and put her penlight away. "I need to get with Adam later and create a list of medicines and how different paranormals react to them."

Gavriel leaned forward. "Not to ruin anyone's good mood," he turned to Aiden, "what do we do now?" Everyone got quiet.

Aiden leaned back in his chair. "The council has reclaimed the remaining necklace from

Adam and has it under guard. Now that they know what they are dealing with they are starting a new barrage of tests."

"You're kidding me, right?" Amelia said, feeling her blood pressure rising.

Aiden winced. "I wish I were."

"Aiden, it's no longer just a necklace. Those beads are people! They are trapped in a moment of pure terror, we have to destroy the necklace and set them free!"

Aiden turned to her sorrow on his face. "If it was up to me, it would have been done yesterday. But the council has taken over the investigation; it's out of my hands."

"So what do we do?" Meryn asked quietly.

"We do what we always do. You and Beth will take over my office to do your computer magic. Penny will go to school. Rheia will head to the clinic, and the men will begin our morning drills." He looked at Amelia. "You are to rest. I'm exhausted today just from watching you yesterday."

Rheia nodded. "I agree, Amelia. You stay put today."

Amelia snuck a glance at her mate. While getting ready this morning, she had noticed that he was even more withdrawn than normal. He felt emptier now than before they had made love.

"I'd like to watch you all train if that's okay? I'm comfortable on the training field. I grew up on one." She gave Aiden her ten thousand megawatt smile.

He smiled back at her. "Of course, but no joining in. I heard you hold several speed records in Storm Keep."

"I'll just watch," she promised.

Aiden stood. "Okay people, let's start our day."

Amelia turned to Darian and grabbed his hand. When he looked down, his eyes were devoid of emotion. "I'll cheer you on, okay?"

He nodded and extricated his hand from hers making his way toward the foyer. She had to do something. She was losing him! But she had no idea what to do or who to turn to. She debated going to Aiden when the conversation with Caiden popped into her mind. Darian had a brother! Maybe Oron could help. Taking a deep breath, she went to the hallway and grabbed her coat out of the closet. If Oron couldn't help, she didn't know what she'd do.

She went outside and searched the faces of the men. What if he wasn't here today? She took a chance and walked up to the first fae warrior she saw. "Oron?"

The warrior looked down at her and smiled. "No, I'm Larik Li'Milerlen of the Beta Unit. Oron is the one working the ropes." He pointed to the shirtless warrior doing battle rope exercises.

"Thanks!"

"Anytime."

She crossed the training field to the brother of her mate.

"Hello," she said.

"Hello, little one. I was wondering how long it would take before you sought me out. Did Darian tell you about me?" Oron asked, setting the thick ropes down.

She shook her head. "No, I heard about your relationship from my brother, Caiden."

"Brothers are funny things, aren't they? The only people in the entire world you would gladly die for, but they are also the only ones in this world who can drive you crazy." He grinned at her, his brown eyes full of life and light.

She couldn't help her reaction. She felt her face crumple as tears sprang to her eyes.

Oron looked around in a panic. "Whatever I said to upset you, I'm sorry." He wrapped an arm around her and cuddled her in a way that reminded her of her brothers. That thought brought on a fresh wave of tears.

"Shhuush honey, it's okay. Tell me what is wrong. I'll do whatever I can to help." Oron picked up his discarded shirt and started patting her face, accidentally poking her in the eye.

"Ow!" She took the shirt and dried her tears. His dejected expression made her smile. He was very bad at this.

"Excuse me while I go ask my Unit Commander to kick my ass." Oron sighed and went to walk away.

She laughed and pulled at his arm. "I'm sorry, I didn't mean to scare you. Though I find it highly amusing a few tears put you in such a tizzy."

Oron's face softened. "My mother always taught us that a woman's tears were priceless and should only be shed in times of great joy."

"Is that Darian's mother, too?"

Oron nodded. "In a way."

"Would she be able to help him? He's so very close. This morning he looked right through me." She shuddered at the memory.

Oron was suddenly all business. "I don't mean to get personal, but has he claimed you?"

She shook her head. "He won't chance turning and destroying my soul. We have been intimate though." She blushed furiously. "It seemed to help for a little while, but today it's almost as if he's worse because of it."

"There may be a way, but he won't like it," Oron hedged.

"I don't give a rat's ass if he likes it. I'll have Aiden and Colton tie his huge ass up if I have to," she fumed.

Oron chuckled. "Mother will like you." He pulled his shirt on before kneeling down to reach into his gym bag. He pulled out a small leather pouch, opened it, and turned it upside down. A large, ornate, silver ring dropped into his hand. "Normally, a fae returns to Éire Danu every thirty or forty years to replenish their light. We absorb the light and magic from the city. It's one of the main reasons the city is closed to outsiders. About six hundred years ago, Darian got into an argument with our mother. He had had a dream where he joined the Alpha Unit and supported the new Unit Commander here in Lycaonia. Our mother was furious, mostly because she was terrified. Darian was always the gentle one, the poet. He was a competent swordsman, but he didn't wasn't a warrior."

"He disobeyed her, and she banished him from Éire Danu. One of the main reasons his light is almost gone is because he hasn't been home in nearly six hundred years."

Amelia felt confused. "Then why doesn't he just go home now? Surely it's okay after all this time."

Oron shook his head. "Discounting the fact that my mother and brother are two of the most stubborn creatures on the face of this green earth, for some reason, Darian's light is dimmer than it should be. No fae has ever been so dark without having committed a great sin. If he tried to go through the portal to Éire Danu as he is, it would reject him. It's a security measure to keep ferals out of the city."

"Then what can we do?" Amelia felt as if there was no hope.

"That was before he found you. We can try something that has never been done before. Like I said, no other fae has ever become so dark without committing a sin, so we've never had this type of scenario before. But because you are his mate, if you were to go through the portal with him, it might recognize your light and see him as a mated fae, and let him through."

"And if it doesn't?" she asked quietly.

"It could kill you both."

"I'm not scared for myself, but he'll never go for it." She rubbed her face with her hands.

Oron cupped her face. "How much time does he have?"

Amelia was about to answer when she heard an inhuman roar to their right. Oron looked up and had just enough time to shove her out of the way before Darian tackled him to the ground.

"She is mine! Mine! Mine!" Darian growled and spat.

"Guess that answers that question," Oron said and grunted as Darian's fist made contact with his stomach.

"Darian, stop!" She didn't move in time and was knocked to the ground by their flailing bodies.

"Quinn! Tangled Web!" Oron yelled wrestling with Darian trying to keep him under control.

Amelia watched as a warrior ran over already reciting a spell. She felt a rush and her magic sung! He was using earth magic.

Trunculi Laqueumin!

Oron jumped out of the way as hundreds of thin tendril roots shot from the ground and wove themselves around Darian. Her mate snarled and hissed, his eyes completely black. She pulled her knees to her chest unable to face the reality that she had lost him.

"Oron!" Aiden yelled running up to them.

"I have to take him home sir. It's his only chance."

Aiden helped her to her feet. "Don't give up yet. I don't make it a habit of losing men, and we're not going to start now." He kissed her forehead.

Oron searched the ground for the silver ring he had pulled out earlier. He picked it up and slid it on his right ring finger. He easily picked up Darian and slung him over one shoulder. He held a hand out. "Amelia, hurry!"

Startled, she took his hand.

He looked down at her. "Think of him, and in your mind, keep him in the light. "

She closed her eyes and remembered how he looked walking with her in the fae gardens. Him trying not to smile at something she said. The look on his face when he finally admitted his feelings and the way he seemed to glow as he stared down at her while they made love.

She felt her body wrench and jerk. Darkness and ice seemed to pierce her body, and just as she was about to give in to the pain, it was gone. She opened her eyes and blinked.

She looked around. They were in a large courtyard. A warm sun was overhead and hundreds of flowers bloomed around them. Sprites of every shape and size flittered around screaming their heads off.

"Halt! Who dares to trespass in Her Majesty's royal garden?"

Her Majesty?

Amelia looked at the group of very large fae warriors dressed in identical uniforms bearing down on them.

"Oron!" she whispered urgently.

Oron set a still hissing and spitting Darian down on the cobblestones and rose to his full height.

"Seize them!" The guards surrounded them. A set of hands grabbed her and pulled her away from Oron. She watched in horror as a guard lifted a radiant, silver sword over Darian's neck.

"Oron!" she screamed.

Oron grabbed the warrior by the throat and lifted him off his feet. "I know you weren't about to hurt my baby brother, were you?" He swung his eyes over to where she was being restrained by a guard. "And get your hands off my sister!" he ordered.

"You have no authority here. How dare you bring this feral filth into the Queen's gardens!" A guard said removing his helmet.

"Malcolm, you're Captain of the Guard? Mother must have been desperate after I left." Oron said, his tone insulting.

The captain stopped in his tracks. "Prince Oron?"

Prince?

Around them, the guards froze instantly. The hands holding her let go in shock. She immediately returned to Darian's side.

"What is going on here?" A soft feminine voice demanded.

"Your Majesty, Prince Oron has returned, bringing a feral and a witch with him," the captain reported.

"Oron? Feral?" A tall, willowy figure stepped into the light. Amelia had never seen a more beautiful woman in her life. She embodied every human fantasy of what the fae looked like. This woman was the Queen of the Fae and the heart of their race.

The queen looked down at Oron's feet and gave a low wail. "Darian! My son!" She hurried over and dropped to her knees.

"Prince Darian?" the men around them whispered.

Oron knelt beside the queen. "Can you help him, Mother? This is his mate, Amelia. She is the reason we were able to get him through the portal."

The queen didn't answer. She waved a hand over Darian, and he quieted instantly. Seconds later, the roots were gone and she was pulling him into her arms. She rested his head against her breast and rocked back and forth, keening softly. "This is all my fault! I never should have said what I did. Please Goddess, do not punish my son for my foolishness. Take my light, let it pass to him." A warm light enveloped them.

Oron stood and walked over to Amelia who watched in shock. He wrapped an arm around her and held her close. "If anyone can save my brother, it's her."

Wiping her tears, she also prayed to the Goddess.

Please. Please don't take him from me. We have only just found each other, I need more time.

After a few minutes, the queen looked up confused. "I don't understand. This should be helping." She looked back at them. "Has he claimed you?"

Amelia shook her head. "He didn't dare. He knew how close he was."

The queen shook her head. "It's as if a piece of his light is missing altogether."

Amelia's heart stuttered. "What did you say?"

The queen blinked. "He has a hole in his aura, the core of his light is gone, not dim, gone. Normally, that wouldn't be so critical as fae return regularly to Éire Danu to recharge their magic, but he hasn't been home." Her voice broke.

Amelia stepped forward. "I have it! He gave it to me when I was a child, so he could find me." She clutched at her chest.

"Come here!" The queen ordered.

Amelia knelt down beside Darian.

The queen hesitated. "This may hurt."

"I don't care, help him!"

The queen nodded and lifted a pale, slender hand. Amelia looked down as a small sphere of golden light was lifted from her chest. She felt its loss, but knew she could live without it, Darian couldn't.

Amelia watched as the queen gently pushed the sphere into Darian's chest. His body jerked once and slammed back down. He gave a shuddering sigh of relief, and his face became peaceful.

"Thank the Goddess! It's working!" The queen continued to bathe Darian in light. Amelia felt a wave of dizziness. Oron was at her side immediately helping her to lie flat.

"Amelia, Amelia can you hear me?" A soft voice called.

Amelia nodded with great effort.

"You need to stop fighting and let your body rest. It has to adjust to the absence of Darian's light. Sleep daughter of mine, and when you wake, your mate will be waiting for you."

"Promise?" Amelia asked.

"I promise, dear one, now sleep."

Amelia learned that when the Queen of all the Fae tells you to sleep, you sleep.

CHAPTER ELEVEN

Amelia woke slowly and instinctively turned toward the beautiful masculine voice. The words were familiar; she had heard them before. Soft words sang of a candle's flame and a love that would endure wind and rain. Stepping from his dreams and into his life. When she opened her eyes, the singing stopped.

"How do you feel?" Darian asked, his voice soft and gentle.

She looked into his enchanting lavender eyes and began to cry. He was the prince from so long ago. She must be dreaming.

"Oh, my love, don't cry. I can withstand anything except the sight of your tears. Why are you so distraught?" He pulled her into his arms and rubbed her back.

"You're my dream prince, which means I must be dreaming." She sniffed. "You're probably really dead, and I've snapped, and this is a hallucination!"

"You really are related to Meryn, aren't you?" he asked before tilting her head back. Slowly and deliberately he began to kiss her face—her forehead, between her brows, each eyelid, her nose, and finally, her lips.

She blinked up at him. "This is real?"

He propped himself up, resting on his hand, and grinned. "You and my brother managed to achieve the impossible by bringing me home. Mother returned the light I gave you, and by being in Éire Danu, I was able to restore my inner light." He smiled. "I remember now, that dream from so long ago. After I gave you my light, I woke up, and the memory of you and the dream were gone. I thought I was turning feral, but in reality, I was adjusting to the loss of my light."

Amelia gasped and sat up in bed. "Oh my Goddess, this is all my fault! If I hadn't..."

Darian quieted her by placing a finger over her lips. "I remember feeling completely panicked as you stared up at me, so tiny and innocent. When I saw the fear in your eyes at the idea of being forgotten, I didn't even stop to think, I gave you my light. If we're placing blame, it should be placed solely at my feet. But in my defense, I had no idea that losing my light for such a short amount of time while I was unable to visit Éire Danu would almost turn me feral. "

Amelia couldn't believe the difference in him. He was smiling and joking; he seemed to exude congeniality. She didn't like it. She had dreamed of her prince and thought he was the one she longed for, but she had fallen in love with her dark and surly warrior.

"You're frowning." He sat up and the sheet pooled at his waist.

Blushing, she realized that she had been stripped, too. She turned away, embarrassed.

"Hey, what's this? Why are you turning from me?"

She couldn't meet his eyes. It felt like she was in bed with a stranger.

"Amelia?" Darian's voice was no longer so affable. It held an edge of concern.

When she looked up, his brows were knitted together, and he was frowning. She threw her arms around his neck. "You're you!" she cried out.

"Of course I am." His arms went around her, and he pulled her into his lap to sit between his legs. "What's going on?"

"I feel like I don't know you when you're smiling. I like your frowny face better." She sniffed and used the sheet to wipe her nose.

"My frowny face? Gods above, what a mangled mating I have given you where you don't recognize me unless I'm a sullen bastard." Darian cradled her head to his chest.

"I like you grumpy," she mumbled.

He pulled back and glared at her. "How's this?"

She giggled. "Much better."

His features softened. "I'll have to introduce you to my smiling face so you recognize both."

Amelia shrugged. "You seem shifty when you're smiling."

His eyebrows shot up. "Shifty? Shifty! I'll give you shifty!" He started tickling her mercilessly.

"I give! I give!" she shouted.

"I even serenaded you," he grumbled, pulling her down to lie beside him.

"It was Michael Bolton."

"I won't begrudge a fellow bard who happened to have written the words to describe my feelings perfectly." He turned on his side and slowly began to trace his finger down her body. "How are you doing, really?"

Her breath caught in her throat, and all of her attention was on the tip of his finger making lazy circles around her breast. "Fine," she managed to squeak out. She felt moisture begin to pool between her legs. He was barely touching her and she could barely think.

"Amelia, I'd like to claim you, if you're willing," he said, laying his hand flat over her heart.

"There's nothing I'd like more!" She had been dreaming of this moment all her life. She was finally going to be claimed.

His fingers trailed down her body until they brushed her opening. He teased her while his mouth suckled and nipped at her breast.

When he moved over her, she smiled up at him. He reached down and eased himself forward. She gasped and threw her head back. There was no pain, just the pleasurable sensation of being full and complete.

"For every tear I made you shed, I promise you a million smiles," he whispered, thrusting deep.

"For every moment of doubt and pain, I will give you hours of pleasure." He kept eye contact as their bodies merged.

"I cannot change the past, but I give you my future." Slowly, he sunk himself to her very core. He was stringing out each moment until it collided with the next, each wave of pleasure unending.

"I promise to be your best friend, your lover, and the father of your children, placing your needs and their needs above my own." He stopped, now completely inside of her, and leaned down to kiss her gently.

Just when she thought she couldn't take the slow pace anymore, he began to glow. He threw his head back, the muscles in his neck pulled tight. When the sphere of light widened to include her, her body detonated. Small explosions of pleasure ran down her spine causing her to scream her satisfaction.

She felt her soul lift up and merge with his. Where they had been two incomplete pieces, they were now whole. When they separated, the light that was the piece of their combined souls drifted back into her chest, carrying a piece of him with it.

Breathing heavily, Darian withdrew from her body and collapsed to one side. "Thank you, my love."

Amelia couldn't quite catch her breath. She lay on her back staring up at the plant-covered ceiling. "Anytime."

He chuckled once then groaned as he sat up in bed. On unsteady legs, he wobbled to what she assumed was the bathroom. She was sure when he came back a few minutes later with a cream-colored linen cloth.

He stood at the foot of the bed, a smug expression on his face as he stared down at her body. "Gods, you are beautiful."

"So are you." She smiled at him.

He gently cleaned her up and returned to the bathroom with the cloth. He sat on the edge of the bed and stroked her hair away from her face.

Amelia looked around the room. It reminded her of his room back in the Alpha estate only fancier. All the furniture here was white with accents in silver and gold.

"Where are we?"

"My quarters in the palace."

"Didn't you leave almost six hundred years ago?"

He nodded, a sad look on his face. "My mother must have kept this room up all this time."

"She was very distraught earlier when she thought you were dying."

He nodded. "I can't wait to meet with her. We've been invited to an early dinner."

"Dinner? What time is it?" She blinked and looked around for a clock.

He grimaced. "I think you mean, what day?"

"Get the fuck outta here."

Darian laughed. "It's the day after you brought me here. I woke up a couple of hours ago. Someone was kind enough to leave a tray of food by the door so I ate while I sat with you. If you didn't wake up in time for dinner, I was going to send for a healer."

"How soon before we have to go meet your mother?" she asked, sitting up.

He looked out the window for the sun's fading position. "In about thirty minutes."

"What!" she shrieked and flew out of bed. "Where's the shower? Where's my clothes? I need my makeup!"

He stood and placed his hands on her shoulders to stop her frantic circling. "Calm down. There's a dressing robe for you hanging up in the bathroom. On the counter, there is a basket; all you have to do is say what you need, and it will appear."

"Even makeup?"

He nodded, and she could tell he was trying not to smile. "Even makeup."

She twisted away from him and ran to the bathroom.

"Amelia?" He sounded concerned.

"Twenty-eight minutes until I have dinner with you mother who happens to be the queen of all the fae, and I have some of your cum dripping down my leg! Why am I even explaining this?" she slammed the bathroom door.

Men!

She could hear his unrestrained laughter from behind the closed door. She took a second to appreciate that he could laugh before she jumped in the shower.

She got out and quickly dried off. She was sorry she didn't have more time. The towel felt like a cloud from heaven. She wrapped herself up in its softness and padded over to the counter. She looked at the plain, white basket. She picked it up and turned it over. On the underside, written in fae, was a spell. Grinning, she set it back down. She took a deep breath and began reciting all the things that she would normally use to get ready. One by one the items started to appear.

She was just finishing her makeup routine when she heard a knock at the door.

"Come in."

Darian opened the door and she temporarily forgot what she was doing. He was dressed in a cream silk dressing robe, and his hair had been pulled back in a half-pony and braided. He wore a crown of gold and silver leaves, which accented the gold and silver threads in his robe perfectly.

"Gods, you're exquisite," she breathed.

"I was about to say the same thing about you." He pointed to her towel-wrapped body.

Laughing, she let the towel drop and watched with satisfaction as he swallowed hard. She reached past him to grab her robe. It was a grayish-silver color accented in emerald green. She slipped it over her head and had a moment of surprise when underthings appeared under the robe.

"All fae garments have a bit of magic in them." He held out his arm. "Shall we?"

Amelia turned to look in the mirror one last time. Her brown curls were behaving for once, and the robe made her eyes look like liquid silver. She turned back to him and laid her hand on his elbow. "Let's go."

"Darian!" The queen threw herself into Darian's arms.

"Hello, Mother."

Amelia watched as Darian laid his cheek on top of his mother's head and held her tight.

"I'm so sorry!" The queen sobbed into his chest.

"There's nothing to be sorry for," he assured her.

A man every bit as tall as her mate stepped forward and gently extricated the queen from her son.

Darian held out his forearm and the man clasped it. "Brennus."

The handsome fae smiled. "Darian."

Darian turned and held a hand out to her, motioning her forward.

"Mother, Brennus, I have the pleasure to present my mate, Amelia Ironwood. Amelia this is my mother, Aleksandra Vi'EireDan, and her mate and consort, Brennus Vi'Eirlea, the unit leader for Tau Unit and commander of all the units in Éire Danu. His half brother Celyn Vi'Ailean is the fae Elder in Lycaonia. " Darian scooted her forward with a gentle push.

Remembering her deportment lessons, she curtsied low. "Your Majesty."

"Call me Aleksandra, or preferably, Mother." Aleksandra pulled her into a warm hug.

"Brennus is fine for me." The warrior winked.

"And you can call me Super Big Brother," Oron joked.

"Come. Cord has made all your favorites, Darian." She turned to Amelia. "Cord is my squire. He has known Darian and Oron since they first came to the palace."

They walked into a smaller dining room where the table was set for five. Amelia couldn't stop looking around. She thought there was a lot of magic in Storm Keep, but even the city of the witches couldn't compare to the palace of the fae. Everywhere she turned, spells were used to light hallways, turn fans, and keep fresh flowers from wilting. It seemed as if every surface glowed.

Once seated, a fae with the darkest hair she had ever seen stepped into the room, tears in his eyes. Most fae had blond hair in hues ranging from white to gold. This man's hair was like burnt umber and just as beautiful.

"Prince Darian," he said, his voice breaking.

"Cord! It's so good to see you again! I have missed your cooking." Darian stood and abandoned all formality to pull him into a hug.

Aleksandra turned to her. "I was mated to Brennus only seven hundred years ago. Cord acted as a father to both Oron and Darian before then," she explained.

Darian released his old friend and sat down.

The squire wiped at his eyes. "How embarrassing."

"Think nothing of it, old man. We're all glad Darian has come home," Oron said, patting the man on the back.

"Cheeky youngster." Cord swatted at Oron's hand, making him laugh.

Amelia turned to Darian's mother. "I don't know if it's okay to ask, but how are you all related?"

Aleksandra looked at Darian and Oron, and the three of them started laughing. She turned to Amelia. "It is a bit of a puzzle, isn't it?" She looked over at Darian. "Would you like to explain or shall I?"

"You tell the story best, Mother." Darian wrapped an arm around her shoulders, getting comfortable.

Aleksandra thought for a moment. "I suppose it all started right after the Great War. It was dark times; so many people had lost family. There was no victor in that war, just losers. The fae returned from the battlefields to find that things at home had changed as well. People were giving more deference to the families that had proven themselves in battle instead of established noble lines." She paused and looked at Darian and Oron before continuing.

"Before the war, House Eirson had been the closest to the throne, but they had made some bad decisions and lost favor with the people, whereas House Alina gained the people's trust by bringing home so many fathers and sons." She paused, again looking at Oron.

He nodded. "I know the story well Mother, you won't hurt my feelings in the telling of it."

"I love you, darling."

"I know."

The queen continued. "One night, the members of House Eirson decided to completely eliminate all of the family members of House Alina and blame it on a smaller house, House Liordon." Amelia gasped. Aleksandra looked at her. "You know that family?"

Amelia nodded. "Yes, Aedan Li'Liordon serves in my eldest brother, Caiden's, unit in Storm Keep."

The queen smiled. "His brother, Aeson, serves here in the Chi Unit. They are very good boys."

"They are," Amelia agreed.

"Since House Liordon wasn't a prominent house, the head of House Eirson figured no one would question his word when it came time to report the deaths of House Alina."

Amelia leaned forward. "What happened?"

The queen smiled at Oron. "He hadn't counted on the noble heart of a ten-year-old boy, his own son. Oron overheard the plans, but was caught trying to sneak out of the house to warn someone. He was locked away in the cellar until almost morning when he was able to break free. He immediately ran to House Alina and snuck in through a back window, which happened to be the window to the nursery. Oron gently picked up the baby and climbed back out the window. He heard the sounds of screams and men's shouts and decided to run and get help. He arrived at the palace carrying the only surviving family member of House Alina."

Amelia turned to her mate. "You?"

He nodded. "If Oron hadn't come to check on the house first, I would have been murdered with my family. He really is a super big brother." He winked at Oron.

Amelia smiled gratefully at Oron. She knew that hearing this story had to bring up painful memories for the warrior.

"Of course he is, he has always taken care of you." The queen took a sip of water. "Due to Oron's testimony, the members of House Eirson were banished from Éire Danu, forever denying them the light of the fae. Deciding their fate was the easier of the two tasks I had before me. After the rogue fae had been banished, I was still left with two little boys who had no family and no home. I interviewed countless families willing to take in baby Darian, but none would take Oron. They didn't want to be associated with such a treacherous House. I watched Oron and Darian closely, and what I saw made my decision for me."

"What did you see?" Amelia asked.

"I saw one little boy dedicated to a baby that he insisted was his brother. I asked Oron which family should have Darian and he said..."

"You can only give him to a family that has lots of boys. He'll need a big brother." Oron said quietly.

The queen nodded. "And I said, it's a good thing I have decided to adopt you both. You can be his big brother."

Oron leaned back. "It was the happiest day of my life. I swore that night that I would never let anything happen to my baby brother. And Gods, did he ever put that oath to the test! I never saw a kid get into so many fights and dangerous situations in all my days." He turned to Amelia. "It looks like I have blond hair, but it's really white. That's what he did to me."

Amelia laughed.

"I wasn't that bad," Darian scoffed.

"I started drinking at an early age because of you," Oron argued.

"Boys!" The queen clapped her hands.

"Sorry," they said together.

The queen looked at Amelia and winked, and they both laughed.

"I'm sorry to interrupt, but dinner is ready," Cord announced as server after server carried in bowls of hot soup and plates of grilled vegetables. To Amelia, everything smelled incredible.

"Brothers can be the biggest gift and the biggest pain in the ass," Brennus said as he lifted his spoon.

Amelia, Darian, and Oron nodded. The queen looked shocked. "Brennus, language."

Brennus grinned. "I forgot my love, there's no way two unit warriors like Oron and Darian, or a woman raised by unit warriors like Amelia have ever heard the word 'ass' before."

Aleksandra sighed. "I wanted to at least give Amelia a good impression."

Amelia waved off her concerns. "He's right. I was raised by my brothers and pretty much all the warriors in Storm Keep. There isn't much that can shock me."

The queen became thoughtful. "That's right; you're an Ironwood...hmmm... that must mean you also know the Ashleighs?" she phrased it as a question.

Amelia nodded. "Despite actual blood ties, I consider the Ironwoods my brothers and the Ashleighs my half-brothers."

"Maybe if Amelia stayed here for a while, we could entice the Ashleighs to make their home here," Brennus suggested.

Amelia shook her head. "With what we discovered, they'll be needed by the council and Aiden McKenzie now more than ever."

The queen looked at Oron who shrugged. "What do you mean, dearest, by with what you've discovered?"

Amelia quickly looked at Darian. Was she not supposed to say anything?

Darian leaned forward. "Mother, a soundproof spell if you would."

Looking shaken she ordered most of the servants to leave and then folded her hands in front of her. A silver white light shone from her body and filled the room.

"Done." She nodded at Darian.

"The day before we arrived here, my unit was investigating the feral necklace for the council," he began.

Brennus nodded. "We have all read Aiden's report that the necklaces can halt the decay of a feral, mask their scent and give them abilities."

Darian's jaw clenched. "What we discovered that day, thanks to Amelia's amazing empath abilities, is that each bead in those necklaces is a soul."

Oron stared as the queen gasped.

Brennus shook his head. "We would have had a report from Aiden if that was true."

Darian exchanged looks with Oron. "We don't know what new information could have been revealed while we were here or what the orders from the council are."

To Amelia, it seemed like the light in the room dimmed just a little with the sad news, like the sun going behind a cloud. She turned to Darian. "I want to get home and check on Meryn." She hadn't been a big sister-cousin for long, but she couldn't stand the thought of anything happening to her quirky baby sister-cousin.

The queen turned to her a questioning look on her face. "You're concerned for Meryn McKenzie. What ties do you have to her?"

Amelia smiled. "She's my baby sister-cousin! Technically, my cousin, our mothers were sisters, but since I've never had a sister before, I claimed her as my baby sister-cousin."

Oron burst out laughing, hooting loud, and banging the table with one hand.

"Shut up, Oron!" Darian growled.

"Oh, this is rich! You mated into that craziness! Has she tried to electrocute you yet?" Oron heckled.

"You've mated into the craziness, too, Super Big Brother," Amelia teased.

Oron's laughter stopped immediately. "That's not funny. Seriously? That crazy little human menace is my sister now?"

The queen smiled. "Menace? I really do have to meet this woman. I don't think I've laughed harder than when Oron was telling me about her mating Aiden McKenzie."

Oron chuckled. "Trust me, the unit warriors enjoyed every second of watching those two come together."

The queen turned to Darian. "You would have missed knowing the Unit Commander. You would have never known Meryn or met your mate had you listened to me." She looked away, ashamed.

Darian strode over to her chair and dropped to one knee beside it. "I felt like I had betrayed everything you had done for me the day I left. I just couldn't explain the push I had to leave. Will you forgive me for the worry and heartache I caused you?"

The queen held him close. "Only if you forgive me for telling you that the only choice you had was to stay or forever be banished, I never should have given you that ultimatum. I just couldn't see how my gentle son could last as a warrior. Oron yes, but you my sweet boy, you couldn't stand to see people get hurt."

"Hey!" Oron protested.

The queen pulled away from Darian as he stood and looked at her eldest son. "You've always been a warrior my son, from the day I met you until this very second."

"Yeah, you brute," Darian teased.

His mother nudged him in the ribs. "Be nice to your brother, as memory serves me, he saved your butt more than once."

"Mother!" Darian protested, turning red.

"You tell him, Mother." Oron nodded.

The queen stood shaking her head. "Thousands of years old, and you still act like children." She stood on tiptoe and kissed Darian's cheek. "As much as I want to keep you here for months catching up, you're clearly needed back in Lycaonia. I think it's about time you have this." She reached into her skirt pocket and pulled out a silver ring. When Darian looked down, he paled and stepped backwards.

"Mother, no." He shook his head.

"I have already had this conversation with Oron. He knows he cannot inherit since his family name has been stricken from our records..."

"You could have children of your own," Darian interrupted.

The queen shook her head, and Brennus rose to stand behind her. "We've consulted every witch with the gift of premonition; I will never conceive."

Brennus wrapped a supportive arm around her shoulders and looked at Darian then Oron. "Besides, we do have children of our own. Fate does things for a reason, do you think it coincidence that your mother adopted you, unbeknownst to her at the time that she couldn't have children?"

The queen stepped forward and took Darian's hand. She put the ring in his palm and closed his fingers around it. "You are my heir. This ring can take you to any pillar city through the fae portals along with select human cities. It will also act as a signet ring allowing you to speak for me and be recognized as my heir."

Darian shot a desperate look at Oron who raised his hands up grinning. "Don't look at me, baby brother, we both know I am not suited for diplomacy. I would, however, like a promotion to personal guard when you take over."

Brennus walked around his mate's chair to kneel in front of Amelia. He took both of her hands in his. "Just breathe darling, being a consort isn't so bad. For the most part, I just stand beside her and look pretty. I know you can do that."

Amelia looked past Brennus to Darian, and they shared a moment of pure panic. She took slow deep breaths as Brennus instructed and was able to smile reassuringly at her mate. "Think about it this way: is there anyone else you trust to do it?" she asked.

He immediately started to grin. "I think I can do anything if you're at my side."

"Even face the council regarding possible charges I may or may not be facing for attempting to kill a shifter family matriarch?" she asked smiling brightly.

Darian blinked. "Seriously?"

Amelia shrugged. "She was threatening Meryn."

Oron turned his face away, his entire body shaking with laughter. Darian let his head drop back as he mentally counted.

"Five...six...seven..." she said out loud.

He scowled at her, and she giggled. "There's my frowny face!"

Brennus stood and Amelia stood with him.

The queen laughed and then her eyes filled with tears. "Oh dear, I told myself not to cry. You can visit any time now."

Darian pulled her into a hug. "We'll visit every week. How's that?"

Aleksandra nodded and stepped back. "And bring the crazy human, too."

Oron stood. "That I have to see."

Darian slid the ring on his finger and turned to Oron. "You do the honors?"

"Sure thing." Oron stepped away from the table, held up his hand, and a portal of silver light appeared. "Ready when you are."

Darian kissed his mother's cheek and clasped forearms with Brennus. "I'll send an update as soon as I can." Brennus nodded.

Darian held out his hand to Amelia and they walked over to Oron who held out both hands. Darian took one and she the other. Together, they stepped through the portal.

CHAPTER TWELVE

Unlike the journey to Éire Danu, returning to the Alpha estate was much easier. There was no jarring or cold sensation. It was as easy as stepping from one room to another. One second they were in the royal dining room, the next they were stepping out onto the training field from where they had left. The men were doing evening drills before dinner.

Darian turned to Oron and Amelia. "Let's keep recent developments to ourselves for a while," he said, looking down at his ring. Amelia and Oron nodded.

"Aiden! Darian's back!" Keelan yelled before running over.

Amelia watched as Darian pulled the young witch into a brotherly hug. "Thank you. Thank you for everything you did to save me, even when I didn't want to save myself." He released Keelan and ruffled his hair.

Blushing furiously, Keelan ducked away from Darian's hand. "Don't be ridiculous. Of course, I'd try and save you. You're the only one who takes my side."

Darian grinned. "I'm back."

Keelan smiled wide. "Good!"

Aiden, Colton, and Gavriel clapped Darian on the back. Aiden exhaled, looking relieved. "I'm glad you're okay."

He turned to Amelia. "So how was your first trip to the fae city?"

"I got to meet the Queen."

"Don't tell Meryn; she'll mope for days." Aiden rolled his eyes.

"Where is she?" Amelia looked toward the house.

"She and Beth are upstairs in the nursery trying to decide where to put a Tardis, whatever that is." Aiden shrugged.

Amelia laughed. She couldn't wait to see the nursery. Immediately following that thought was the realization that this was truly home now. Grinning, she turned to Darian. "Guess I can officially move in now, huh?" she teased.

"You better." He pulled her close and kissed her passionately.

The men around them began to cheer and whistle.

Everyone quieted and looked around when a phone began ringing. When all eyes turned to Keelan, his eyes widened. "Crap! That's your phone, Aiden!" He pulled it out and handed it to Aiden.

"Aiden here. ... Say again? ... On our way." Aiden hung up and cupped his mouth with both hands. "All units report!"

Amelia stood close to Darian as the men began to crowd around. Aiden held out his phone after placing it on speaker. He looked up. "Ferals are attacking the city," he said shortly.

"Hello?" Sascha yelled.

"What's your status?" Aiden shouted into the phone.

"It's a clusterfuck out here, sir! We're getting hit from every direction. Requesting backup, ASAP!" Gunshots and screams nearly drowned out Sascha's voice.

"We're on our way!" Aiden hung up the phone, and he had just turned to face them when a huge explosion rocked the group. Amelia would have fallen if Darian hadn't had his arm wrapped around her.

Coughing and waving the dust away from their faces, the men ran to the back of the house. A huge fire was climbing up the side of a small building.

"Meryn!" Aiden roared.

"Wasn't me!" Meryn replied. Everyone turned and looked up; Meryn and Beth were staring wide-eyed out an open window.

"Gods, they were trying to take out the armory." Colton said.

"Those four foot thick walls looking worth the effort now?" Aiden asked. The men scrambled for water hoses and fire extinguishers.

Aiden roared loudly getting everyone's attention. "Epsilon, Delta, head to the city to back up Gamma. Their backs are against the wall, and there are a ton of civilians in the crossfire. Gavriel, check in with Zeta; they were on perimeter patrol. Colton, get my father on the phone. We need every man he can muster in the city, and I'd like him to come here to guard the estate. Everyone else, let's get this fire out!"

Amelia turned to Darian. "I bet Ryuu has a fire extinguisher in the kitchen."

He nodded and worked with Oron, unraveling the hose. She leaned up and kissed him quickly. "Be right back."

She ran up the back steps and through the door, looked around the kitchen, and decided to check under the sink first. As she knelt down, the hairs on the back of her neck stood straight up. As she turned, stars exploded behind her eyes, then nothing.

***

"Sir, Kade has checked; the fire's out." Lorcan, the unit leader for Beta, reported.

Darian stood back and wiped his forehead. It had taken nearly half an hour to put the blaze completely out. Aiden wasn't satisfied until the fire witch confirmed it was out.

"Good work," Aiden said, his face just as smudged as everyone else's.

"Looks like you're having fun without me," a deep voice said. Darian turned around and smiled. Byron and his old unit members were walking around the side of the house.

"Father, thank all the Gods! What do you know?" Aiden wiped his hands on his pants before pulling his father into a hug.

Byron clapped his son on the back and let go. "Gamma, Epsilon and Delta are doing the best they can in the city. The ferals are coming in waves, which means they aren't being overwhelmed yet, but they have been fighting non-stop." Byron nodded to his old friends John Younger and Abraham Carter. "They came from the city. Most streets have been blocked off, but there are still a lot of people trapped in buildings."

Gavriel walked up. "I checked in with Zeta. They haven't seen a thing."

Aiden cursed under his breath. "Gods damn those necklaces! Have them abandon the perimeter and head into the city. Patrols are useless at this point."

Gavriel nodded and reached for his phone and walked away to redeploy the Zeta Unit.

Byron turned to Aiden. "I have activated all retired or inactive unit warriors in the city. Most had already suited up and jumped into the fray with Gamma."

Aiden looked relieved. "We'll take all the help we can get." When Gavriel rejoined them Aiden looked at the men. "Let's check in with the ladies and head to the city."

Darian didn't have to hear that twice. They all jogged to the front of the house and headed inside.

"Meryn!" Aiden called out.

Meryn, Beth, and Ryuu came down the stairs. "Is it true there are ferals in the city?" Meryn asked.

Aiden frowned. "How did you know that?"

Meryn held up a military-issue walkie-talkie.

Aiden sighed. "Yes, we're about to head there now."

Darian looked around. When he saw Jaxon and Noah come out of their office and Amelia wasn't with them, he started to get nervous.

"Where's Amelia?" he asked.

Everyone froze.

"Amelia! Amelia!" Darian yelled, his gut twisting painfully.

He ran for the kitchen, that was where she said she was going. His entire world crashed around him when he saw the cabinet doors under the sink open and the rug bunched and twisted. He looked toward the door, and his heart stopped when he saw drops of blood on the floor.

He threw his head back and roared. His mind narrowed to a single purpose: he had to find his mate. Strong arms wrapped around his chest and wrestled him to the floor. He fought and snarled, trying to break free.

"Darian, brother, you have to keep it together! You're not going to help her by losing it like this!" a voice yelled in his ear.

Slowly he regained his senses. He looked around, and his fellow unit members were standing around him looking worried. Meryn peered down at him, scowling. "Get your giant ass up and go find my big sister-cousin!"

He patted Oron's locked hands at his chest, and his brother released him. He stood and pulled Meryn into a hug. "I'm going to bring her home."

Darian watched as Oron disappeared down the hall. Where was his brother going?

She stepped back. "Of course you are, now get to it." She made a shooing motion with her hand.

Aiden turned to his father. "Can you take over as Unit Commander?"

Byron nodded. "You didn't have to ask, but you know son, that the rest of the council won't like you leaving Lycaonia when the city is under attack."

Aiden growled. "I am in charge of the units, not them. Alpha Unit move out. Beta, you're to report to my father. You're on guard duty here until we return."

The men drew their sidearms at the sound of heavy boot treads in the hallway. Oron was the first to appear in the kitchen doorway. He grinned at Aiden. "I brought some backup."

Everyone walked out to the foyer where sixteen fae warriors stood in burnished gold plate armor. "Her Majesty, Queen Aleksandra of The Fae has offered the assistance of her personal guard." Oron winked at Darian who'd never been more relieved in his life. Sixteen fae warriors could do a lot of damage. Closing his eyes, he focused on his bond with his mate. He let out a breath slowly and concentrated on her light. He opened his eyes and looked around. The room seemed brighter to the east.

"Yum," Meryn said ogling the warriors.

"Meryn, stop looking!" Aiden barked.

"No."

"No?" he asked incredulously.

"No. Because I have to focus on something or I am going to get real upset, real fast about someone breaking into our house *again* to kidnap my big sister-cousin!" Meryn roared back at her mate.

"Aiden..." Colton began looking anxious.

Aiden turned to John Younger. "Can you lead half of these men to the clinic and escort Rheia and my brother to the city?" John nodded and led half the fae out the door.

"Aiden, they should come here," Colton protested.

"They should, but they won't. You know as well as I that they will insist on going where they are needed, at least this way they'll be protected," Aiden countered.

Aiden turned to Oron. "Go with them and catch up with Gamma in the city."

Oron shook his head. "No."

Aiden threw up his hands. "Why is everyone telling me no?"

Oron checked the clip in his gun and holstered it. "Normally, I would obey any command you gave, but I'm going with my brother to get my sister back." Oron's tone booked no argument.

"Fine! Darian, do you have a direction yet?" Aiden asked.

"East. We head east," Darian replied.

"Okay men, move out!" Aiden yelled.

Hold on my love, I'm coming!

⁂

Amelia blinked as she slowly came to; she had no idea how long she had been unconscious. Every time she had tried to wake up it had felt like she was trying to climb a slippery slope. Each time she thought she could open her eyes, she slipped back down and lost track of time. When she was finally able to open her eyes and keep them open, panic-induced adrenaline burned away any lingering traces of sluggishness.

"Ah. She's awake." A male voice said to her right.

She looked around and couldn't see anyone. She tried to move and realized she was strapped against a steel plate. Metal cuffs secured her in place around her neck, waist, wrists, thighs, and ankles. She twisted and pulled, but it was no use. She was trapped.

"I wouldn't try to escape if I were you. The metal edges on those cuffs can be sharp." The disembodied voice cautioned.

"Who are you? Where are you?" she called out.

"No need to shout, dear. Look to your right. Do you see a small box?"

She nodded.

"Good. That speaker is projecting my voice. If you look up and over the doorway, you'll see a camera. That is how I can see you."

She looked up and saw a white camera mounted to the wall over the door.

"Why am I here?" She wanted to keep him talking while she summoned her magic. With any luck, she could call some vines from the earth to break her free.

"You're here because you're valuable. Moreover, if you're thinking of using your magic to break free, I feel like it's my duty to tell you it won't do any good. In fact, it will help me enormously. I would say look above your head, but, well, you can't." There was light male laughter. "What you can't see is that you are strapped into a metal tube. There's a large crystal above your head that collects and stores magic. In less than an hour, it will be ready to suck you dry. By that time, your mate and his fellow unit members should be here to rescue you."

"Is that why you brought me here, to get the Alpha Unit? Because that was the dumbest thing you could have done. They are going to kick your ass!"

"Tsk, tsk dear, language. It will be very hard for them to kick my ass when I'm not even in the vicinity. The entire complex you're in has been abandoned for the sole purpose of destroying the Alpha Unit.

"As for why we brought you here, let's just say, you were always going to end up here. In fact, we had a team ready to run your car off the road just outside of Lycaonia."

"Why? There's no way you could have known my mate was in the Alpha Unit."

"We didn't bring you here to get the Alpha Unit. They're just the icing on the cake."

Amelia swallowed hard. "Who did you bring me here for?"

There was more laughter. "Your brothers dear, all six of them. There isn't anything they wouldn't do for their little sister."

"You sonofabitch! You leave them alone!" she screamed.

"I'm afraid that just isn't an option. We've made huge strides refining our techniques. Your brothers represent a very valuable resource, one we simply cannot do without. It makes perfect sense to cull the decedents of the two strongest remaining witch families. When your mate gets here, we'll detonate a spell that will rip the souls from the bodies of any living person in the facility. We'll swing by, collect them, and be on our merry way. The Alpha Unit will be no more. The remaining units will be without a commander. The shifter Elder will be grieving the loss of a son, and I will have gained the perfect bargaining chip to negotiate with your brothers."

"But you said that spell will rip the soul out of everyone in this facility, how can you negotiate with my brothers then?"

"Because they will be negotiating for your soul. Do you have any idea how hard it is to keep a hostage? Souls are much easier to work with. Now, you'll soon feel a slight pinch before pain will explode through your entire body, I personally haven't experienced what you're about to, but previous witches screamed a great deal so I imagine it's very painful. Goodbye, my dear."

"Wait! Wait!" She struggled against the metal as she heard the machine over her begin to power up.

Darian stay away!

"I don't like it." Meryn grumbled. Beth agreed. Something didn't feel right.

Meryn turned to Lorcan. "Go help Aiden. We have Byron and Abraham here, not to mention Ryuu and some kick-ass fae warriors. We'll be fine; Aiden will need you more than we will."

Lorcan looked torn. Beth could tell he was itching to follow Aiden. He looked around and met Byron's eyes. "Do you think you'll really be okay here?"

Byron nodded. "Yes, Meryn's right. We have enough men here. Go help my son."

Looking relieved, Lorcan barked out the order to leave. He and the rest of the Beta Unit quickly headed for the door.

After they had left, Meryn turned to her and smiled. "Phase one complete."

Gods help them; she was scheming something!

Meryn picked up her walkie-talkie. "Gamma Kitten One, Gamma Kitten One, this is Menace come in, over."

Beth looked over at Byron who started to rub his chin and smile. He knew she was up to something, too.

"Menace? Why are you using the radios?" Sascha demanded.

"Gamma Kitten One, you didn't say over. Anyway, I was letting you know that me, Papa Bear and friends, Bunny, Wheels, Pretty Boy, and Baby Girl will heading your way, over."

"Like fucking hell you will! Listen to me Menace, stay put! It's dangerous here!"

Beth could just imagine the veins in Sascha's forehead sticking out.

"What was that Gamma Kitten One? You're breaking up. We're on our way. Menace over and out." Meryn clicked the walkie-talkie off before turning to Byron.

"I assume you approve."

He nodded. "It makes sense to get everyone together so we don't have split resources."

Meryn smiled. "That's why you kick ass playing strategy games." She turned to Jaxon, Noah, and Penny. "Let's roll."

Beth shook her head and picked up Meryn's bag. Ryuu had already gathered their coats and was waiting in the hallway. They ended up taking three SUVs to the city. Beth had never been so scared as when they made their way to the city center. Gamma, Delta, and Epsilon Units, along with volunteer warriors, had created a large barricade in front of Council Manor lit by spotlights. This is where the city had held the Midwinter Ball in December. Families from nearby houses and businesses had come here for protection.

When Sascha saw them approaching, Beth could see him cussing from where she stood.

"Dammit Menace! Are you trying to get us both killed?" Sascha yelled.

Meryn crossed her arms. "Where are the Delta and Epsilon Units? Why is Gamma defending this barricade alone?"

Sascha shot a look at Byron who simply raised an eyebrow. Sascha turned back to Meryn. "They are helping to defend checkpoints throughout the city, there are a lot of scared people out there."

"Exactly!" Meryn said.

"What?" Sascha asked looking between Meryn and Byron.

Byron stepped forward. "I've learned a thing or two from Meryn here about urban combat from a strategy game we play online. Meryn's methods are extremely simple, but they work every time."

"What method?" Sascha asked.

Meryn picked up her walkie-talkie and turned it back on. "Goldilocks, Santa Claus, and Quarterback come in, over."

Sascha grinned at the other's call signs. Seconds later, Graham Armstrong, Santiago Diaz, and Markus Aiken answered.

"Menace, who gave you permission to create these crazy call signs?" Graham grumbled.

"Quiet down, Goldilocks. Here are your new orders. Coordinate with the volunteers working with your units and start herding civilians to Council Manor. I have Wheels and Pretty Boy setting up a mini command post inside the manor; they will guide you in using the surveillance system to avoid pockets of ferals."

"I fucking love you, Menace," Santiago said, making Meryn smile.

"Divvy up the streets and start moving, gentlemen," she ordered.

"Yes, ma'am," they replied.

Sascha shook his head. "What did we do without you?" He looked around. "Where's Beta?"

"Drag your knuckles and beat your chests. I sent Beta to back up Aiden." Meryn looked around. "Where's Rheia?"

Sascha pointed to the Council Manor. "She's in there with some of the injured."

Meryn turned and went to Penny. "Head inside kiddo, your mom is waiting for you." She looked up at one of the fae warriors. "She is your only responsibility. You're her new shadow, got it?" The warrior banged his fist on his chest and held out a hand to Penny and escorted her inside.

Meryn looked at the remaining seven fae warriors. "The rest of you decide who will guard Beth and me, and the rest are to report to Sascha. Our main focus is getting as many people here to safety as possible."

One of the warriors stepped forward. "My name is Doran Ri' Eirlea, brother to Brennus, our Queen's consort. I will stay and guard you. My queen was very clear in her orders that nothing was to happen to you." He also raised a fist and banged his chest making the armor ring like a bell.

"Well, all righty then. Doran you're with me. Everyone else, get your orders from Sascha." Meryn turned to Byron. "Can you watch over the barricade?"

He stared down at her unblinking. "What are you going to do?"

She shrugged. "Nothing."

Ryuu cleared his throat. "*Denka,* I think we all know that is a lie."

Meryn sighed. "No explosives, that's all I can promise."

Byron pinched his nose the same way Aiden did when he got aggravated. "Fine, but if anything happens to you, Adelaide will skin me, and use my fur as a rug. No putting yourself in danger, young lady."

"Pffft, would I do that?" She held up a hand at their dubious expressions. "Never mind." She turned and darted away with Ryuu and Doran in tow.

"She will either save us or be the death of us all," Byron said, heaving a great sigh. He turned to Beth. "And what will you do?"

"I'll head inside. I'm used to coordinating large groups of people from when I worked with my uncle in Noctem Falls. Pretty soon, we'll have a lot of scared people looking for someone to tell them what to do." She said looking at the small groups already arriving.

Byron clapped a hand on her shoulder. "Gavriel is very lucky to have you."

She smiled. "I feel the same way about him."

Beth blinked as she watched Meryn bounce past them wearing a green army helmet and carrying a gun slung across her back.

Dears Gods in heaven!

"Meryn, what in the hell are you doing? Where did you get that helmet?" Sascha roared.

"I'm helping, and I got the helmet from one of the duffel bags behind the sandbags, cool, huh?" she asked, rapping her knuckles in it.

Beth didn't have the heart to tell her she looked like a child playing soldier. The helmet kept sliding down over her eyes.

"Help? Help how? Dammit, Menace, that gun is bigger than you!" Sascha said, trying to pull the gun off her back.

Meryn backed up. "I got this!" She ducked behind Ryuu then ran inside the Council Manor, Ryuu, and Doran following.

Sascha grimaced and held a hand to his midsection. "My stomach hurts. How does Aiden do this all the time?"

Beth patted him on the arm. "She'll be fine. She's been practicing with Penny and Colton. Aiden forbade her to use handguns after she accidentally shot him, but he was okay with her learning how to use a rifle."

Sascha gave her a sour look. "A high power sniper rifle?"

They heard men shouting to their right. Beth and Sascha turned to see a small group of three ferals bearing down on them.

"Shit! They must have gotten past Delta!" Sascha brought up his gun, but before he could fire the three ferals went down, one right after another.

Sascha's walkie-talkie crackled. "Gamma Kitten One, did you see that? I got em! Over."

Beth laughed. Sascha shook his head in defeat. "Good work, Menace. I owe you one."

Slowly, in small and large groups the entire city was evacuated to Council Manor. Beth stayed outside to help give them direction trying to keep neighbors together. Since all the units had now fallen back to the manor, she was about to head inside when she looked up and saw a thick white mist begin to roll in toward them from every side street.

She hurried over to Sascha. "What is that?"

Sascha shook his head. "I have no idea."

"Gamma Kitten One can you let everyone know that I've borrowed some of your peeps and we're creating that mist. Over." Meryn's voice broke the silence.

Sascha picked up the radio and looked up at the roof. "What is it, Menace?"

"I haven't seen any ferals in a while. That's when I remembered some of them could be invisible. So I had two of our witchy friends use earth magic and water magic to make a flour-based, glue-like mist. That shit will stick to everything. So if you see a blob of white coming at you with no face. Shoot it. Over."

"Shoot faceless, white blobs. Roger that Menace, Gamma Kitten One over and out."

Beth smirked at him. "You know, now that you used that call sign, you're stuck with it for eternity."

Sascha shrugged blushing. "It's grown on me."

Beth looked down the street. "Not to ruin your night, but you have faceless white blobs appearing in the street."

Sascha gave an evil grin and turned to the men around him. "Light those motherfuckers up, gentlemen!"

Beth put her fingers in her ears as dozens of different caliber guns started going off all around her. She hurried inside to help keep the people calm. She couldn't let Rheia and Meryn do all the work.

CHAPTER THIRTEEN

Darian checked his gun and stood with his back against the wall. Amelia's light had led them to an abandoned clinic.

"Darian, you sure?" Aiden whispered.

He nodded.

"You'll get her back, I promise," Keelan whispered.

Darian looked down at his friend. "Did you have a premonition?" he asked, keeping his voice low.

Keelan's smile was sad. "Something like that. When the time comes, don't hesitate. Make sure Aiden leaves."

"Keelan, what..." Darian started.

"Move out!" Aiden whispered loudly.

Colton took point and checked the door. Luck was on their side; the door was unlocked. Stealthily, they made their way down the dark hallways. Darian could tell it was making everyone extremely nervous that there was no resistance. He was about to concentrate on Amelia to get a direction when they heard screams.

"Amelia!" Darian hissed. The men ran toward the sound of the screams. It took everything in Darian to resist the urge to run into the room. Aiden held up a fist and peeked in the open door. He nodded and they ran inside.

Darian watched in horror as his mate writhed in pain under a glowing crystal. Keelan darted forward and pressed a series of buttons. The crystal dimmed, and the straps holding his mate were released.

Gavriel turned to Keelan. "How did you know how to do that?"

"Saw it in a dream," Keelan said, pulling a lever down that shut off the entire device.

Darian caught Amelia as she slumped forward. When she opened her eyes and saw him she began to cry.

"It's okay my love, you're safe now." Darian lifted her up into his arms.

Her eyes were unfocused as she shook her head. "Trap. It's...a...trap," she whispered.

Keelan grabbed Darian's arm and shoved him toward the door. "Run!"

They had only made it about halfway down the hallway when a bright light appeared behind them. Darian looked back, and a large, glowing sphere appeared in the middle of the hall.

Keelan stopped and planted his feet. Lifting up his left hand, he started casting.

"Keelan, come on!" Darian yelled.

Keelan raised his head, and the look on his face was peaceful. "Remember what I told you, don't hesitate. Colton, get Aiden out of here." Behind him, Darian heard Aiden fighting Gavriel and Colton as they practically carried him down the hall.

Keelan smiled. "Goodbye, my friend. Tell my brother he was right, but this was the only way I saw where you all lived. Tell him I'm sorry for what I've done, but I'd do it again." Behind Keelan, the sphere pulsed. He turned back to Darian, tears in his eyes. "Go!"

Darian held tight to Amelia as he turned and left his friend behind him. Outside, Gavriel and Colton had tackled Aiden to the ground to keep him from going back inside. Out of nowhere, Lorcan and the Beta Unit ran up to them from the parking lot.

"Where are we at?" Lorcan yelled.

"Bomb!" Colton shouted.

Kade, the Beta Unit witch, had just enough time to raise a shield when a pulse wave slammed into it. It threw the men to the ground, shoving them back several yards.

It took a couple minutes for the ringing in his ears to stop. He gently laid Amelia on the ground. She wept uncontrollably into her hands. He stood on unsteady legs and blinked, trying to clear the dark shapes from his vision.

He could just make out the forms of the other men standing and shaking their heads.

Lorcan turned to him. "Where's Keelan?"

"Guard Amelia!" Darian yelled.

He didn't answer Lorcan's question, because he didn't want to say it out loud. If he said it out loud, it would become real. He pushed past Lorcan and ran with Aiden back into the building. They turned the corner and skidded to a stop. There, in the middle of the hallway, lay Keelan's crumpled body.

"No! No, Keelan! You idiot!" Darian ran over and pulled his friend into his arms. "Aiden, help him!"

Aiden sat on the ground, his elbows on his knees his face in his hands. Was their commander crying? He couldn't be crying, because that would mean they'd lost Keelan.

He shook Keelan. "Wake up!"

Behind him, Oron tried to gently pull Keelan from Darian's hands.

"No!" he pushed Oron away.

"He said he'd been having the same nightmare for weeks, and every night he tried to change the outcome. This must have been the only series of events that he would allow to happen. He said this was the only way we'd all live," Amelia said, tears streaming down her face.

He pulled Keelan up and yelled in his face, "You knew! You sonofabitch! You knew and sacrificed yourself anyway!" He heard his voice crack and didn't care.

"Get him up! We need to get Keelan back to Lycaonia, maybe we can figure out the spell to undo whatever this was," Lorcan said.

"The voice over the speaker said that the spell would rip the soul from the body of any living thing in the building, creating soul spheres. He said that they would collect the souls of all the Alpha Unit members." Amelia shuddered.

Aiden looked up from his hands. "They have his soul?" His voice was almost unrecognizable. Amelia could see the image of a bear semi-imposed over his body. Aiden's anger was almost palpable.

Lorcan looked around, confused. "Why didn't they just kill us in the parking lot when we were all stunned for a few minutes?"

Amelia looked up, her eyes distant. "I don't think they would have risked a fight with two units. Besides, I think they have plans for your souls."

Colton pulled Aiden to his feet. "We'll get his soul back."

Aiden nodded. "Yes, we will, right before I destroy every single one of them," he promised.

The men nodded looking at each other.

Oron helped Darian stand, but Darian refused to hand Keelan over. He carried his friend's body to the car and gently laid him in the backseat.

Aiden turned to Lorcan. "How did you know to come?"

Bishop, Beta's vampire, shook his head. He turned to Gavriel and Aiden. "Your mates. They were uneasy and said something was wrong. They sent us after you."

Aiden looked shocked. "She never ceases to amaze me."

Lorcan clapped Aiden on the shoulder. "Wait until you hear this. Sascha kept us updated as we drove out here. Meryn moved everyone from the Alpha estate into Council Manor, evacuated the city, then proceeded to set up on the roof as a sniper before working with the witches to release this particle spell that made all the invisible ferals visible."

Aiden opened his mouth and closed it.

Gavriel shook his head and turned to Bishop. "How'd you find us?"

Bishop rubbed the back of his neck. "GPS locator beacons that Meryn made us install on all the vehicles."

"Let's go help my baby sister-cousin," Amelia said, her voice sounding flat.

Darian turned to his mate. "Love? Are you okay?"

She nodded absently.

Kade walked over and laid a gentle hand on her shoulder; he immediately pulled it back as if he had been burned. "Gods above, her magic is completely unfettered. It's as if something stripped her of every discipline or restraint that she built to control her magic. What in the hell did they do to her?"

Darian cupped her face in both of his hands. "Baby? Do you know what that machine was that you were in?"

She nodded, her eyes unfocused. "He said it would steal all my magic."

Kade turned to Darian. "We need to get her to Quinn. He uses earth magic like Amelia. He can help her get her magic under control."

All at once, the men were moving.

Oron took the seat next to Keelan's body. He met Darian's eyes and nodded. Darian knew that his brother would look after Keelan while he helped his mate. Once Amelia was well, he'd face what had happened. Later, he'd face it later.

Just outside the city, Darian heard Colton start cussing.

"We have company," Gavriel said from the drivers seat, keeping an eye on the rearview mirror.

"Maybe they changed their mind about a fight." Aiden cracked his knuckles.

Colton's phone buzzed, and he answered it putting it on speaker, it was Lorcan.

"What do you want to do, Commander?"

"Punch it. Let's put some distance between us. Then I want to pull over and transfer Keelan and Amelia to your vehicle. Your only objective is getting them to Adam and Quinn as quickly and as safely as possible. Alpha Unit will handle our guests," Aiden said, his face dark with emotion.

"Roger that," Lorcan confirmed before hanging up.

Aiden turned in his seat to face Darian. "I'd understand if you wanted to go with Amelia."

Darian looked over; his poor mate stared into space, tears trailing lightly down her cheeks. He kissed the top of her head then turned to Aiden. "No. I owe them for what they did to my mate and for what they did to Keelan. With any luck, Keelan's soul is with them, and we can set him free."

Aiden nodded and turned back in his seat. Gavriel pushed down on the accelerator, and the van behind them became smaller and smaller. After about ten minutes, Gavriel brought the SUV to a stop, and the men moved quickly. Darian had time to kiss Amelia before Lorcan picked her up and carried her to their SUV. Larik, Beta's fae warrior, nodded at Darian, his eyes flicking to the silver ring on Darian's right hand. Larik raised his fist to his chest in salute before picking Keelan up. Darian trusted all of his unit brothers equally, but he felt relieved that it was another fae looking after Keelan and Amelia.

Doors slammed and the SUV carrying the most important person in his life, his mate, turned left and sped toward Lycaonia. Everyone, including Oron, got back in the SUV.

Aiden looked around. "Let's take this off the main road. I don't want any innocents to get hurt."

Gavriel nodded and turned left down the same road where the other SUV had just disappeared. They drove slowly for about five miles before they saw the dark van coming up fast behind them. Gavriel pulled off to the side of the road, and the men got out. They stepped into the road and watched as the van got closer and closer. Less than a mile before the van reached them, it came to an abrupt stop, and the front of their car collapsed in on itself like an accordion. Steam from the radiator created a cloud that was barely seen in the grey pre-dawn light.

"Well, you don't see that every day," Oron said, squinting at the wreck.

After a few minutes, the van doors opened and men stumbled out. They looked up and saw the five unit warriors standing in the middle of the road and ran forward. Seconds later, like their car, they slammed into an invisible force, and blood spraying, their bodies fell to the ground.

"Well, I'll be a sonofabitch; Elder Airgead must have figured out a perimeter spell." Colton whistled his admiration.

Gavriel tilted his head and watched as the completely dazed ferals tried again to run at them only to be knocked senseless against the barrier. "As much as I would love to watch them do this all day, we do have ferals attacking the city." He pulled out his gun.

Colton looked over at the men on the ground and sighed. "Doesn't seem right. They should be frothing at the mouth and trying to bite us."

"Think of it like killing a mouse in a mouse trap, it's just a quicker way to exterminate," Aiden said, pulling his gun out.

All five men walked over and took aim. The sound of gunshots shattered the tranquil winter morning. They checked each body and the car for Keelan's soul. Not finding it, one by one, they dragged the bodies into the ditch for burial detail later and got back into their SUV.

"I bet you it was a witch in the city that freaked out during the attack that created the perimeter," Colton said, looking out the window.

"We need to find out who it was so we know the conditions. No perimeter is perfect, we learned that with..." Aiden swallowed hard.

"With Keelan." Gavriel said, finishing their commander's sentence.

"One thing at a time, Aiden. Let's secure the city and make sure our mates are safe first. Then we'll let your father try to figure out who broke the law and cast a spell over the whole city while we get some rest," Colton said, resting a hand on his friend's shoulder.

Aiden just nodded.

Everyone was quiet for the rest of the drive to the city.

Amelia stared out the window as Lorcan maneuvered their SUV through the parking garage. No one spoke as they pulled into a spot and got out. Larik picked up Keelan and gently lifted him out of the vehicle. Amelia watched; to her, it looked like he was sleeping. She recalled his smile, the way he teased Darian, his concern for his friend, and the way he would wink at her, making her feel like she belonged. He was the sweet one, the kind one. Why? Why had this happened to him?

"Amelia, time to go." Lorcan said, holding out his hand to her.

Wordlessly, she took it, and he helped her out of the SUV. "Can you run?" he asked.

She looked up at him and blinked.

"I'll take that as a no. Come on, sweetheart, let's get you to Quinn, he can help you get that magic under control. You'll feel more grounded then." Lorcan easily lifted her and began to run with his men down Lycaonia's cobblestone alleys.

Just a few days ago, her only concern had been whether or not she would have enough time to go shopping. Now, she had lost a friend and was being carried through what sounded like a war zone.

She looked ahead and saw unit warriors running toward them. They met up with their group and surrounded them, acting as an escort.

"We heard you were bringing in precious cargo," Ben said to Lorcan.

"Amelia needs Quinn, and Keelan... I don't think anything can be done for him. But I promised Aiden we'd try," Lorcan said.

The blond pulled out a walkie-talkie. "Gamma Kitten One, this is Adonis, have Foxy Boy on standby to receive Big Sister-Cousin, over."

"I really fucking hate that you got Adonis and I got Gamma Kitten One!" a male voice complained.

"Take it up with management," the blond said flippantly. "Over and out."

"Ben, who's Foxy Boy?" Lorcan asked as they ran.

"Quinn, that's the name Meryn gave him because his last name Foxglove."

"Gods, I can't imagine the call sign she's given me," Lorcan said.

"Lorelei," Ben said with a grin.

Lorcan grimaced. "I had to ask."

The group ran into the city square. Two warriors broke off to intercept four attacking ferals. Lorcan slowed down and finally stopped after they had gotten behind a tall barricade. He set her down on her feet. "You okay to stand?"

She nodded. All around her, the men started barking orders. Gunshots were almost non-stop, filling the air with the acrid smell of gunpowder.

"Gamma Kitten One, what happened to Key Largo? Why did he have to be carried into Council Manor, over?" Meryn's voice demanded to her left.

She watched as Sascha picked up his walkie-talkie. He took a deep breath. "We'll talk about it later, Menace, not over walkie-talkies."

"Let me talk to my big sister-cousin" Meryn ordered.

Sascha handed her the heavy black walkie-talkie.

"Hey, are you okay?"

Amelia nodded.

"I can see you nodding only because I'm peeping you out with my scope; you have to press the button to talk," Meryn said.

Amelia just stared down. She couldn't muster up the desire to speak.

"Gamma Kitten One, what's wrong with her!" Meryn sounded frantic.

Sascha gently took the walkie-talkie from her and looked up at the roof. "She went through a bit of an ordeal. We have, what in the hell is his call sign..."—Sascha scrunched up his face—"...Foxy Boy, that's right. We have Foxy Boy coming in to help her with her magic. She'll be okay, Menace, I promise."

"You better not be bullshitting me."

Sascha scowled up at the roof line. "Would I bullshit someone who's looking at me through the scope of a sniper rifle?"

"Good point. Menace over and out."

Sascha rolled his eyes and reattached the walkie-talkie to his belt. He steered Amelia over to the steps leading up to the Council Manor. "Let's head inside, Quinn will be here soon."

She nodded followed him docilely. With every step she took, the pressure built in her mind. All over her body, she began to feel cuts, broken bones, bullet wounds, and concussions. She staggered back causing Sascha to stop. "What's the matter?"

Mothers' fear for their children, fathers' impotent anger, children crying, all flowed through her as if the emotions were her own. Anger and fear flooded her heart.

"Gamma Kitten One, come in, over."

"Not a good time, Menace," she heard Sascha say.

"Make time. The ferals are congregating just outside the square. I think they are going to make one massive attack on the building." Meryn reported.

"Gamma Kitten One, this is Adonis. I can confirm that report. Also, the streets are empty. The ferals are no longer getting reinforcements, over."

"Attention all units, fall back to the Council Manor steps. All reconnaissance groups return to base."

Sascha turned to Amelia. "I have to go back."

She nodded. "Okay."

Sascha turned and ran back to the barricade, lifting his weapon. One by one, the unit warriors ran into the square from side streets and jumped the barricade to get in position.

Amelia took a step closer to the Manor. The emotions washed over her, but instead of drowning, she focused on her own anger. She turned the peoples' despair and fear into her own strength. When the dam burst inside her, she let it happen. The swirling confusion stopped, and there was only blessed emptiness. For once, her empathy would help, not hinder her.

She walked down the steps to the barricade. She watched the ferals begin to surge forward.

She climbed the barricade and began to walk leisurely across the square, as if she was going from one shop to the next.

"Amelia!" she heard Meryn scream.

She stared at the approaching ferals. They were the ones stealing people's souls. They were hurting and killing innocent people. They were the ones that hurt her and killed Keelan. Calmly, she raised her right hand, her power hand, and for the first time in her entire life, she let her magic go.

The very machine they had used to try to steal her magic had broken every binding put in place to restrict her magic. She was able to use it against them now; she would make them pay.

Under her feet, she felt the earth begin to shift and undulate like a rising wave. She coaxed it, called to it like a beloved child. Cobblestones flew in the air as large mud hands reached up and grabbed the ferals, their once terrifying advance stopped dead in its tracks.

Amelia. Sweetheart, you have to stop. A familiar voice said in her mind.

No, I don't want to.

I know you don't want to, but you have to. If you don't stop, you'll hurt someone, and I know you don't want that.

Yes, I do, Athair! I want to hurt them all! I want them dead!

Calm down and let me help you pull your magic in. Something has removed every protection I put in place for you.

No!

Amelia Violet Ironwood, you will do as I say. The voice was firm, uncompromising.

They killed Keelan!

She screamed and her earth magic began to tighten and twist the bodies it held in its mud hands.

Seconds later, a tremendous surge of magic flowed through her. Fire erupted out of the mud, incinerating the ferals almost instantly. She let her hand drop. Kendrick's fire magic had drained her of power. She knew he had somehow inadvertently used her to channel his own magic to destroy the ones that had killed his little brother.

She stood alone in the square. The ferals were now macabre statues of ash. A small body slammed into her back, and she felt arms wrap around her waist.

"Amelia, Amelia, Amelia! Don't leave me alone! You're the only family I have," Meryn begged, soaking her back with tears.

"There's too much pain, Meryn, everyone's pain." Amelia let her head drop forward. She didn't have the strength to go on any more. What would be the point?

"Give me five minutes. I'll go and knock all those fuckers in Council Manor out so you don't feel their pain," Meryn pleaded.

"Share your pain, my love."

Amelia looked up and saw her mate walking toward her. The early morning sun was rising behind him and seemed to set his hair ablaze, giving him a golden halo. Around him, the Alpha Unit entered the square. Aiden gently pulled Meryn away from her. Darian cupped her face with both hands and looked down.

"If there's too much pain, let me share it. If you find it too hard to take a step forward, I'll carry you. You didn't let me give up; I'm returning the favor." He leaned down and gently kissed each eyelid.

Just being near him made the horror of the night fade away, like the stars fading with the rising of the sun. She sighed. "I'm so tired."

"Then let's go home." Her mate's voice was the last thing she heard before she closed her eyes and let the darkness sweep her away.

Amelia slept until late afternoon and was shocked to see that she was still in Council Manor when she woke. She looked around from the cot where she lay, trying to find Darian, but he was nowhere in sight. She got up and folded the gray wool blanket, leaving it on the cot. She glanced around the crowded ballroom before she spotted a familiar face.

She saw Sascha helping a couple with their children and jogged over to him.

"Where is everyone? Why are we still here?"

Sascha growled as the small family walked away. "Aiden has been in with the Council since this morning, and none of the unit members are leaving here without him. They haven't even let him get any rest.

"Meryn and Beth woke up about an hour ago and have been helping to get the last of the families reassured and back to their homes. Rheia has been at Keelan's side since she woke up. The last I heard, Gavriel finally hit his limit, and he and the Alpha Unit barged into the council session to get Aiden. They should be coming out soon." Sascha nodded his head toward the heavy wooden doors.

"Thanks, guess I better go find Meryn."

"Hey, Amelia," Sascha called.

"Yes?"

"We're all real sorry about Keelan. He... he was like a kid brother to all of us. I'd do anything to have him up and electrocuting me again." Sascha turned his head, his eyes filling up with tears.

"Thank you," she said simply and walked away to find her baby sister-cousin.

After a few minutes, she felt tendrils of her empathy begin to flare to life. All around her, people's emotions were riding high. Taking advantage of nearly depleted magic, Amelia took a deep breath and easily shoved her empathy back into the mental box where she normally kept it. She didn't know what to do about her earth magic, but considering she had destroyed the city square, she didn't think it would cause problems any time soon. She looked out at the setting sun. She was beginning to think they would never be able to go home.

She walked around until she found Meryn and headed over to where she, Beth, Penny and Rheia stood around the gurney where Keelan lay. Meryn wept quietly as she brushed Keelan's hair back from his face. Ryuu stood behind her, a comforting hand on her shoulder. Penny looked on with sad eyes, reaching out occasionally to pat Keelan on the cheek.

"I can keep him alive, but I don't know for how long. A body isn't meant to live without a soul," Adam explained. They all nodded.

"We'll take care of him," Meryn promised fiercely.

The large wooden doors creaked open, and with faces like thunderclouds, Aiden, Gavriel, and the rest of the Alpha Unit walked up to the small group.

"We're leaving. Adam, can you arrange for transport to get Keelan back to Alpha Estate? He is not, I repeat *not* to be transferred to the medical quarters here in Council Manor for study." Aiden growled out the words, his upper canines peeking out from his lips.

Adam's face darkened with anger when he heard of the council's plans for Keelan and he nodded. "We'll be right behind you. Where do you want him set up?"

"In his own room," Aiden answered.

Ryuu stepped forward. "When you get to the estate let me know, I will do all I can to help."

Aiden looked at the squire with a sour expression. "And where were you when my mate was shooting ferals with a damn sniper rifle?" he demanded, exhaustion adding a bite to his words.

Ryuu gave him a flat look. "Holding her ammunition."

Aiden growled again in frustration. "Let's go home!"

They ended up taking two SUVs back to the Alpha estate. Darian held Amelia's hand tightly as everything suddenly seemed to catch up to her. Once back home, the couples separated, each heading to their own suite to mourn Keelan's loss and recover from the previous day's traumatic events.

Darian led her up the stairs to their room. He opened the door, and she walked inside.

"This is the first time I've been in here since becoming your mate." So much had happened in just a few days.

"Blessed Imbolc," he whispered, walking up to wrap his arms tightly around her. She leaned her head back to rest on his chest.

"I don't feel very blessed. Keelan..."

"Is alive. As long as he's breathing, there is hope."

"It's not the same. He won't be at the dining room table scared of Meryn or giving me a thumbs up." Amelia let her tears drop.

She felt Darian's shuddering breath. "We'll have to remember everything that happens so we can tell him when he's back."

Amelia held his hands where they were clasped together at her waist. "You're right. He's not gone, just not here right now." She turned to face him and wiped her eyes. She looked up into his lavender eyes as an idea began to form. "Let's get everyone together."

Darian's expression was doubtful. "I think everyone needs time alone right now."

Amelia shook her head. "Get everyone together and tell them to leave their lights on. I need to find Ryuu!" She jumped up, grazed his chin with a kiss, and ran out the door and down the stairs.

"Ryuu," she called.

Ryuu stepped into the foyer from the front room. "Yes, *itoko-sama?*"

"We need candles, lots of candles! It's Imbolc!" she decreed. She felt a burst of energy that she was sure came from being completely overwhelmed but she didn't care.

Smiling, Ryuu bowed. "Of course, that's a wonderful idea." He hurried away as everyone started coming downstairs looking puzzled.

"Did you leave your lights on?" she asked the group.

Everyone nodded, but she saw that Rheia and Meryn looked confused.

She walked over to Meryn as Ryuu began passing out the candles. "Imbolc or what is sometimes called Candlemas, is a celebration of light. It marks the passing of winter to spring and the rebirth of the sun. We turn on all the lights of the house and light candles to welcome the warmth of the summer." She turned to the group. "I know that it's not easy to feel cheerful right now, and that's okay, but I thought that if we light up the Alpha Estate, maybe Keelan could find his way home easier."

Around her, a little at first, everyone began to smile. "Me, too! Me, too!" Penny said jumping up and down. Ryuu handed her a flameless LED tea light. Everyone eagerly started lighting the candles.

"We'll keep one light burning until he comes home," Aiden said, tears in his eyes.

Darian stood behind her. He leaned down and whispered. "You're my light, my savior." He pointed to the group. "Only you could draw people out of their pain like this."

She turned her face to look up at him. "In my darkest moment, you came to me like a golden angel. You're my prince and my own savior."

Amelia turned back and looked around their small circle. Everyone held their lit candles and took comfort in each other's company. As a family, they held vigil for the one who was missing among them, the fallen warrior that had sacrificed so much so that they could live.

EPILOGUE

Later that evening, everyone had retired to the front family room. After their candlelight vigil, it had felt too lonely to separate. In the background, cartoons played as Jaxon colored with Penny.

Aiden looked up from the latest copy of the *The Observer*. Daphne Bowers had had a vaginoplasty! What was their world coming to? He heard the front door open and close. A bit of movement caught his eye, and he looked up to see a very guilty-looking Noah dart past the doorway with something large tucked under his arm.

"Aiden..." Gavriel murmured.

Aiden sighed. "I saw." He was especially aware that his mate was nowhere to be seen.

A few minutes later, Noah walked into the room and headed straight for Jaxon. He sat down, picked up a crayon, and began coloring as if his life depended on it.

Aiden set his paper down and crossed his arms over his chest. He faced the doorway and waited.

What in the hell is she up to now?

He didn't have to wait long. Seconds later, Meryn strolled by the doorway trying to look casual, too casual. Under her arm was a large wooden board.

"Meryn," Aiden called. His mate stopped in her tracks.

She turned and smiled brightly. "Yes?"

"What do you have?"

"A Ouija board." She turned as if to keep walking.

Aiden frowned. "What are you doing with a Ouija board?"

Meryn shrugged. He was beginning to learn her shrugs. This was the 'I probably shouldn't be doing what I'm about to do, but I'm going to do it anyway' shrug. "Amelia gave me an idea about shining a light for Keelan to find his way home. I'm going to use the Ouija board to call his spirit back."

Aiden heard Amelia snicker. "It was a metaphor."

Meryn shrugged again. That was her 'I don't care' shrug. "Whatever." She turned and headed toward the stairs.

Colton cleared his throat. "I'm no expert on spirits and the occult, but this is Keelan we're talking about. If by some miracle his soul did find it's way back to the Alpha Estate, Voodoo Meryn with a Ouija board doing incantations would scare him back the way he came."

"*Denka,* let me carry that for you." Aiden heard Ryuu's offer. Just once, he would like that damn squire to keep his mate out of trouble.

Aiden stood and was heading for the foyer when he heard knocking on the door.

"I'll get it!" Meryn yelled.

"Meryn stop. Let me answer it. It could be dangerous!" Aiden rushed forward, the other men and their mates behind him.

Meryn gave him an exasperated look. "Bad guys don't knock."

Heavy pounding on the door shook not only the doorframe but also the wall around it. Meryn swallowed and backed away from the door. "Okay, maybe they knock like that."

Aiden looked behind him. Colton had his gun out; he nodded at Aiden who turned back to the door and opened it. He looked out at the visitor. Unable to believe his eyes, he felt his stomach drop and his heart clench. It couldn't be.

Meryn flew by him to hug the stranger. "Keelan!"

Aiden pulled her back and shoved her behind him into Ryuu's arms.

"Aiden! What are you doing? That's Keelan!" Meryn said pounding on his back.

Behind him, Amelia gasped. "Kendrick?"

The man shoved back the hood to his cloak his eyes full of power and anger.

"Where is my brother?"

Thank you for reading!
I hoped you enjoyed My Savior.

For a full listing of all my books please
check out my website:
www.alaneaalder.com

I love to hear from readers so please
feel free to follow me on :
Facebook , Twitter, Goodreads,
AmazonCentral or Pinterest.

**If you liked this book please let others
know. Most people will trust a friend's
opinion more than any ad. Also please to
leave a review :) I love to read what y'all
have to say and find out what your favorite
parts were. I always read your reviews.**

Don't forget to sign up for my newsletters so
you will receive regular updates concerning
release information and promotions.

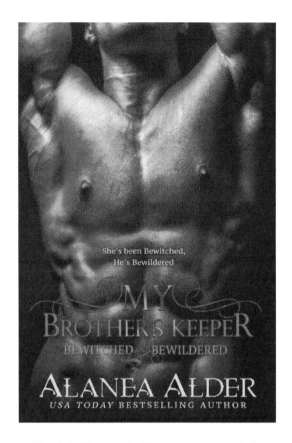

She's been Bewitched,
He's Bewildered

MY
BROTHER'S KEEPER
BEWITCHED BEWILDERED

ALANEA ALDER
USA TODAY BESTSELLING AUTHOR

Get My Brother's Keep as soon as it is
released on November 17th.

Two hundred years ago Kendrick Ashwood
had a premonition that showed him the
gruesome image of his baby brother being killed
in the line of duty while serving with the Alpha
Unit. When centuries go by and Keelan is still
alive and well, he begins to relax. He believes
that his prayers sent to the Gods to make him
wrong this one time have been answered.

As Kendrick feels his godsdaughter's magic flare out of control he immediately merges with her in an attempt to rein it in. That is when he learns of the tragedy that has taken his only family away from him.

Using every resource at his disposal he immediately heads for Lycaonia to find out for himself who would be suicidal enough to harm his brother. What he finds shocks him to his core.

Anne Bennett gets a phone call that changes her life. Her new best friend Keelan has been hurt and his commander is asking her to move in with them to help take care of him. Her heart breaks when she hears from his family that the dreams she has been having of them together were shared by Keelan and that he was meant to be her mate.

Upon meeting Kendrick, her entire world is shaken. His more mature appearance and perpetual frown makes him look more like the man from her dreams than Keelan ever did. When she can no longer fight her attraction for him she confesses her feelings only to have them rebuffed. Kendrick is adamant that he would never steal his brother's mate. But Anne is almost positive that she was never Keelan's mate to begin with.

As the Alpha Unit races to find the enemies who have stolen Keelan's soul and covered Lycaonia in black magic, Kendrick begins to uncover dreadful truth behind the necklaces.

When turning to Anne feels more natural than it should, Kendrick faces the fact that Anne truly is his mate.

As the paranormal world teeters on the brink of darkness, he finds himself protecting not his brother's mate, but his own.

OTHER BOOKS BY ALANEA ALDER

Kindred of Arkadia Series

This series is about a shifter only town coming together as pack, pride, and sloth to defend the ones they love. Each book tells the story of a new couple or triad coming together and the hardships they face not only in their own Fated mating, but also in keeping their town safe against an unknown threat that looms just out of sight.

Book 1- Fate Knows Best
Book 2- Fated to Be Family
Book 3- Fated For Forever
Book 4- Fated Forgiveness
Book 5- Fated Healing
Book 6- Fated Surrender

Book 7- Gifts of Fate
Book 8- Fated Redemption

Bewitched and Bewildercd Series

She's been Bewitched and he's Bewildered...

When the topic of grandchildren comes up during a weekly sewing circle, the matriarchs of the founding families seek out the witch Elder to scry to see if their sons' have mates. They are shocked to discover that many of their sons' mates are out in the world and are human!

Fearing that their future daughters-in-law will end up dead before being claimed and providing them with grandchildren to spoil, they convince their own mates that something must be done. After gathering all of the warriors together in a fake award ceremony, the witch Elder casts a spell to pull the warrior's mates to them, whether they want it or not.

Each book will revolve around a unit warrior member finding his destined mate, and the challenges and dangers they face in trying to uncover the reason why ferals are working together for the first time in their history to kill off members of the paranormal community.

Book 1- My Commander
Book 2- My Protector
Book 3- My Healer
Book 4- My Savior
Book 5- My Brother's Keeper

Printed in Great Britain
by Amazon